Dead In The Dirt

ALSO BY EMMY ELLIS

MORGAN YEOMAN
Book 1: Dead In The Dirt

DETECTIVE ANNA JAMES
Book 1: The Pig Pen
Book 2: The Lion's Den
Book 3: The Copy Cat

DETECTIVE TRACY COLLIER
Book 1: Gutted
Book 2: Crushed
Book 3: Skinned
Book 4: Grabbed
Book 5: Sunk
Book 6: Cracked

DI BETHANY SMITH
Book 1: The Cold Call Killer
Book 2: The Creepy-Crawly Killer
Book 3: The Screwdriver Killer
Book 4: The Scorched Skin Killer
Book 5: The Street Party Killer
Book 6: The Candy Cane Killer
Book 6.5: The Secret Santa Killer
Book 7: The Meat Hook Killer
Book 8: The Blade Killer
Book 9: The Sledgehammer Killer

DETECTIVE CAROL WREN MYSTERIES
Book 1: Spite Your Face
Book 2: Hold Your Breath
Book 3: Guilt Burns Holes
Book 4: Best Served Cold
Book 5: Blood Runs Deep

DETECTIVE MORGAN YEOMAN

DEAD IN THE DIRT

EMMY ELLIS

JOFFE BOOKS

Revised edition 2025
Joffe Books, London
www.joffebooks.com

First published in Great Britain in 2020 as
The Woman on Mulberry Lane

This paperback edition was first published
in Great Britain in 2025

Cover art by Dee Dee Book Covers

ISBN: 978-1-83526-992-3

PROLOGUE

David burst into Old Man Cossack's house, shoving the silly bastard backwards down the hall, kicking the door shut behind him.

"Buying from Phil now, are you?" David asked.

Another shove.

He'd waited so long to do this, scaring all his former customers. Maybe too long, what with the rage siphoning all the goodness out of his blood, the goodness Mum said all Jamaicans were born with. Well, he was only half Jamaican, so that put paid to her silly sermons, didn't it? The other half of him was pure wanker.

He'd had a great business before Phil fucking Flint had barrelled up, saying, proud as you like, that he was running the estate now, and if David didn't back off, he'd get what was coming to him. Seemed he'd said similar to Cossack, maybe to everyone, scaring them into being loyal to him instead.

Cossack stumbled into the living room, rubbing his chest, his long grey beard wobbling. "Please, he sent a kid, a lad, said I had to get my gear from him, not you. If I don't, there'll be trouble."

"But there's trouble anyway." David advanced, fist raised. He'd punch this duffer's lights out and then some.

Cossack let out a strangled sound and clutched his arm, his arthritic fingers digging in. The fabric of his beige cable-knit cardigan ruched beneath his wrist. "I swear to God, I'll buy from both of you, just not say owt to Phil. I don't need the aggravation . . . Oh shit. God, that hurts."

What was he doing, having a bloody heart attack in David's moment of being famous for fifteen minutes? That was just rude.

"Give over, you stupid div." David took another step forward. "No one believes you've got a dicky heart, so you can cut this crap out."

"My tablets . . ." Cossack wheezed, his normally red face going puce. "On the mantel."

David went over there. Yep, there were the tablets all right. Shame he wouldn't be giving them to him. Cossack could damn well fetch them, seeing as he thought himself Pinocchio.

David walked to the phone, took the handle off the cradle, and handed it to Cossack, the dial tone humming from the earpiece, the grubby, wiggly cord stretching. "Best ring for an ambulance really. Tell anyone I was here? Well, you'll see what you get."

It'd be a struggle for Cossack to use the phone if he really was having some trouble. Nine-nine-nine would take ages on the circular dial with a weak arm.

David strutted out, leaving the front door ajar, checking the street for nosy bastards. He crossed the road to stand behind some tall bushes, hiding in the shadows to wait for the ambulance to turn up. He wanted to watch the outcome of his visit, see whether Cossack died. That'd be a notch on David's reputation post, murder, even though he hadn't actually killed him and no one would know he'd been there anyway, but in his head, he'd *know. He'd be a murderer, someone to be reckoned with.*

It took about ten minutes, and the show continued. Paramedics hurried inside, and David's chest tightened with the excitement of it. Blimey, what a rush. Two neighbours came out for a looksee, of course they did, speculating in loud voices as to whether Cossack had fallen or he'd finally had the heart attack that had threatened him for so long.

Stupid of him to sniff cocaine then, wasn't it? That couldn't be doing his ticker any good. Served himself right.

You play with fire, expect to be fucking burnt.

"He's always having that young lad here lately, did you notice?" one woman said, hair all backcombed brunette, a flower of some sort jabbed in there, the petals a murky grey-orange in the light of the amber streetlamp. The hue of her clothes gave her the air of starring in a sepia photograph.

"I did. And we all know who he works for. So, either Cossack is a nonce, or he's taking drugs."

"Hmm, might be weed. For the pain. He's got aching joints an' all. Have you seen his knobbly fingers?"

Sod his aching joints. Sod his heart as well. Cossack deserved to die if he was fiddling with kids. David would have to find out more regarding that. He could move his business to beating people up. He'd be good at it, too. Bully for Hire had a nice ring to it.

The young lad in question turned up and stood behind a tree. He was a weird little shit, off his rocker, David reckoned. Definitely not all there up top. And to be honest, he unsettled David. Kids with vacant eyes gave him the creeps, although some said David's were like that.

Funny.

The ambulance crew came out, carrying Cossack on a stretcher, an oxygen mask over his mouth and nose, a blanket covering his spindly body.

"What's up with him?" Backcomb called out to the ambulance crew.

"Heart attack. Can you get hold of his next of kin if you know them, please, love?"

"Will do! That's Florrie Dorchester on Mulberry Lane. His sister." Backcomb toddled off with her neighbour, clearly happy to be of some service. Needed.

David wished people needed him. They had when he'd sold them drugs, so desperate for what he had to give, so happy and relieved to see him on their doorstep, and now look, all of it taken away by Phil.

Prick.

The ambulance drove off, and the lad came out from behind the tree. He scooted over the road, down the side of Cossack's. David had a dilemma. Leave the kid to it or confront him? The freaky brat was probably robbing, stuffing jewellery into his pockets. Old Man Cossack had a nice gold watch, left to him by his mother. He'd offered it to David as payment once, but what good was a watch at the pawnshop if he'd get asked a million questions as to where he'd got it from?

The lad came out, legging it down the road, head bent.

David walked along the pavement, slower, hands in his pockets. He had the mad urge to kick the shit out of something — or someone, namely Phil fucking Flint. Things had really gone tits up, David on the dole now, still living with his mum. She was a nice enough old dear but got in his face about getting a job, making himself useful.

"You shame your heritage," she always said. "We work hard, we're decent people, but you . . . ?"

Ah, get lost.

Three streets along at the top end of Mulberry Lane, David scuffed past The Tractor's Wheel pub and debated going in for a pint. He could do with one, but then all his neighbours from Elderflower Mead might be in there and expect him to chat and have a laugh. He didn't feel like laughing. Mum might be there, too, as it was quiz night, and he couldn't be doing with her bending his ear. Instead, he entered Cost Savers next door, known locally as Wasti's after the man who owned it.

Shite, the twatty lad was in there, buying a load of sweets — probably with money he'd pinched off Cossack. David moved down the alcohol aisle and picked up a six-pack of Heineken, the green cans giving him comfort once clutched to his chest in his welcome arms. He'd be pissed up soon, more than merry, and could think better then. He had to do something with himself, had to find a way to make easy money, and lots of it. Drunkenness always gave him nifty ideas.

The teenager left the shop, and David put his cans on the counter.

"He's a wrong 'un," he said. "Watch him."

Zuhaib Wasti raised his eyebrows, as if what David had said was ironic. "Yes, he's destined for trouble, as are you."

David didn't know how to answer that. Wasti was no different to Mum, all righteous, and David was sick of being told what to do, how to behave. But no matter how hard he tried, he couldn't be mean to Wasti. Everyone round here had grown up with him as the shopkeeper. There were some people you just didn't upset.

He paid for the beer. "I've been going straight."

"So your mother said. No more drugs, eh?" Wasti handed over the change.

"Nope."

"Probably because of Phil Flint, no other reason."

So, everyone knew his shame, did they? Bet they all laughed behind his back at how David Ives hadn't been able to get the younger Phil Flint off his patch. Well, David had new pastures to roam, and they'd soon see he was worth something. He wouldn't be buying Heineken then but Wasti's finest champagne.

He left the shop and went to the derelict street, Vicar's Gate, all with empty, boarded-up houses, plus a block of flats. He'd get peace there, could sit on the bench outside the flats and think.

Laughter floated out, probably that annoying gang of kids the lad hung out with, inside the squat on the second floor. Well, they could get on with whatever it was they were doing. David had plans to make.

He parked his arse on the bench and popped the first can. The liquid went down a right old treat, the bubbles fizzing. He got a bit of a buzz from necking it so quickly, but that was all right. He intended to get pissed as a fart.

On his fifth can, he started at the sight of a kid from his street walking down the road, a studious type, the sort everyone else called a square. Brainy. His skinny frame didn't seem strong enough to carry him along, and he had a flat cap on, like some old man, something Cossack would own.

David huffed out a laugh. Hopefully Cossack would die and never wear a cap again. And if Cossack liked little lads, he'd definitely like Jacob Everson from Elderflower Mead, innocent and trusting. Maybe the kid had already been there and that was why he had the cap, a gift for services rendered.

"Hey, Jacob!" someone called from the flats behind.

David turned, his vision fuzzing, but he made out who was up there all right. Several of the gang leant on the balcony railings. They all appeared spaced out, drunk probably, just like David.

"Come up here," one of them shouted. "We've got some sweets."

David faced forward. Jacob hesitated, hope lighting up his elfin face, the streetlamps still on down here, even though the homes were deserted. He was maybe wondering whether the gang were taking the piss, and if he did *take them up on their offer, it might be more hassle than it was worth. They probably bullied him at school, and he was well-versed in steering clear of them.*

"Hurry up then!" a girl said.

Jacob must have made up his mind to take the risk, the lure of friendship, however fragile, strong inside him. He crossed the road, spotted David, and jumped.

"Not all black men bite," David slurred, "just like not all white men do. Remember that when you get spooked by dark skin." He was away with the fairies, his head spinning. "Like my mum says, we all bleed red blood."

Jacob moved closer.

"You worrying about those kids up there?" David asked.

Jacob nodded.

"Well, don't. I'll be sitting here for a while. Got another can to drink and a spliff to smoke. Any trouble, you just shout for me."

"Thanks."

"That's a nice satchel." David reached out and took hold of the top, bringing the bag and Jacob towards him. "I could have done with something like that for my gear." The leather was cold beneath his fingertips. "Maybe I'll buy myself one for my new business, whatever the hell that'll be."

"Mum got it off the market."

"Then maybe I'll go there and fetch one for myself. Go on now, they're waiting for you."

Jacob darted off, and whoops of delight rang out from the balcony. David peered over his shoulder. Jacob disappeared into the dark stairwell, his footsteps ringing out on the concrete stairs.

David shrugged. Time to roll his joint. He had an extra high to obtain, more than booze gave him. Funny how he smoked Phil's weed. Funny how David's dole money lined that bastard's pockets.

He smoked, he finished the joint, and he zoned out.

Until screams came from behind, piercing and awful. David shook off his lethargy and got up, leaving his cans on the bench. Someone jogged past with their dog, Walkman headphones clamped to his ears, the foam the same weird colour as Backcomb's hair flower. Everything was odd, out of sync, and David swayed, wondering if Phil had discovered a new strain of weed, stronger, more likely to trip David out.

The jogger continued, as did the screams, and then laughter, other screams from other people, shrieks of horror, or maybe that was just David's imagination. Nauseated, he plopped back onto the bench, telling himself he was hallucinating, that the sounds were just those in his head, the ones from his nightmares. They always came out for an airing when he was off his nut.

Eyes closed, he breathed deeply.

The screams wailed on.

Then footsteps, running, lots of them, loud clanks on the balcony.

The clatter of them down the stairway.

The more muted thuds on the expanse of grass in front of the flats.

"Fuck," someone said. "Oh fuck."

David opened his eyes. The gang sped towards him, and he reached out to grab one of the girl's wrists.

She screeched, staring at him as if he were a monster. "Piss off. Get your hands off me."

"What are you lot up to?" He gave her arm a twist.

"Help me," she called to the others who now ran down the road. "There's a fucking demon with blue snakes coming out of his head." She tried to step away. "You bloody dickhead," she said to David. "Pervert snake man."

What the fuck was she on about? "No need to gob off." He stared at her.

She screeched again. "I can't stand this — or you. Get off me! He needs help . . ."

"Who?"

"Jacob . . ."

David let her go, and she pinwheeled away, shooting after her friends. David knew them by sight, so if they'd messed about with Jacob, he'd find them. Problem was, he didn't know if they'd all been there. When they'd come towards him, he hadn't concentrated.

He ran to the stairwell and rushed up, guilt pricking him for letting the lad down. He'd told him to shout if he got into bother, yet David hadn't done a thing, blaming the racket on his mind playing him up.

He pelted along the walkway and barged into the squat. The gang had been smoking, drinking. Cigarette stubs and alcohol bottles — gin and vodka — had been left on the windowsill in the living room. An old brown cupboard stood to the left, one of its doors open.

And Jacob, on the concrete floor, his satchel beside him.

David vomited at the state of the lad, at all the blood, and he knew, if he called the police, they'd say he'd done it. Blame the black man. He checked for a pulse, concentrating hard in his intoxicated state and, sure no throb flickered beneath his fingertips, he reversed. Out of the living room. Out of the squat.

On the balcony, he stared at the jogger coming back.

The jogger stared at him, too.

Shit.

David got a move on and vacated the scene, belting out of Vicar's Gate towards home in Elderflower. He thought of the Eversons living a few doors down from him, how they'd be wondering where their son was now. He thought of their faces when they were told he was dead. And he thought of the gang. They'd killed that boy, that much was obvious, and he'd make it his business to find every one of them and get them to admit what they'd done.

That was his new venture. Making them pay.

CONFESSION

You know when you see someone who needs a serious kicking, but you can't because you're a copper? That. Do I or don't I? Cross the line or stay behind it? The thing is, I don't want to stay behind it, not anymore. I need results. Now, not next week. If I don't push for them, he might kill again. Bastard.

—DI Morgan Yeoman

CHAPTER ONE

"DI Morgan Yeoman, over here, please."

Morgan glanced across the incident room at Jane, a blonde prissy sort who played it by the book, never a wayward step off the police track as far as he was aware. She was all right as women go, didn't favour makeup or tarty clothes like some he could mention when they all met up for drinks after closing a case, but something about her got on his nerves all the same.

She was too clean. Too . . . good. No grit to her. Seemed to always peer down her nose at the rest of the team.

He walked to her desk. "What's up?"

"See this?" She jabbed at her monitor, her stubby nail tinking on the screen.

The photo of a man filled the top-right corner, a mug shot, his details to the left. Yes, some aspects fitted the profile Nigel Stansford had cobbled together, but this fella, he'd only just got out of the nick last week. He'd been banged up in Rushford Prison for armed robbery, did a fifteen stretch, and had barely got his arse settled in Halfway House on Mulberry Lane, so to go straight out and off someone? Doubtful. Although he could have asked a mate to do it; plenty of scallywags in his circle who'd kill for a grand. Desperate folks in need of quick money. Delia, the deceased, had known the victim and played a part in him going down.

"Yep, we're already aware of him," Morgan said.

Jane knew this. They'd had him on their suspect list from the start. Was she bringing Gary Flint up again to wind Morgan up? Wouldn't be a surprise. She liked doing that. Seemed she always wanted to rile him or trip him up. Maybe she didn't like him. He probably got on her nerves.

"I'm paying him a visit today." Morgan scratched his stubbled chin. "Keep looking, Jane Blessing."

He'd called her by her full name on purpose. Childish, but he tended to be sometimes when the fancy took him, although he liked to think of himself as stubborn, a man who made a point whenever the opportunity arose. She always insisted doing it to him. Couldn't just say 'sir' or 'Morgan' or even 'Yeoman', always 'DI Morgan Yeoman'.

Weird bird. He'd work her out one day, see what made her tick.

He turned and went over to Nigel, who sat with his head bent, also searching through files to see if anyone stood out as a potential suspect. Whoever they were after knew his onions, wasn't a novice, unless you counted footprints left at the scene, so there was another reason to discard Flint, who was a bit thick, hence getting arrested for doing the robbery.

"No one's quite right." Nigel leant back and sighed. He ran a hand through his floppy brown hair. "Like searching for a hymen in a whorehouse."

Morgan stared at the bloke on Nigel's screen. Black fella. Similar to Morgan's cousin, which gave him a bit of a jolt until he peered closer and saw it wasn't him. "Could be an out-of-towner, someone we don't have on record."

Nigel pinched his bottom lip. "Hmm. Flint, though . . ."

"I know, but come on, he's a skinny runt and isn't the brightest button. Still, when Shaz finally shows her arse, I'll go and see him."

Shaz — Sharon Tanner, his DS, a hard-nosed type who fitted his way of policing perfectly. She didn't mind bending the rules a bit if it got them what they needed, although she wasn't prepared to go as far as Morgan. She wouldn't punch anyone, for instance, but give her time. Maybe if she watched him doing it, she might come out of her shell.

Morgan wandered off to the whiteboard. Photos of the dead woman, notes about her, people she knew, lived with, loved, hated, all of them listed, and all of them struck off as innocent yesterday — for now. Alibis, they were handy things. Everyone had one. They'd been spoken to, questioned, and none of them had struck him or other officers as dodgy. All right, a couple of them were weird, but then so many people were, and weird in a quirky way, not sinister.

But that poor cow. Delia. Long dark hair. Blue eyes. Naked, dirty where she'd been thrown into a ditch in Queen's Wood. That strange murder weapon looped around her neck.

It had rained a lot recently, bucketloads, the ground unable to soak it all up, its belly full. Muddy puddles. Beige grass, drenched at the roots. A bit of a mess really, the crime scene. Footprints, size eleven — Flint was a seven. Wellies, so Jane had discovered from searches on treads. So, they were after a big-footed bastard then. Tall. Maybe with a bit of brawn to him.

That wasn't Flint.

Shaz stormed in, all scrunched eyebrows, black arches in that insane style some women opted for these days, filled in daily with one of those pencils. She'd shoved her bottle-red hair into a ponytail so tight it stretched her eyes. "That bloody traffic . . ."

"Same excuse every day," Morgan said, bored with her justifications. "Like I've said before, *we* all manage to get in on time. It's called leaving home earlier."

"Get lost." She dumped her bag by her chair and took her phone out. A scroll through Instagram, then, "What's on the list for today?"

"You know this. Gary Flint." Morgan sniffed. "I don't think it's him, but we need to check."

"Right." Shaz slid her mobile in her pocket. "Now?"

Morgan glanced at the clock on the wall. Nine a.m. "Half an hour late today, Shaz, not the usual ten minutes."

She shrugged. "I do enough overtime."

"Don't we all," Jane piped up.

Shaz gave her a shut-your-trap glare then raised her facial caterpillars at Morgan. "Are we going then or what?"

Morgan nodded. "Yep."

They left the incident room, Shaz whinging about not being caffeined up to her tits yet.

"Forgot to make my to-go cup for the journey. My alarm never went off."

"So it wasn't the traffic then . . ."

She strode ahead of him and pushed past some twat or other who was being booked in by Graham Vale, the daytime front-desk sergeant.

"Got your hands full there, Gray?" Shaz said.

"Nothing I can't handle." Gray waved her off. "Mind your own."

"Arseholes to you," she muttered and shoved her way outside into the car park.

Morgan smiled. Shaz was a bitch without enough coffee in her.

"We'll stop off at Costa," he said. "Can't be doing with you being a mardy cow all day."

She turned and walked backwards, grinning. "Love you, Morg."

"No, you don't, you're just being a creep so I don't dob you in to the DCI for keep showing up late. I'll be picking you up in future, quarter to eight. Now get in the car." He blipped the fob to open the doors. "We haven't got all day."

He had a man to see about a dead body, although whether Flint knew anything or gave up information was anyone's guess.

Time to find out then, wasn't it?

CONFESSION

There are only so many times you can spread your legs or open your mouth for strangers without hating yourself for it. But you do these things for money, don't you, to feed your son. I wouldn't ordinarily have gone down this route, of course I bloody wouldn't, but with no other income, my options were limited. A supermarket doesn't pay enough, and the dole wasn't an option. I work for my money. Hard. God, that wasn't meant to be a pun.

—Val Hoskins

CHAPTER TWO

"Will you bloody well get a move on, you're late!"

Val had a bit of a panic on. If that son of hers didn't bugger off to college any time soon, he'd catch her first customer of the day arriving. Times past, she'd nearly got caught on a few occasions, leaping out of bed and shoving the blokes down the stairs then out of the side door, instructing them to "Fuck off, I'll make it up to you next week." They'd scuttled up the ginnel, shirttails flying, waiting at the end until Karl had come into the house via the front.

It wasn't good for her nerves, this Russian roulette lark. Karl being eighteen now, well, he had a mind of his own, didn't he. She couldn't force him out of their home like she had years ago, taking him to school, him staying there while she conducted her business. Maybe today was one of those where he didn't have to be in until later. The college alternated weeks, so was this A or B? Was Karl only meant to be there from twelve onwards on a Monday?

"Shit, I don't have a chuffing clue." She raced upstairs, out of breath on the landing, a sheen of sweat erupting on her face. That'd be the makeup ruined then. She waited until she'd calmed, flung Karl's door open, and poked her head inside his room, greeted with the scent of stale aftershave and Lynx Africa body spray. "Oi, you. Get up."

He rolled onto his side and dragged the quilt over his head. It crackled, what with it being filled with down, and he groaned. "Ugh. What time is it?"

"Quarter past nine."

"Bollocks! I've got a mock exam at eleven." He jumped out of bed, boxers all ruffled, and brushed past her to go into the bathroom.

Val nodded as if congratulating herself, glad she hadn't lost her marbles regarding the college schedule. She needed a printout of it so she'd definitely know the score in future. There'd be none of this worrying then, would there.

Downstairs, she popped some thick-sliced bread in the toaster and sorted him a coffee in his ceramic to-go cup. It had his name on the side, something she'd had done online for a Christmas present the previous year. He could eat and drink on the way. Her client was due at ten.

Blimey, her heart pitter-pattered, sent even more haywire once the toast popped, too much noise and too much vigour added to the mix. She wasn't up to working today, to be honest, but the bills didn't pay themselves, did they, and besides, Harry wasn't a chore. He got too excited and finished inside a couple of minutes. An easy eighty quid, that one.

She'd pay the veg woman later. Olga Scrivens, her name was, and she lived at number one. She grew all sorts in her back garden, even had a greenhouse. The stuff was fresher than a kid's outlook, cheaper than Tesco, too.

Karl appeared, hair wet, his jeans and T-shirt slung on if she was any judge. She handed him his breakfast and coffee, silently urging him to leave. He rammed a corner of toast in his mouth, the butter soaked in, and some dripped down his little finger.

"Got to study before the exam. Going to my mate's place after, so I'll be back about ten when his mum kicks me out." He waved and left the house.

Val released a long breath. Cutting it fine wasn't on her agenda. She couldn't handle hassle anymore and needed everything to run smoothly. In her forties now, she was no spring chicken.

She cleaned up and managed to peg some washing out quick sharp. It was a nice day, the sun belting heat out, and her sheets would dry in no time. She owned a few sets, considering what she did for a living, all the same so Karl didn't ask why she kept changing them. Now he was getting older, it wouldn't be long before someone let something slip down the boozer: *Your mum's a tart, didn't you know?* She needed to stop before he found out, but what else could she do? What was she good for other than sex?

Inside, she looked in the gilt-framed mirror in the hallway to make sure her makeup was all right. Wouldn't do for Harry to get an eyeful of smudged kohl and mascara. God, the things she had to do for work.

The doorbell rang, and she checked who it was from the living room window, standing behind the cream-coloured voiles so she wasn't clocked. If Harry hadn't gone round to the side door, she'd brain him. They all knew the rules, and using the front wasn't on.

Olga stood there, arms folded beneath her vast tits, chubby hands curled against her sides. She had her usual flowery apron on.

Balls, she's here for the veg dosh.

Val owed her for two weeks. She sighed and opened the door, telling herself she'd use some of the rent from her tin in the larder and replace it with Harry's payment later.

Door open, she smiled. "Two seconds, Olga, and I'll get your money."

Olga shook her head and glanced up and down the street, a poor imitation of Miss Marple acting surreptitious. "I'm not here about the money."

Val frowned and stared at Olga's feet. No carrier bag beside them, leafy greens poking out of the top. No bulge in it from the roundness of a cabbage or a marrow. So, if she wasn't delivering the goods or collecting her tenner, what *was* she doing? "Eh? Are you all right?"

"I know I don't usually mingle, but I should come in." Olga gave the lane another once-over, as though she didn't want anyone to see her, but everyone was nosy, so she was shit out of luck there. "I've just seen that copper of yours going to Halfway House."

"What's that got to do with me?"

Val thought of DI Yeoman. He was due here later, two o'clock — *if* he could get away from that Shaz he worked with. He paid for an hour, but they never *did it*. He was married to some fancy piece Delia and Olga used to know, who had ideas above her station. He'd never touch the likes of Val. Yeoman came for information, simple as that.

"Haven't you heard?" Olga arched her bush-like eyebrows.

"Heard what?"

"Sodding well let me in and I'll tell you."

Val stepped back, surprised Olga wanted to come in. She rarely did that. Something must have kicked off, and while a good natter about other people's misfortunes passed the time, Val didn't have any to spare. She'd keep this short and to the point, then send Olga on her way.

Olga entered, breezing through to the kitchen, huffing and puffing, her fluffy slippers slapping on the dark laminate.

Val peered down the lane. Yeoman's car sat outside Halfway House. It was no surprise he was there, what with all those blokes staying in rooms after being in the nick. Maybe he needed to check on a new resident. She'd seen someone carrying a suitcase in there last week, his back to her.

She shrugged and closed the door, joining Olga in the kitchen.

"What's going on?" Val opened the larder and took her tin out. "Do we need a cuppa for this or what?" She counted out ten quid in fivers and handed them to her neighbour.

"Could do." Olga stuffed the cash in her apron pocket. It was streaked with mud — she must have been gardening, changing from her cerise Crocs into her slippers to nip here. "The runner beans are ready if you fancy some. A pound'll do."

Val dug out the coin and put it on the table. "Karl likes those with a bit of sausage and mash. They go down well with Bisto." She sorted the cups and got on with putting coffee granules in them, then lifted the kettle. "So, out with it."

"Delia's been murdered."

Val almost dropped the damn kettle, which was still hot from when she'd made Karl's drink. "What?" She placed it back on its base, hand shaking. Her heart galloped, the beats too hard and too fast. "Fucking hell, pour that, will you?"

Olga trundled over and did the honours. "She was found yesterday morning. Didn't the police come and ask if you'd seen or heard anything?"

"No, but then I was round Mum's for Sunday dinner." Val's eyes stung. Who on earth would want to kill Delia?

"Nice. What did you have?"

"Beef." *Who cares what I bloody had when our mate's dead?*

"Lovely. Hope you used my veg. Guess what?"

"What . . ." Val gritted her teeth.

Talking to Olga was difficult. The woman changed subjects at random, probably because she was such an introvert she didn't know how to converse properly.

"Gary Flint's out."

Val's knees threatened to buckle. She'd been the one to encourage Delia to grass on him after the robbery. Yeoman had come round, and together they'd gone through it — what Delia had seen, how she'd have to go to court and testify, and if she liked, she could go into hiding while Flint awaited trial. He had acquaintances who'd hurt her, but thankfully, none of them had, even after he'd been banged up. Val suspected his brother, Phil, had sorted that.

"I can't . . . Oh God." She stumbled over to the table and sat.

Olga brought the coffees over. She plonked them down on shiny white coasters and parked her arse opposite. "Delia was out on the corner, if you catch my drift."

Val caught it. Delia worked out there, didn't use her house, preferring the alley behind Halfway House for a quick fifty quid. She was a good sort, always smiling. Well, apart from when she'd gone through everything regarding Flint and her mum dying. They'd swapped notes on who the bad punters were and watched each other's backs. Val couldn't believe she was gone. And murdered to boot.

Is there a prosser killer out there? Am I next?

"I only saw her about eight Saturday night. She was under the streetlamp on her phone." Val picked up her coffee and jumped at a knock on the side door. "Shit, that's Harry."

"I hate that man. Do him in the garden. I'll wait in here; I don't want to risk seeing him. Your coffee'll still be hot by the time you get back. I heard he's a one-minute wonder." Olga grunted.

"I can't work after this! He'll have to wait until I've come to terms with it." Val walked to the side door and opened it, her mind swimming with images of a dead Delia, blood everywhere.

Harry crouched beside the blue wheelie bin, peering up at her, the corner of a pizza box poking out, resting on his head. His sparse, dyed-black combover was liberally drenched in wet-look gel, as usual, and his nose was getting worse. He had the strawberry type associated with drinkers, all red with the air of cauliflower about it, too many small lumps and bumps. Grey streaked his long sideburns. The years hadn't been kind to him. Like Olga, most people disliked him, but money was money, and so long as he didn't get funny with Val, things would be fine.

"For Pete's sake, get up, will you?" She shut the door and stood on the step. "People round here know what I do, and they see you here every week, you daft git. What's the point in hiding, unless it's so your wife doesn't spot you?"

"Not long seen your lad, have I, and Yeoman's about." He stood, checking down the ginnel between her house and the next. He leant against the fence behind him, ferreting in his pocket, for her fee, most likely.

"So? Karl's off to college, and Yeoman knows what I do, he just happens to keep his mouth shut. I can't sort you out today anyway. Had some bad news. Plus, I have a mate in my kitchen. Us two going inside is rude."

"But it'll only take a minute." He held the cash out. "I'm desperate, like. My missus isn't in the mood lately, and I like the way you let me pinch you."

"Jesus Christ." Val glanced up at the side window in Florrie Dorchester's house. The blind was down. "All right then, but not the full works. I can't be doing with getting caught with my knickers around my ankles." She snatched the notes and stuffed them down her bra.

Harry was done and gone in seconds, and she wondered if the dangerous element of Yeoman being about helped matters. Harry might well have got off on it like he did with the 'dirtiness' of going with a sex worker. He said some strange things whenever they did business, and muttering about her being 'just like that slapper I used to know' was only one of them.

She returned inside and washed her hands with disinfectant soap to get the condom residue off them, her arm hurting from where he'd pinched and twisted the skin.

She really ought to pack this in. Find a different job. What, though? Yeoman's weekly informant money wouldn't cover all her bills. Fifty pounds was nothing these days, went nowhere.

"Told you." Olga nodded. "There's still steam coming off your coffee, look."

Val sat and sipped some. "The perv liked the fact Yeoman's in the lane, I swear."

"Did you know his wife's up the duff? Harry's, I mean."

"No, he's not one for sharing anything about her, and it's no wonder, seeing as she's so young and there's a suspicion he was perving around her when she was underage. Some men do like to chat after, though. I could write a book about all the goings-on. Make a fortune. Chapter one, older man fathers a baby with young wife." Guilt hit her for joking at a time like this, and she blushed, hating herself for momentarily forgetting her friend was gone, dead. "So. Delia. What the hell?" Tears pooled, itching her eyeballs.

"I know. They reckon it was a punter. Her bag was found in the alley Sunday morning, her purse inside, a wedge of cash in it."

"So not a robbery."

"Which is Flint's specialty." Olga closed her eyes for a long blink.

"So do you think he topped her because she grassed on him?"

"Probably. Word has it he's got one of the front bedsits and would have seen her standing on the corner."

"Why the hell was he put in Halfway House then? The coppers know Delia lives here."

"Lived."

"Shit. I can't get over this. So, was she found in the alley as well? And how the heck do you know so much anyway? Did one of your customers dish the goss?"

"No. It's online, and the Pinstone Facebook page is full of chatter. She was dumped in Queen's Wood, probably Saturday night. Naked."

"Bloody hell . . ." Val's heart thumped away, and a cold sweat broke out. A chill rippled up her spine, spreading into a flurry on her scalp. "Naked? What about her clothes?"

"They're missing, although her shoes were left behind." Olga scratched her nose. "Got any bourbons or custard creams?"

"In the larder."

While Olga fetched them, Val imagined Delia left in the woods. Had she been alive when she was there or dead beforehand? Had she suffered?

"What . . . what did the killer do to her?" She dreaded the answer but needed to know.

"Strangled her by all accounts." Olga flumped down and opened a packet of Wagon Wheels. "With a rubber snake."

"Pardon?" Val stared, open-mouthed. "A rubber snake?"

"Yeah. It was left around her neck, a blue one."

"And that was in the news?"

Olga nodded. "Shocking, isn't it. You can't even get murdered without the world and his wife knowing all the ins and outs." She slid the pound coin towards her and dropped it into her apron pocket. "I'll pop the runners round later. After that copper's been to yours."

Val nodded. She gave Olga her schedule every week, the names of who'd booked an appointment, what times they were arriving, for safety, in case something happened to her. And thank God she did, what with a killer on the loose. She'd have a word with Yeoman, see if she was in danger. Like she'd thought earlier, she couldn't be doing with any hassle, least of all being strangled.

Poor Delia. This was going to hit the street hard. Everyone knew everyone, and the community spirit was high. One of their own being topped wouldn't go down well. Val wouldn't be surprised if they gathered outside her house later, waiting for Yeoman to arrive.

The poor sod would have a job on his hands if they did. The folks on Mulberry Lane didn't take kindly to being brushed off. They'd want answers, and want them now.

Same as Val did.

CHAPTER THREE

Delia placed her purchases on the counter in Cost Savers, tired from being out on the lane until way past midnight. She'd managed about four hours of sleep after a good soak in the bath, and now, at eight in the morning, she was dying for a coffee. The milk had gone sour, lumps in it and everything, and she'd had to dash up the end of Mulberry Lane to buy some more. A bar of Dairy Milk had found its way into her basket as well, along with some pickled onion Monster Munch and KP salted peanuts. She'd have a morning relaxing and snacking in front of the telly. David Suchet was on This Morning later, and she wanted to watch it. She'd loved him in Poirot.

Zuhaib Wasti bagged the items while jabbing at his old-fashioned till. He hadn't moved on to scanners, preferring to input the amount himself, so he'd said. Delia loved him to bits, having known him all her life. She'd grown up on the lane, and the council tenancy had gone to her after Mum had died. Dad had come back on the scene, wanting money Mum might have left, but there hadn't been any. If there had, Delia wouldn't be working the corner, that much was certain. Her old job at the pub hadn't paid enough.

"Nasty day out there." Zuhaib put the milk in the bag.

Delia turned to look outside. "Shite. Trust me to come out without a brolly. I thought the rain would hold off until I got back."

Zuhaib smiled, his teeth bright inside the swathe of his dark beard. "I have one you can borrow. Bring it back next time." He shuffled off through the doorway marked PRIVATE.

The chime at the entrance jangled, then came a crash, someone opening the door with a bit too much force, banging it into the chewing gum rack on the counter. She turned, and Gary Flint stood there, all in black, a beanie perched on his blond head, the hem rolled up in a sausage on his forehead. Legs bowed, one arm curved at his side, the other stretched towards her, a gun in his gloved hand.

It took a moment for her to register the gun properly and why he'd be pointing it at her. She stared, a ragged gasp coming out of her, and stepped to the side behind the stand of cornflakes, out of shooting range.

"What the fuck, Gary?"

"Tits," he said. "Bloody Nora!"

She peered round the stand. The beanie was a balaclava, the rolled hem now pulled down to cover his face. The stupid prat must have forgotten to disguise himself before coming in. He peered through two holes, and maybe because she knew it was him beneath the fabric, she'd say she'd recognise those eyes anywhere. His mouth, too, his fleshy lips sticking out.

"Shut your fucking face about this, like about the other thing, you hear me?" He waved the gun in her direction.

Her legs weak, she nodded. What else could she do? And shit, Zuhaib would be back in a minute with the brolly. Should she run for it out the back and warn him?

"If you let me go through that door there" — she gestured to it — "you can do whatever it is you want to and leave."

He waggled the gun. "Go on, piss off then. And keep your gob shut if you know what's good for you."

She rushed there, pushing through into the storeroom, bumping into Zuhaib, chest to chest. "Is there a lock on this door?" she panted out and turned to check. A shiny silver Yale stared back at her, so she secured them inside, her heart clattering away.

"What's the matter?" Zuhaib moved to peer through the square of glass in the door.

"Keep back. Someone's out there with a gun." She'd said 'someone', which meant her brain had decided to keep Flint's identity a secret. She

stood to the side and peered through using one eye. "He's locking the shop door." Oh God, what if he shot at them? What if he shot another customer if they tried to get in? "Ring the police." That'd take the decision out of her hands then. They'd catch him, see who he was.

"I'll do more than that." Zuhaib pressed a button on a panel beside the door.

A clunk sounded, and the metal grate came down in front of the main door and windows. An alarm went off, piercing, and Delia covered her ears.

Zuhaib patted the private door. "Bulletproof glass," he shouted over the din, "and this has a steel panel. The police will be here soon. Two minutes."

Delia stared out into the shop. Flint stuffed money from the till into a backpack, his movements quick. He turned and grabbed some cigarettes off the shelf behind him, packs of two hundred. A glance Delia's way, then he scooted around the counter, slinging his backpack on, and yanked open the front door.

"Fucking let me out, Wasti, or I'll come back for you in your sleep," he yelled.

Delia stared at Zuhaib. "Do as he says."

"But he has my money, my cigarettes."

"They're not worth it. If he comes for you . . ." Delia had always known Flint was a bad 'un, right from when they'd been younger.

Zuhaib nodded and pressed the button. The metal grate seemed to take forever to rise, then Flint was off, outside, turning to stare over his shoulder, rain lashing down on him. He made eye contact with Delia, and for a split second, she thought he was going to lift the gun and shoot her after all. Then he ran out of the lane, probably to a car parked on the corner.

She pressed her back to the door. "Bloody hell . . ." The shakes overtook her, and she slid to the floor, bringing her knees up and hugging them. Her teeth chattered.

"We need tea. That will make it all better." Zuhaib was calm as anything and moved over to the kitchenette hidden behind a stack of boxes bearing brand names. PG Tips, McVitie's Rich Tea, and one at the bottom marked Kellogg's All-Bran.

Tea wouldn't fix this. It wouldn't fix the fear rattling her bones. She knew who Flint was, and he knew she knew. Would he come for her in her sleep, like he'd threatened Zuhaib? "Jesus . . ."

The rumble of the kettle gave her some sense of normality in this strange moment, but things would never be normal again. She'd watched Flint rob the shop, and while there might not have been much money in the till, what with it being early and only the float in there, he'd probably intended using the gun to chivvy Zuhaib to the safe in the storeroom. There may well be a couple of thousand in there.

What if she hadn't come in and needed a brolly? Zuhaib would have been behind the counter, alone, and Flint could have done all sorts to him.

Zuhaib held out a cup. "It's coffee. I remembered you don't drink tea."

She stood on shaking legs and accepted the drink. He didn't appear fazed at all, and she supposed he lived with the fear of being robbed every day and had got used to it.

A commotion from behind caught her attention, and she looked through the square of glass. The police were here. The question was, should she tell them it was Flint or keep her mouth shut, as he'd demanded? Would his face be on CCTV anyway?

"Do you have cameras in the shop?" she asked.

Zuhaib sighed. "No, just mirrors."

"Any outside?"

"No."

So no one but her knew it was Flint.

And that was a burden she really didn't want to carry, not on top of the other one they shared, but if she didn't, she'd be in trouble.

Maybe even dead.

CHAPTER FOUR

Morgan and Shaz had spent a few minutes talking to the woman who ran Halfway House, finding out whether Flint had stuck to the rules and been a good boy. Seemed he had, although she had heard a car out the front, but it could have been anyone living in Mulberry Lane.

"How do you know who went out? How do you keep track of curfews?" Morgan had asked.

Emma Ingles, about fifty with wrinkles most likely brought on by scowling rather than smiling, sniffed. "I had a new system installed. Each resident has their own code, and they have to key it into the panel inside to get out, outside to get in. It registers on my computer."

She'd shown them the data. Flint hadn't left the building since he'd moved in, but who was to say whether he'd forced another lag to give him their number? He might be shite at robbery, but he could threaten well enough. One other man had been out on Saturday night, leaving at ten and returning at two. A decent window of opportunity.

Morgan and Shaz would speak to him after Flint.

Now, Flint stared at them from the doorway to his bedsit, blond-grey hair tousled, eyes piss holes in the snow, as if he'd drunk too much alcohol since leaving prison and it'd sent his liver funny. Yellow eyeballs, muddy-brown iris splodges in the centres, his skin a pasty cream. He'd had a shock, seeing Morgan, as well he might if he'd killed Delia.

"Oh, bloody hell, it's you. What do you want?" Flint's armpit hair stuck out, his black vest top displaying more limp flesh than was tasteful. The skinny bastard needed a meal or two in him an' all. Food at Rushford clearly hadn't stuck to his bones. "I've been on the straight and narrow since I got out, so there's no need for you to check up on me."

"Being on the straight and narrow for a few days is nothing." Morgan glared at him. "Aren't you going to be polite and ask us in? Didn't you learn any manners in Rushford?" He pushed Flint's chest and stood in the middle of the bedsit. "Not too bad here, is it. I see you've got a PlayStation. Come with the room, does it?"

Flint sighed at Shaz barging past him. "You know it does. Your lot did that charity thing to pay for them. The Ingles woman told me. Like I need to be grateful to a few coppers, probably the ones who helped put me away. Not on your nelly."

"I was just checking. You might have robbed it from some poor kid who'd got it for his birthday."

"Piss off." Flint shut the door. "What do you want? I've turned over a new leaf, so if you're here to pin something on me, you can knob off."

"Piss off and knob off inside sixty seconds." Morgan laughed. "What a polite chap."

"I've never claimed to be polite, but I'm telling you, nothing's gone on." He sat in a clothes-covered armchair, a pair of dodgy-looking Y-fronts falling off the wooden arm onto his lap. He threw them to the floor. "Come on then, what am I accused of this time?"

"Where were you Saturday night after ten?" Morgan asked, even though he'd been assured Flint was home.

"In here. Playing *Resident Evil*."

"If the cap fits," Shaz muttered.

"What are you on about?" Flint frowned and swiped his bony wrist over his nose.

"You're an evil resident," Morgan explained. "Got to be if you robbed poor old Wasti."

"I didn't rob Wasti. That Delia bitch got it all wrong."

"That Delia bitch is dead. Murdered. Abducted from the alley beside this house."

Flint shot up and paced, gripping his thinning hair. "What? You can't put that on me. I was in here, I swear."

"Like you swore you didn't empty Wasti's till and nick his fags?" Morgan quirked his eyebrows.

"You fucking cheeky n—"

"If you call him the N-word," Shaz interrupted, "I'll arrest you."

"All right, dickwad then," Flint said.

"Still cruel," Shaz said.

"And he's still a cock, whatever way you view it." Flint flung himself on his bed, staring at the ceiling, hands behind his head. "D'you know, there were times in my bunk I dreamt of killing you, before I saw the light and put such musings behind me." He looked at Morgan. "You coerced Delia to say it was me who robbed the shop, you got her to point her finger in my direction."

"Hmm. There are times I've thought the same about you over the years an' all, except I did it from my nice warm bed while I was free. Now . . ." Morgan took two steps and grabbed Flint's vest. He hauled him to his feet and slammed his back against the door. "You can either fuck me about or tell me what I want to know. Someone killed Delia, and if it wasn't you, I want to know who it was. Don't mess me about. Tell me."

Flint shook his head. "I can get you done for this. Harassment with violence, that's what it is."

"Who's going to believe you?" Morgan twisted the fabric in his fist. "The minute I tell my colleagues you spouted racial slurs, no one's going to give you the time of day."

Flint held his hands up. "Listen, I don't know anything, all right? Ask Ingles, she'll tell you I was here."

"You might not have done it, but did you use another bloke's code or ask someone else to stab her?" Morgan was testing him, seeing if he knew a stabbing wasn't the method of murder.

"I didn't get anyone to do nothing."

"Anything," Shaz said.

"What?" Flint blinked, his cheeks getting redder by the minute.

"Forget it." Shaz poked through some documents on the TV unit. "You clearly didn't go to school."

"I bloody well did!"

Morgan bent close, so his nose almost touched Flint's. "If I find out you're bullshitting me . . ."

"I'm not. And anyway, what are you going to do, frame me again?"

Morgan counted to five in his head. The urge to punch him out was strong. "Now isn't that a good idea."

"Fuck you." Flint struggled to get away.

Morgan pinned him with his body. "Remember, I'm watching you."

Shaz came over. "And me."

"Bent coppers, the pair of you." Flint raised his hands and gripped Morgan's wrist. "Get off me, or I'll—"

"You'll do nothing." Morgan let him go and pushed him away from the door.

Flint staggered sideways and landed on the bed. "Police brutality or what."

Morgan chuckled. "If you think that's brutal, wait and see what I do next time I lay eyes on your scrawny arse if I find out you're lying."

He walked out, Shaz behind him, and climbed the stairs to bedsit twelve. A knock on the door produced an overweight bloke, chest on show, navy-blue trackie bottoms. His light-coloured hair was slicked back, wet, clouds of shaving foam over his cheeks and chin, raw meringue.

"Yeah?" he said, his teeth yellow amid all that white.

Morgan held his ID up. "DI Morgan Yeoman and DS Sharon Tanner. We need a word." Without waiting to be allowed entry, he pushed past the man and stood beside his bed with its smoothed quilt, probably a soldier's corners on the sheet beneath.

Rushford had taught him something then. It had also taught him to eat everyone else's leftovers by the look of him. Shaz came in, and the fella closed the door.

"Is this some kind of parole check?" he asked.

Morgan shook his head. "No. Oliver Elford, isn't it?"

"Yes . . ."

"Where did you go between ten Saturday night and two Sunday morning?" Morgan eyed the room. Neat as a bloody pin, no dust anywhere.

"Fuck." Oliver sat on the only chair by the window.

"Fuck indeed." Morgan sighed. "Deary me. Breaking curfew, eh? Even though Emma Ingles explained the rules, as did your probation officer."

"I needed to get out." Oliver rubbed his forehead. "It does my head in, being locked up. Can't go anywhere. I had this massive urge to be free, came over me all of a sudden, like, so I fucked it and went out."

"Where?"

"To The Tractor's Wheel for a few. They had a lock-in, but I didn't stay for that. I had three pints, then wandered outside, and the fresh air hit me. Felt more pissed than I had in the pub, and I can't remember how I got there, but the next minute, I was down the alley beside this place, waking up. That was at five to two."

The hairs rose on the back of Morgan's neck. "So, you're telling us, and expecting us to believe, that you left The Tractor's and flaked out in an alley?"

"Yeah, because that's what happened."

Morgan huffed out a breath. "Right. Going along those lines — let's just say we believe you — did you see a woman standing on the corner under the streetlamp when you left at ten?"

"What, that dark-haired bird, the one on the game?"

"Yes."

"I did as it happens. Once I'd got down the road a bit, I glanced back, and she was talking to some bloke in a red car."

Morgan's hackles went up. "Why didn't you tell this to the officers who came round yesterday?"

He recalled Oliver's name being on the whiteboard, the info beside it saying he hadn't seen a thing. And why hadn't Emma Ingles mentioned he'd gone out until Morgan and Shaz turned up?

Maybe Jane and Nigel hadn't thought to ask.

Fuck's sake.

"Because I knew you lot would think I'd killed her," Oliver whined.

"So why tell us now?"

"You're a big bastard, scary. You're frightening me."

"What, by just being here?"

"Yeah. Plus, you look like that fella in Rushford, the one who beat me up."

"Right . . ." Morgan didn't need to employ the same tactics here as he had with Flint. Oliver would roll over and offer his belly any second, the wimpy shite. "So, this red car. Get the make, did you? The number plate?"

Oliver shook his head, his man boobs wobbling. A blob of shaving foam landed on a nipple. "No. It was just red."

"Four doors? Two?"

"I don't know."

"The driver. See him?"

"No."

Jesus Christ. "Okay. So, you can't even remember going down the alley. Pointless me asking if you saw the woman that time, or her bag, so what *did* you see when you woke up?"

"Oh, I saw her bag. I was tempted to nick it but remembered the shit I'd be in if I did and got caught. I don't want to go back to prison."

"You weren't bothered about getting caught by going out, though, were you?"

"No, but . . ."

"So you left the bag where it was."

"Yeah."

"And you didn't think it was odd that it was there? You know, some lady's handbag, on the ground, when you know a woman had stood on the corner earlier and it could be hers."

"My head was all over the place. Fuzzed by the drink. I promise you, I didn't do anything to her. Those coppers came round, and that was the first I heard she'd been offed. Then there was the news. I don't own no blue snake."

Morgan closed his eyes for a moment. Having a go at this prat because the local rag had printed the specifics wouldn't help matters. Still, the need to wallop the fucker came over him. He clenched his fists by his sides.

"If your fingerprints are on that bag," Morgan said, "because we'll have them on file . . ."

"I didn't touch the bloody thing, I swear."

"So you say. Forensics will tell." Morgan didn't think this was their man. He was too . . . well, he just wasn't the type. "We'll be in touch if anything crops up, and someone will be round to take a proper statement off you, not the 'didn't see anything' bullshit you gave our colleagues." He moved closer to Oliver and pointed. "Don't break curfew again, got it?"

Oliver's whole body wobbled. "I won't. I'm telling you, I won't."

"Make sure you mean that, otherwise, I'll be back round here so fast . . ."

"Shit. Okay. Yes, I get it."

"And buy a bra," Shaz said. "Because you bloody well need one."

"I can't help having tits." Oliver covered them.

Morgan sighed. "For fuck's sake, this isn't a body-shaming visit. Do me a favour and take that muck off your face." He wanted to see Oliver properly without the shaving foam.

The man swiped it away, and Morgan imprinted his features into his mind, plus took a picture with his phone.

"Right. We're off."

They left, waving to Emma on the way out. Morgan couldn't be arsed asking her why she hadn't mentioned Oliver going out to Jane and Nigel. He'd get the gist of things when he next spoke to them.

In the car, they laughed a bit too hard about what had happened in Flint's bedsit. Sometimes, suspects got to you, and showing them who was boss tended to take over. In Morgan's case anyway. He couldn't imagine Jane Blessing stooping to such lows.

"Did you see Flint's *face* when you gripped him up?" Shaz said.

"Yeah, well, he had it coming. I wanted to cross the line and punch the bastard but held off at the last minute."

"I'd have turned a blind eye if you had."

"Hmm." Morgan drove off, asking himself why she'd do that.

He'd slipped up back there at Flint's. He didn't usually manhandle people while Shaz was with him, although she'd probably guessed he resorted to any means necessary when she wasn't there, considering he'd had a few complaints lodged over the years, all successfully swept under the carpet. "I want to go and see Delia's father again."

"Why?"

"He appeared like a bad bloody penny for her mum's money when she died. My grass told me. Maybe he thought she was lying when she said there wasn't any. He could have bided his time, waited for Flint to get out so the finger pointed away from him."

"Killing your own daughter is a bit much, though, isn't it?"

Morgan shrugged. "People do it. Money is a big draw, and besides, he left the family home when Delia was about two, so he hasn't got emotional ties to her."

"We spoke to him yesterday, though."

"Briefly, and I know that, I was there." An eyeroll laced his words, and he regretted that. "But he was off. One of the weird ones we talked to. And we didn't really have a proper chat, did we. All we had time for was a visit to all her family and friends, telling them what had happened and asking them where they'd been at the time."

Val hadn't been in when he'd called on her, though, but she always went to her mum's on a Sunday, so that hadn't come as a surprise. Morgan would get hold of her soon, but if she knew something, she'd have texted him.

Uniforms, plus Nigel and Jane, were part of that questioning process, visiting some while Morgan and Shaz dropped in on others. At least there hadn't been a mother to tell, her being gone already. He could only hope, if Heaven existed, that Delia was with her old dear now.

"I get you," Shaz said, "but his alibi checked out. He was in The Tractor's Wheel all evening, and they had a lock-in. Maybe he saw Oliver in there." She reached into the glove box and took out a bag of Scampi Fries.

"Really? Now?" Morgan have her the side-eye. "You'll stink."

She shoved them away again. "But I didn't have any breakfast."

"Your problem. Like I've told you before, get up earlier. And I *am* going to be picking you up of a morning, you know. I wasn't joking."

"You're a wanker sometimes."

"Thought you loved me."

"I do but . . ."

"And you don't need to stick up for me every time someone says bad shit. I appreciate it, but I can handle myself."

"I saw that."

"What, with Flint?"

"Yeah." She elbowed him. "You're lucky it was me with you. Imagine if Jane was there. She'd have reported you, the brown-noser."

They continued in silence, nothing more to say. Morgan knew what she'd meant. She'd keep quiet about his method of gathering info. He hadn't expected anything else. She was on the cusp of being that way herself, he sensed it.

He turned on to Elderflower Mead and parked outside number six. The street, a scabby affair, told an immediate story. People down on their luck, old mattresses and fridges in the front gardens more often than not, cracked paving slabs on the paths, weeds reaching for the non-existent sun from their homes in the fissures. Delia's father's place was no different. Dirty red front door, windows in need of a wash, and the curtains hung from some kind of wire, visible as it bowed from the weight of the material. No wonder he'd been after money. He probably wanted to buy curtain poles.

They got out of the car. Roger Watson appeared at the window, drawing the curtain back. He scowled then disappeared, and the front door opened, revealing the man who'd walked out on his little girl without a backward glance.

"What do you two want?" He scratched his arse. "Bit early, isn't it?"

"Inside," Morgan said.

They gathered in his gross living room, cats everywhere, their fur clustered in balls on the carpet. The place hadn't seen a good clean in years, and Morgan's skin crawled, same as it had yesterday. Roger limped over and sank onto the saggy sofa. A puff of animal stench wafted up.

"Come to tell me her body's been released, have you?" Roger's ashen belly peeped out between the hem of his dirty black T-shirt and his eighties satin shorts, shiny red with a white trim.

These things were still available to buy? Christ.

"As we said last night, she won't be released for a while yet." Morgan breathed through his mouth.

"She's just evidence to you, isn't she." Roger grabbed a packet of Superkings off a manky cushion and lit a fag. Smoke shrouded his face. "Nothing more than evidence."

"Like she was to you?" Morgan cocked his head. "Delia was just evidence you'd fathered her. You didn't give a toss about her."

"Not true. Her mother wouldn't let me see her."

"Fuck me, you live in the next street." Morgan shook his head in disgust.

"You could have applied for a visitation order," Shaz said.

Roger shrugged and blew smoke out. "Yeah, well, I didn't."

"How did it go when you saw Delia after all those years?" Morgan asked.

"What do you mean? Last time I saw her, she was two." Roger splayed his legs.

The alarming visual of his saggy bollocks peeking around the shorts seam left a bad taste.

"No, you visited her when your ex-wife died. After money, so the story goes." Morgan shoved his hands in his pockets.

"Says who?"

"Delia."

"How? She's fucking *dead.*"

"Before then, you prat." Morgan wanted to grip him up like he had with Flint but resisted. "How well do you know the landlord and the regulars in The Tractor's?"

"What's that got to do with you?"

"Everything if they're lying for you." Morgan moved to the window and shifted the curtain across. Some woman had come out to wash the glass in her front door. An excuse, he reckoned, because this lot down here sensed the police a mile away.

"You saying I wasn't in the pub?" Roger asked.

Morgan shrugged. "CCTV will let us know. Someone's on that job." He turned to face him. "So if you weren't there, you might want to say so now, before we get too far down the road."

"I *was* there."

"Did you see this man?" Morgan held out his phone, the photo of Oliver on the screen.

Roger laughed. "Yeah, drinking pints like they were going out of fashion."

"Notice what time he left?"

"I did. Before last orders. I know this, cos I counted how many drinks he had — four — all inside an hour, and I thought he was more than half cut when he staggered out." He paused. "So when can I go into Delia's place?"

This bloke was an out and out bastard.

"What?" Shaz shook her head. "Are you seriously after going in there and having a dig about?"

"Someone's got to deal with her stuff, and I'm the next of kin, the one who needs to do it."

"Not in her documents you're not," Morgan said. "She's got someone else down to deal with her things if something happened to her. She must have known, had a sixth sense, that you'd roll up again with your begging hand out, or maybe, because you didn't have anything to do with her, she didn't act like you existed."

"Who's she picked?" Roger ground his fag out on a saucer.

"I won't be answering that. So, if we watch the CCTV from The Tractor's, you'll be seen leaving it *after* Delia was abducted, yes?"

"Yeah."

"Good, because if you're not on it, you really don't want me on your doorstep again."

"What are you going to do, duff me up?"

"Don't be silly. I'm a copper. We don't do things like that." Morgan glanced at Shaz.

She smiled. "Suggesting such a thing is ridiculous."

"Is that all then?" Roger stood. "Only, I've got a bacon sarnie to make."

Morgan left before he did something he wouldn't regret. Roger was a piece of scum, but Shaz was right in asking why they'd come round here again. Like with Oliver, Morgan didn't think Roger was their man, but someone was, and he'd find them eventually, and when he did, they'd better hope he wasn't alone.

Lines would be crossed if he was.

CONFESSION

I've been a right rum bastard in my time, apparently a weird little kid, always up to something. I hadn't thought about what I'd do when I grew up until Mum and Dad died. My brother, Phil, took over my care, and I ended up selling his drugs. There are some paths you can't reverse on, just continue onwards, hoping for the best. Sometimes, the best never happens.

—Gary Flint

CHAPTER FIVE

Crapping his pants, Flint had watched the detectives drive away. What should he do? He hadn't killed Delia, no way, and he *had* turned over a new leaf in Rushford, like he'd told them, but those coppers, they thought: *Once a criminal, always a criminal.* That wasn't the case here. He'd worked hard educating himself inside, and them thinking he was the same man who'd walked into the prison didn't sit well.

He could hardly blame them, though. He'd been a dick in his younger days, wanting shit for nothing, and getting a job was a laugh, something only dickheads did. He'd rather have pilfered stuff than earn money to buy it, but now he'd seen the light, as it were. If someone robbed him now, he'd be well upset, so why had it been okay for him to do it?

Flint slid his finger over his phone screen. His brother, Phil, had bought it for him, sending it via courier the other day. Flint had one hell of a time trying to work out how to use the thing.

He was going to have to speak to Phil, see if he'd organised for Delia to cop it. If it was him, why hadn't he done it while Flint was inside? He'd had fifteen long years to kill her, yet someone had chosen to do it now, when Flint could get the blame.

Bloody hell.

He jabbed at Phil's contact icon and waited.

"Who's this?" Phil said, all mean and whatever, his usual voice for those he didn't know or like.

"Gary. Didn't you put this number in your mobile?"

"Fuck me, bruv, you could have warned me with a text you were going to ring. Sorry I haven't got hold of you yet, been a bit busy. There's this bint with a nice rack on her, and I've been caught up playing with it the last week. Besides, thought you'd like to settle on the outside in peace until you got used to it. Things have changed since you went in. Smartphones, all sorts."

"I noticed." The lack of care from Phil got on Flint's nerves. In all the time he'd been inside, Phil had only visited twice, and getting him to talk on the phone for longer than two minutes had been a miracle. "Delia's been murdered."

"Yeah, heard something about that."

Flint gritted his teeth. "I've had Yeoman sniffing round with that bitch of his, wanting to know where I was Saturday night. I was here, thank fuck, but I don't need them on my arse."

"Not my problem, mate. If you will go and get caught . . ."

"What are you saying?"

"Next time, put the balaclava on *before* you steal."

"I'm not into that anymore."

"Right, and my knob hasn't been exercised lately. Pull the other one."

Flint closed his eyes. Held his breath then let it out. "Is this anything to do with you? Delia, I mean."

"Is it fuck."

"It's just that you said you'd get her back one day."

"Yeah, that was in the beginning, but then you went all righteous on me, told me not to bother, so why would I spend money on getting a hitman? Cash down the drain. I'm worth a few bob but I don't waste it."

"Do you know who did it?"

"Nope. Like I said, I had a rack entertaining me."

"Can you find out?"

"Why don't you?"

"Because I've got a curfew for six months and can't be seen doing anything dodgy, not that I would now."

Phil sighed. "I'll put the feelers out but won't promise anything."

"Cheers."

"Whatever. Got to go. Don't contact me, I'll contact you, save your number and whatnot."

"Right. So no brotherly chats in the meantime then?"

Phil laughed. "Why change the washer on a tap that doesn't leak? Laters."

Flint stared at his phone, the CALL ENDED message laughing at him on the screen. No wonder he'd turned to crime, having the family he did. None of them kept an eye on him or cared what he got up to. Even Mum and Dad hadn't bothered with him much while Dad sold hooky gear out of his car boot and Mum stood watch, ready to whistle if a copper came along.

What sort of role models were they?

He stared outside, to where Delia had stood on the corner. He'd resisted going out there, thinking the police had put him in Halfway House as a test, to see what he'd do with her living on the lane. And anyway, like he'd said, he wasn't into bad shit anymore, so he wouldn't have gone out there to ask her why she'd dobbed him in.

So, if he hadn't killed her, and Phil or his crew hadn't, who the hell had?

He needed to find out. He wasn't taking the rap for this. Even though he had an alibi, that wouldn't matter to Morgan. Flint also had one for robbing Wasti's crappy little shop, and that hadn't made a blind bit of difference. All right, it *had* been him going in there with a toy gun, but that was by the by.

He was in deep, an easy scapegoat.

He just had to hope Phil found out who'd strangled her.

Flint released a wry laugh. Strangulation with a snake. It fitted. Delia *was* a snake, slithering through the long grass, waiting to bite him with her venom. And if Flint *had* murdered her, he'd have stabbed the bitch. Five thousand, four hundred, and seventy-five times.

One jab for every day he'd spent inside.

CONFESSION

Having the responsibility of bringing up your wayward little brother wasn't something I thought would happen, know what I mean? I'd expected to bury my parents, just not so early, and to have the care of a kid who went off the rails before he'd even got his train fully on the fucking track . . . I wanted no part of it, but duty called. It was what Mum and Dad would have wanted. Sometimes, you did stuff because you felt you had to. A bit like when I popped someone or smacked the shit out of them with a claw hammer in the early days. Suppose you could say I was wayward, too.

—Phil Flint

CHAPTER SIX

Phil Flint knocked on Val's side door. While he'd had fun with the bint who had nice tits, he'd always had a thing for Val. He got bored easily with the others, see, and anyway, Val was the main stem of the grapevine around Pinstone, and while he was meant to have been narked back then about her helping Delia to frame Gary, she was a good shag, a kind woman, and not someone he was prepared to keep away from.

She opened the door, her pretty face going pale. Probably thought he was here for a bust-up now Delia was gone. Well, she was mistaken, wasn't she, and he'd soon put her right.

"What do you want?" She clutched a tea towel, white, red stripes, and some bubbles from washing-up clung to the back of one hand.

"What do you think?" He placed a foot on the step. It could have been seen as menacing, considering what he did for a living. He wasn't averse to ordering someone to beat the shit out of people if they didn't pay up. Perks of the job. Kept his crew fit. The thing was, that life was wearing thin.

Val blinked. "I don't want any hassle. You told me I was okay, that you were glad Gary got put away."

"I was. He's a dick and needed reining in. Nothing's changed. Got a spare hour?"

She sighed. "You're meant to book a slot."

"I know, but I fancied a bit, and I was down this way. Need to ask the residents a few questions."

"About Delia?"

"Yeah. Got to show willing. Gary asked me to find out who killed her."

She glanced up at the side of the house opposite.

Phil looked over his shoulder. "Old Florrie being a nosy cow again, I see."

Val tutted. "Get inside, you."

He strode past her into the kitchen, smiling, and flicked the kettle on. He liked a cuppa before he did her. It always made him feel like he was right at home, not here to pay a prostitute. He convinced himself, after he left the money on the table and they went upstairs, that she wanted him here and they were a couple. When she offered him a biscuit, that was it, fantasy complete.

Stupid, the things you told yourself. Val wasn't interested in him, not in that way. Since her old man had walked out, leaving her with a baby, she'd sworn off having a permanent man. Told him so that time he'd asked her if she fancied giving up the game and trying her luck with him.

She'd laughed, thought he was joking.

He wasn't. The candle he held to her . . . well, it burned brightly, always would, the wax forever melting, the wick sturdy beneath the flame. He filled his days shagging younger birds to forget her, and once a week, he came here and played pretend.

It got him through.

She locked the door, took two mugs out of the cupboard. "I only found out earlier. You know, about what happened."

Phil lounged on a dining chair. "Yeah, nasty business."

She spooned sugar into the mugs. "Was it you?"

"That's the fifth time I've been asked that, second time today, and I expect Yeoman will make it a sixth, coming round to bully answers out of me."

"He'll be here at two." She checked the clock then poured boiled water.

"Got anything to tell him?"

"No, but I want to know what's going on. I'm in the same line of work as Delia, don't forget. What if some nutter's got it out for the likes of us? It's common knowledge what goes on in this house."

"You wouldn't have to do it if you'd take me up on my offer. You'd never have the risk of Karl finding out either. Wouldn't have to be Yeoman's grass so he looks the other way regarding what amounts to a brothel, albeit with only one woman working in it."

She took milk from the fridge and added it to the mugs. "Turn the knife, why don't you. I wasn't ready for a relationship back then, wanted to make it on my own, and this, what I do, is handy and pays well."

"That many years is a long time by yourself. I should know."

"Don't make me laugh. You've got a different woman every night."

"Not the one I want, though. They're just a fireplace for my poker, whereas you, you're the bee's knees."

She stirred the tea. "Pack that in. Anyway, imagine us two together and Yeoman coming round on the regular. I'd be asked to grass my own fella up."

"I'd give up the business for you."

"My arse."

"It's a nice one. I'm quite partial to it."

Val sighed and handed him his drink. "Like I said, pack it in." She sat opposite. "Besides, you love the money too much. There's no way you'd drop your business. It'd mean you wouldn't live the lifestyle you've become accustomed to in that big house of yours."

"I've got savings. More than enough to last the rest of our lifetimes. The house is paid up."

She blew on her tea then sipped. "Drugs are that much of a lucrative deal then?"

"You know they are."

"Hmm."

He took a swig. Val always made a good cup of tea. The right shade of brown, the right amount of milk. Fuck, he reckoned he loved her.

"So you don't know anything then?" he asked. "Delia never mentioned anyone was after her or owt?"

"No. Last I saw her was Saturday night. She was out on the corner. Before that, it was probably Wednesday when I went up the other end to Wasti's. She came over as I got to my gate and had a natter. Seemed happy enough."

"Well, someone wasn't happy with *her*."

"Could have been a difficult punter."

"Which is why you need to stop." He thought about the proposition he'd come up with regarding her. She'd probably shoot him down, but what the hell. "I've got a deal to put on the table."

She stared at him with those lovely brown eyes of hers, and he all but melted, like that bloody wax.

For shit's sake.

"What's that then?" She frowned. "If you're going to ask me to sell drugs to the customers, you can get lost. I said no to that before, and I—"

"Nope, I wouldn't do that. I only asked last time to bump up your wages." He took a deep breath. "Here's what I thought. Me, your only customer, as and when I fancy nipping round—and yes, I'll text beforehand. I'll pay you a grand."

She laughed, throwing her head back, sobering quickly. She must have realised he was being serious.

"A grand? What's that, monthly? I can't survive on that, even if Karl moved out, which he's mentioned doing."

"A week." He let that sink in.

She gawped, no doubt asking herself if she could handle him a few times a week and not just once. They had a good old workout together, like they couldn't get enough of each other, and she'd admitted once, she only fucked him like that. She even let him kiss her.

So she felt something for him, despite her mouth saying the opposite.

"You're serious, aren't you." She lowered her mug to a coaster.

"Yep. And I won't shag anyone else either." This was as close as he was going to get to having her exclusively. Later down the line, once she saw he was a decent bloke at heart, at least in their relationship, she might agree to them being proper permanent. He'd move her into his swanky pad, and they'd be well happy.

"I'll think about it," she said. "Fancy a Wagon Wheel?"

CHAPTER SEVEN

Morgan pulled up outside The Tractor's. While the landlord, Terry Collins, had promised to sort the CCTV and drop it off, he hadn't as yet. The man had said it would take too much time to find what they needed yesterday and he'd do it after lunchtime closing. That was Sunday. Now was Monday, noon, and Morgan wasn't prepared to wait any longer.

The Tractor's sat at one end of Mulberry Lane between Wasti's shop and Lenny's Laundry, while Halfway House stood at the other. He imagined Oliver Elford rushing up the road towards the pub, desperate for a drink, for that freedom he'd mentioned, while at the same time hoping he didn't get caught. He was nothing but a cockwomble, needing a sense of normality, no one to be worried about.

It was time to see if he'd told the truth about where he'd been.

Morgan and Shaz stepped inside, past the actual tractor's wheel mounted on the wall in the porchway. They entered the pub proper, the chatter loud, laughter ringing out. Half the people on this estate didn't work legally, and most of the men spent the day in here. A brisk trade then, lots of customers dotted about, some eating the Deal of the Day, fish and chips with a side of mushy peas, all available for a fiver with a free soft drink and pudding thrown in.

It reminded him they hadn't eaten.

"Fancy a bit of grub?" He led the way to the bar, the stench of beer strong.

Shaz stood beside him. "Yep, seeing as I wasn't allowed the Scampi Fries."

"Oh, give over." He ordered them cheese and chips, Shaz's favourite, and a couple of orange juices.

The landlord limped up to them once the server, Heidi, had walked away. "Sorry about not getting the footage to you. Had a bit of a problem yesterday afternoon."

"What's that then?" Morgan rested his hands on the bar. "Something more important than finding a killer? Not many things rate higher on that scale in my book."

"Broke my bloody toes, didn't I."

Morgan grunted. "That's inconvenient."

"It bloody is, considering I had to bottle up afterwards while in pain. Once our Heidi came in, she took over, but I had to go and rest up, put my foot on the pouffe. Took some strong painkillers, and they knocked me out. It ruddy hurts when a crate of beer lands on your foot."

"So that was yesterday," Morgan said.

"Yeah."

"What about today? Plenty of time to sort it."

Terry nodded. "I did sort it, just couldn't get down to the station to drop it off. Can't drive with wrecked toes, can I."

"Is your phone on the blink?" Morgan accepted the orange juice from Heidi. "Cheers."

"What?" Terry's forehead scrunched up. "Of course it isn't."

"Then why didn't you ring me?"

Terry nodded. "Now there's a fair point." He shrugged. "Well, you're here now, so no harm done."

There would be harm done if the pub was empty and Morgan and Terry were by themselves. A punch in the nose would've added to his broken bones, and Morgan would feel a hell of a lot better.

He had to stop thinking this shit, imagining hurting people. He'd lose his job if he wasn't careful, but things were bad at home, and . . . No, that wasn't an acceptable excuse. He should behave. Do things like Jane Blessing, by the book.

"Go and get the footage then," he said.

"What, bring my computer out here?" Terry's mouth gaped.

"No, put the footage on a memory stick." Morgan sipped some juice.

Shaz coughed, probably to hide a laugh.

"Oh. Didn't think of that. I'll do it now, while you're eating." Terry hobbled off, through a door at the end of the bar.

"If he had a brain he'd be dangerous," Shaz said.

Yeah, and if I had free rein, I would be an' all.

He gazed about at the punters. A massive black bloke sat at the bar, staring Morgan's way. He'd swear it was the fella on Nigel's screen in the incident room, the one Morgan had thought resembled his cousin. He squinted to see him better, check if it was his kin, but nope, the eyes weren't right. To close together, too piercing.

"Got a problem, mate?" Morgan asked him.

"Why would you think that?" The geezer sounded hard as nails.

"Because you're staring." Morgan showed his ID. "Want to have a serious chat?"

The man quickly looked away.

"Didn't fucking think so," Morgan muttered.

* * *

Morgan and Shaz sat side by side in the incident room at her desk.

"Got something, have you?" Jane called over.

"The footage from The Tractor's," Shaz said.

While she watched it, Morgan swivelled his chair to face Jane and Nigel. "What went on at Halfway House yesterday?"

Jane raised her eyebrows, as though he didn't have the right to ask such a thing. "We spoke to all twelve residents, and none had anything to say. It's on the whiteboard. The only one who seemed remotely iffy to me was Flint, which is why I reminded you of him this morning."

"So neither of you asked Emma Ingles whether a resident broke curfew?" Morgan glared at her.

Jane reddened. "They all said they'd been inside, so there was no need to ask her."

"In your opinion," Morgan said, "when protocol dictates we must ask that sort of question to all concerned, especially the woman who runs a house of bedsits rented by ex-cons."

Jane glanced at Nigel, lifting her hand in a help-me-out gesture.

"I did say, Jane," Nigel said.

Morgan bristled. "Oh, so you 'did say' but didn't do it yourself, Nigel?"

He shrugged. "We were strapped for time, guv."

"So some woman gets killed beside the house, and your excuse is you were strapped for time?" Morgan got up and walked to the whiteboard. He grabbed a black marker and prepared to write as he spoke. "Oliver Elford left the premises at ten p.m. and returned at two a.m. He went into The Tractor's, so he said. Fancied breaking the curfew for some time out, the poor criminal bastard." The marker squeaked against the board. "He then left after a few pints and walked back down Mulberry Lane, to Halfway House, where he promptly blacked out in the alley, waking to find Delia fucking Watson's handbag on the ground."

He turned to stare at them. They stared back, agog, faces flushed, the skin beside Jane's left eye twitching, as though she held in some snarky retort.

"But that's okay," Morgan went on, "because Oliver told you he'd stayed in, and you were strapped for time."

Nigel held his hand up. "Guv, I—"

"Fuck off." Morgan sat beside Shaz. "I'll keep that info away from the DCI this time, but best you watch yourself in future."

It wasn't lost on him, how he disregarded his own failings, an 'it's all right for me but not you' attitude he needed to shake.

To stop himself giving them another spout of sarcasm, he watched the screen.

Oliver entered and left when he'd said, as did Roger Watson. The pathologist, Lisa Uppington, had informed them the time of death was close to midnight. Both men were in the clear, and so was Flint, unless he'd climbed out of a bloody window to avoid using his code.

No, at the start of their chat, Emma Ingles had mentioned them being alarmed, like the doors.

"Rewind it again so we can see if we recognise any other customers leaving about the time she was abducted," he said.

Shaz clicked the back arrow. "I didn't spot anyone we know."

"First time round we were concentrating on Elford and Watson."

She pressed PLAY, and Morgan leant forward to focus. It was the usual suspects from the lane, plus a few from Regency Road, the street running parallel to Mulberry. While they'd spoken to the Mulberry residents closest to the pub yesterday — uniform doing door-to-door — they hadn't done everyone, nor Regency or Elderflower.

"Come on, let's go and speak to this lot." Morgan rose. "I didn't see any of them in the pub earlier — the ones on the footage are the night crowd."

Shaz sighed. "We've been down Mulberry."

"I'm on about Regency. We'll have a proper word with that knob there." He poked at the still of Phil Flint. "He was nowhere to be found yesterday when we needed a chat."

He glanced at the clock on the bottom taskbar. Shit, he was due round Val's. He'd message her, say he'd be late.

He went over to Nigel. "Found anything on Delia's social media yet?"

"Haven't had the chance. You had us out in the field yesterday, and so far today we've been searching for suspects already on file."

Morgan nodded. "True. Social media now." He turned to Jane. "Switch to Shaz's computer and comb over that footage, right up until Sunday, early hours of the morning, in case someone left the pub and returned after dumping her."

She sighed. "I dislike CCTV."

"And I dislike members of my team being awkward, but there you go, we can't always have it all our own way." Morgan strutted out.

He had to, else he'd say something cutting.

CONFESSION

Sometimes, if DI Morgan Yeoman hangs around after giving me a telling off, I struggle to keep my feelings to myself. One day, if he isn't careful, I'll say something nasty, but I'm a professional and hope it never comes to that. I prefer for him to think of me as a nosy, awkward little cow, a do-gooder, a blot on his complicated landscape, one filled with the anger festering with regards to that trampy wife of his.

There's a lot he needs to learn, like going about his business without all and sundry knowing what he gets up to. I've seen the reports, the complaints about him, heard the rumours, and if he just employs a little finesse, he can get exactly what he wants, no one else any the wiser. The problem is, he wears his angst on his sleeve, there for all to see. It's better, I find, to hold your cards close to your chest. People don't know what you're about then. Until it's too late.

—Jane Blessing

CHAPTER EIGHT

Jane huffed at what Yeoman had just said. God, he thought he had the right of it at all times, but he didn't. She was rubbish when it came to CCTV, and he knew that, so why put her on it when Nigel did a better job? Yes, she knew how to conduct herself with that task, but her mind always wandered no matter what training she'd had in the art of concentration.

And this case . . . Bloody hell, it was close to home. Too close. She'd known Delia, *and* that silly little gang she'd run around with ever since they'd been kids. What they'd all done . . . Jane couldn't think about it without a red mist coming down, suffocating her. Delia deserved what had happened to her, but Jane had kept that to herself. No one knew, even back then, that their antics had affected her to the point that she'd become a policewoman just to stop people like them bullying their way through life.

She hid her true self behind a sharp facade, one that cut people to the quick if she had a mind to turn her acid tongue on them. DI Morgan Yeoman really ought to watch out. She'd teach him a lesson during this case, one she'd waited a long time to produce.

Sometimes, you just had to keep your feelings to yourself until the right time presented itself. He may not know it yet, but this case was personal to him, but he'd find out soon enough. Probably go round roughing people up in the meantime.

Why couldn't he conduct himself like she did?

"Bloody social media," Nigel grumbled.

Now, Jane liked Nigel. He was a decent sort.

"Want to swap?" she asked.

Nigel lifted his eyebrows at her. "What, you'd go against Morgan's orders?"

She almost let out a manic laugh. The amount of times she'd gone against Morgan without his knowledge was classic insubordination and career suicide. Look at that time she'd dressed all in black, tights over her face, and 'bumped into' a certain criminal out the back of The Tractor's, giving him a nudge — with the sharp blade of her knife — to come in and admit he'd assaulted that woman down Rectory Road after a few bevvies.

It hadn't worked with Gary Flint, though. He was the first one she'd had the courage to threaten, and he'd laughed at her, said for her to piss off back to the rock she'd crawled out from under.

Horrible man.

"Hmm. What Morgan doesn't know won't hurt him," she said. "We can switch back if he swaggers in."

Nigel chuckled. "Swaggers. You're not wrong there."

No, she rarely was.

CHAPTER NINE

Phil sat in his living room in Regency Road. His place was three two-up, two-downs knocked together, snapped up cheap with a little persuasion from him. The former residents either side of his original home didn't like people turning up at all hours, rapping on his door. They might have been a bit scared of him an' all, but that was okay, that sort of thing got the job done.

He hadn't bothered going to speak to the Mulberry lot after he'd been to Val's, no need now. He gazed out of the window, thinking about her. That Wagon Wheel she'd offered . . . Did that mean she felt the same way he did, underneath all the rubbish she spouted, the kind that said she wasn't ready for a relationship? Had she secretly wanted him all this time but found it too hard to trust? After all, she'd given that ex-gimp of hers a boatload of it, yet he'd left her anyway.

Shit like that cut deep and affected your ability to move on.

She'd told him she'd let him know by tomorrow if she'd take him up on his offer. A grand a week was nothing to him, and he'd spend more than that if it meant he got her to himself. If she refused him, he'd double the fee, see what she said then, but a thousand quid every Friday wasn't to be sniffed at. She'd live handsomely on it, *and* without the sticky paws of her customers all over her. Had to be a bonus, didn't it? Especially with him buying her presents as well. A nice bit of Jimmy Choo here, a Tiffany & Co there.

She'd be his princess for life.

They weren't getting any younger either. While mid-forties wasn't considered old these days, what about when it came to fifty? Five more years, and the likes of the nippers around here would see them as ancient.

Christ, where had the time gone? One minute they'd been young and free, and the next—

Shit. Yeoman's car pulled up outside. Phil had been expecting it, would be a twat if he hadn't, but nevertheless, he didn't want to talk to that man today. And as for his sidekick, well, she was a sarky little cow. This was going to spoil his post-sex glow.

He got up and opened the front door in the hallway that was once his old front room. He'd had wide stairs built, dead centre, and the houses either side formed wings. He was the earl of the manor, so why the fuck not? Four double bedrooms, the smaller two from before now en suites, the original three bathrooms still there but done out modern. A palace for his queen, who lived directly behind, and if she was in the living room with the light on and the curtains open, he got a good view of her. Not that he was perving or anything.

"Afternoon," Phil said. "No, it wasn't me. No, I don't know who killed her. And no, you can't come in." He had a stash of gear in the kitchen cupboard for his runners to collect later and didn't need these two nosing around.

"So you knew what we wanted to ask," Yeoman said. "Probably because it's the standard line of questioning in your world."

"What, to do with murder? I don't kill anyone."

"Not you, maybe," Yeoman muttered.

"Having a dig, are you?" Phil asked. "Coming to a load of dead ends and taking it out on me?" He checked his watch. "Oh. My, my. You'll be late."

Yeoman glared. Yeah, Mr Detective was due at Val's soon. It pissed Phil off, this copper going there, using her for info, but if she agreed to take that grand, she wouldn't need Yeoman's cash anymore. Unless she liked grassing and carried on doing it. Phil wasn't about to stop her, as long as she didn't grass on him.

"We weren't even here to see you." Yeoman jerked his head at the street. "Other people to see, more important than you. Anyone would think, with you coming to open the door, that you wanted to stall us — or chat to us so it seems like you're innocent, a good boy helping with our inquiries."

Phil didn't even offer them a reply. He shut the door. Fuck them. He knew something, but now Yeoman had been rude, he wasn't going to say anything. Val had let something interesting slip about who'd visited her that morning, which meant Yeoman was wasting his time in Regency Road.

The place he needed to concentrate on was Mulberry Lane.

CHAPTER TEN

Delia hadn't been able to sleep since the robbery last week. Each night she dreamt of multiple people in balaclavas, coming towards the door marked PRIVATE with guns raised. They pulled the triggers, all at the same time, and the bullets ripped through the steel door, the square of glass, and pierced her shaking body. She screamed. Wasti fell to the floor, riddled with holes seeping blood, and the moment she attempted mouth-to-mouth, she woke up.

She knew who all the balaclava people represented. They'd lived in her past and continued into her future. So long as she kept her mouth shut, she'd be left alone.

Her nerves, shot to pieces, grated every time someone knocked on the door. It was usually only Val or Heidi, her friend from work at The Tractor's, but it shit her up just the same. As had the note that had been pushed through her letterbox.

TELL ANYONE IT WAS ME AND FLINT, YOU'RE DEAD.

What? Someone else was involved with the robbery? How could she tell anyone if she didn't know who the second person was? At the time, she'd guessed Flint had got into a car but assumed he'd *driven it away.*

He must have told the driver she'd seen his face, so not only did she have to avoid him, but an unknown as well.

She'd stuffed the note into an envelope and put it in the sideboard drawer so Mum didn't see it. The last thing Mum needed was hassle. She was having trouble with her heart, had to take tablets for it, and the doctor had advised her to remain calm as much as possible.

Well, she wouldn't be calm if she knew someone had threatened Delia, who hadn't even told her about the robbery and what she'd seen. Delia had given a statement to the police at the shop, surprised at Olga walking in a minute or so later. They'd gone back down the lane together after, and Olga admitted to seeing a man in a balaclava getting into a white car.

"Don't tell anyone," Delia had said. "Just don't."

If she did, Flint would think it was Delia, and she couldn't risk that.

The letterbox flapped again.

"Who's that now?" Mum said from the living room.

"I'll go." Delia, in the kitchen, stared down the hallway at the front door.

The fuzzy figure of someone walked away, lit up by the security light in the porch eaves. The flash of a brake light in the darkness, then a car moved off.

This had happened last time a note had come.

She walked to the door and crouched to pick the paper up off the prickly brown mat. Her hand shook, and she unfolded the note, her chest seeming to go hollow.

I SAW YOU WITH OLGA. SHE'S BEEN WARNED, TOO. STAY QUIET.

"Delia?" Mum called. "Who is it?"

Delia jumped. "Nothing. Just a pamphlet for Slimming World."

"Stick it in the bin then."

"Will do." Skin clammy, Delia rushed up the hallway, and she'd swear eyes were out there, watching her through the front door glass. She stuffed the note in the envelope with the other one and hid it in the bottom of the drawer this time, beneath a stack of placemats and napkins.

Olga had been warned. About what? She hadn't seen anything, she'd told the police that, just a man in a balaclava. Or had she seen the second person and had decided to keep her mouth shut, too?

Delia closed the kitchen door and, despite their agreement years ago not to speak to one another unless they absolutely had to, like when she picked up veg, she rang Olga. She needed to know what was going on.

"Hi," Olga said. "You just caught me coming in from the garden."

Olga was weird the way she pottered in the greenhouse at night. She said it calmed her to listen to music on her headphones while she planted and whatever, the shimmery moon watching her through the roof.

"Um, about the robbery," Delia said.

"What about it?"

"I've, um, I've had a couple of letters from someone, and they're—"

"Just keep your bloody trap shut. You don't want to mess with them."

"Them?"

"Bugger . . ." A pause. "Take it from me. We saw nothing, got it? We didn't have this conversation either. Don't talk to me about this in front of Val or anyone, for God's sake."

The line went dead. Delia stared at her phone, blinking, trying to compute what she'd just heard. 'Them.' Flint had an accomplice, that much was obvious, and from the sound of it, they'd definitely got to Olga, too.

Delia threw up in the sink.

"What's the matter, Del?" Mum shouted. "Got a dicky tummy? There's some Andrews in the cupboard. That'll sort you out."

No, Mum, nothing will sort this. Nothing.

CHAPTER ELEVEN

Morgan had lied by telling Phil they hadn't called round to see him. Of course they had, but he wanted the prick to be taken down a peg. The gobby git thought he knew everything, so Morgan insinuating he wasn't important enough to speak to had done the trick. Phil closing the door told him that. While the man was suspected of being a drug dealer and apparently had blokes on his payroll available for hire in the killing department, nothing was ever proved. Uniforms kept an eye out, though, ready to catch him. Phil ran a car lot as a front, paying some dweeb or other to manage it for him.

The residents of Regency Road were a mixed bunch. Some were happy to talk to them throughout the afternoon, others not so much. Those who frequented The Tractor's were obliging, transparent in their movements, seeming to hide nothing. Some who didn't pay taxes to HMRC via PAYE or self-assessment took handouts from the state while working for cash on the side. It was obvious, especially with their nice cars and fancy house interiors, and speaking to coppers meant they might get caught.

One such man, Billy Price, lived at number one, his home in front of Halfway House and with a direct line of sight to Olga Scrivens' place, the woman who sold veg from her back garden. Billy, now he was the local odd job, painting, gardening, you name it. Rumour had it he'd done Phil Flint's houses up, although if the social came round asking, he'd deny it. He was on Universal Credit along with his missus, Sherry, and according to the lies that tripped out of his mouth when asked about it, he'd never dare fiddle the taxman.

Morgan usually collared him for a chat every so often. Like Val, Billy was in contact with a lot of people. While men told Val their business after a quick tumble in the sheets, Billy earwigged to conversations as he worked away in folks' houses. The pair of them gave good info, and Billy had agreed to talking to him so long as it wasn't made known he did it. Fine by Morgan. He could do discreet if he had to.

The thing was, he had Shaz with him today, so he'd have to chat to Billy in an official way. The man himself was stacking scaffolding poles into the bed of his lorry and nodded at their approach.

"Mr Price, we need a quick word." Morgan stared at him to let him know it was all above board, that they mustn't speak like mates but copper to civilian. "We're talking to every resident in Mulberry, Regency and Elderflower regarding the murder Saturday night, early hours of Sunday. Delia Watson. Did you see anything? Hear anything?"

"Nah." Billy tugged his ear. Their arranged signal. He'd seen something all right but wouldn't talk with Shaz there.

"What about Sherry?" Morgan asked.

"Dunno, step in and ask her." He waved at his open front door.

"Go and see her, will you?" Morgan said to Shaz.

She went inside, calling, "Mrs Price? DS Sharon Tanner. Can I have a word?"

Billy closed the door to. "That fucking veg woman. Go and see her."

"*She* did it?" Morgan fiddled in his pocket for Billy's payment. Forty quid should do it.

"No, but whoever was at her house Saturday night might have."

"How do you know?"

"I was watching out the back." He flushed. "I've always liked Delia, know what I mean? I like seeing her on the lane."

Morgan shivered, repulsed at the thought of people ogling her. "Right, whatever floats your boat, you creepy tit."

"I don't watch her like *that*."

"Whatever. So what did you see?"

"Someone leaving Olga's."

Morgan held his hand out to shake Billy's hand. "Man or woman?"

Billy palmed the money. Put it in his pocket. "Couldn't tell. They were just a dark shape."

"What else?"

"They left Olga's and got in their car. Might be a red one. Then they backed up, parked in front of Delia. Spoke to her. She walked along the alley. I came in then, so no idea what went on down there."

"Why didn't you get hold of me about this?"

"Because if Sherry heard me on the phone, she'd ask why I was perving on Delia and get all offended, like."

"As you do. So why not phone me when you were alone — like you were when we turned up just now?"

Billy glanced over his shoulder then back to Morgan. "She's been on me like a rash, hasn't she, since someone told her I was doing some bird a favour with my pork sausage. I wasn't, I was fixing the pipe under her sink, but Sherry's having none of it."

"I'm not a fan of getting involved with domestics." Morgan had enough of that shit at home. "So next time you can't ring, message me."

"Sherry would ask who I was texting. Suspicious mare. I reckon she's been watching me through the window since I stepped foot outside the front door."

"Fuck's sake." Morgan stepped back at Shaz coming from the house.

She shook her head in consternation. "She heard a scream but thought it was someone larking about after coming out of The Tractor's. To be fair, that's not a bad assumption."

Morgan sighed. "Right, and she didn't think to call it in once there was news of a murder?"

"No." Shaz rubbed one of her drawn-on eyebrows. It didn't even smudge. "Are we done here?"

Morgan nodded. "Yeah. I'll drop you back at the station. We may as well call it a day." He didn't plan on doing any such thing. He had Val to see, then Olga.

They left, and in the station car park, Shaz got out.

Morgan leant across to speak to her. "Can you let Prickly Knickers and Nigel know to go home? If they've found anything significant that needs dealing with today, message me and I'll sort it."

She nodded and walked away, saying over her shoulder, "Still quarter to eight in the morning?"

"Yeah. I want you waiting on your doorstep."

She raised a hand. "Whatever, Trevor."

He smiled and drove off, back to Mulberry Lane. Val let him in via her side door, and they sat in her kitchen, drinking tea. Someone had been eating Wagon Wheels, the wrappers left on the table beside the money he'd put there.

"What have you got for me?" he asked her.

"Nothing. I only found out she was dead this morning after my Karl left for college."

"How? Who told you?"

"Olga, the veg woman. I thought she'd come round for her money, but she hadn't."

Olga, eh? Interesting. "What did she say?" He sipped some tea.

Val shrugged. "Just the stuff she'd read in the news. Something about a blue rubber snake. Strangulation." She paused and shot him a look that showed she was more than fearful. "Am I next?"

Morgan felt for her. It had to be frightening, doing what she did. He'd never held with the view that women who sold themselves were scum. They had to make money like everyone else, and if they had to use their body to do it, it was better than starving, living on the streets, nowhere to call home.

He rubbed her arm. "There's no indication at the minute she was killed because of her profession."

Val sighed, relief most probably. "It's all so worrying." She bit her bottom lip.

"It is. How did Olga seem?"

Val tilted her head. "Her usual self. Why?"

"No reason." He wasn't about to let her know Olga needed a good talking to. He couldn't allow her to warn the woman, tell her he was on his way. It'd give her time to make up a story.

"I paid her for the veg, she had a cuppa, then she left."

"How well do you know her?"

"Well enough to give her my work schedule. While she's a bit of a recluse, I trust her."

That was noteworthy. Maybe Olga didn't know her guest had gone down the alley with Delia after they'd left her house. The woman might be innocent in all this. He'd soon see.

"Any other news?" he asked.

"Nothing springs to mind."

"I need you gossiping, out there talking."

"I know, but I've got some things to think about at the minute."

"Which are?"

"Well, Delia for one, and the idea that I might be giving up my job."

He almost snorted. Val, not running a one-woman knocking shop? "Blimey. Never thought I'd see the day."

"I'm tired. Then there's Karl to consider."

"Thought you said he'd be moving out, so he wouldn't catch you at it anyway."

Morgan hadn't told Val yet that her son had got in with a bad crowd. Karl had met them in college. All of them were into drugs and causing a fuss in the pubs in town. Morgan was meant to be having a word with him, scaring him off going down the shitty kind of roads the others travelled on. He hadn't got round to it.

Val sighed. "He is, but . . . I'm still tired."

"Suppose you won't have any tips for me soon then, seeing as the men won't be round, telling you their business."

"You supposed right."

"Sounds like you've made your mind up. What will you do to make money?"

"I'll find something."

"Well, let me know if you need to be off my books, although the gossip you pick up on could still come in handy." He stood. "This Olga. Nice sort, is she?"

"Why?"

"I need some veg. Might as well ask her while I'm here. Is she likely to be off with me, or is she kind?"

"The kindest, although she gets moody sometimes, especially when Delia used to bring up the robbery. She'll be glad of another customer, regardless."

Probably, but not one like him.

He walked down the dark lane, keeping an eye out for red cars. Only one, a Mazda, parked halfway along. If the person who'd visited Olga owned it, why bother driving a few yards to get there? He wrote the license plate down and sent a message to Amanda Cartwright, the nighttime desk sergeant, for her to run it through the system.

At Olga's door, he turned his back to it and surveyed the area. To his left, the alley then Halfway. Opposite, houses. He couldn't see down the alley from here, but he *could* see the corner Delia had always stood on. Now he had his bearings, he swivelled and knocked on the door.

A shuffling sound to his right, then a figure appeared at the side of the house. Olga. She squinted at him in the darkness, and he took his slim torch out of his pocket and shone it at her. She blinked, enhancing the wrinkles beside her eyes. In her forties, he reckoned.

He held up his ID with the other hand. "DI Morgan—"

"I know who you are. Everyone does. You'll have to come round the back. I'm in the greenhouse."

She walked off in a pair of lurid pink Crocs, and Morgan followed, illuminating the path ahead. A large greenhouse stood partway down the garden, lights on inside, so he pocketed his torch. She entered, and he trailed her, stopping in front of a tomato plant on a wooden table littered with compost.

She snatched a tomato off the vine. "Are you here about Delia?"

"That and some veg."

"A fiver for a bagful, pot luck as to what you'll get." She yanked off another tomato. "I didn't see or hear anything going on in that alley, so it's pointless you being here."

"I hear you had a visitor that night who left about ten."

She paused with her hand hovering over some leaves. It shook slightly. "Not me. Must have got me mixed up with someone else."

"Red car. Whoever it was backed up after they left your place and spoke to Delia."

"That'll be her up the road in her Mazda. That's the only red car down here."

"Who's 'her'?"

"Cheryl, number nine." She moved along to fetch a paper bag for the tomatoes. "Want some of these?"

"Please." He liked them with a bit of grated cheese and salt in a sandwich. "So no one was here, you say. Saturday night. Coming to see you."

"Nope." She collected a carrier bag off a hook on the edge of the table and put the tomatoes in. While she bustled about getting a cabbage and a few other things, she said, "The only people who come here are for the veg. And the postman or delivery men. Sometimes Val. She has something she gives me every week, but that's none of your concern."

"Self-employed, are you?"

She hesitated for a split second. "Don't need to pay tax under eleven grand."

"That's what they all say, but if you also get dole . . ."

"Are you here to arrest me?"

"No."

"Shut up then." She turned her back to pick some runner beans. "Damn it, I forgot to take some to Val." She'd muttered it, as if to herself.

"I'll do it on my way back to my car."

"Right." She spun and thrust the carrier at him. "Fiver, like I said."

He fished in his pocket for his wallet. Gave her twenty.

She narrowed her eyes at him. "I'll not grass for fifteen quid, if that's what you're thinking by giving me extra."

"I don't expect you to. It's a tip." *But not that kind. More of a 'tell me the truth before you get into shit' kind.*

She busied herself getting Val's runners. "I liked Delia. Didn't have a problem with her." She blinked a lot while she said that.

"I never implied you did."

"Just saying. In case that was the next question." She reached for another paper bag.

"But a birdy told me you got funny if she ever mentioned the robbery."

"What robbery?"

"The one at Wasti's fifteen years ago."

"Fuck me, that's old news."

"So you didn't get funny with her?"

"Why would I? And to answer your next query, I don't know who'd *want* to kill her either."

"Sounds like you slipped up there, saying 'want'. Like someone you know *had* to kill her, didn't *want* to."

"Don't talk rubbish." She handed him Val's bag. "She's already paid for those."

"Right. Where were you Saturday night? In the house or out here?"

"Out here." She jammed her hands on her hips and nodded to a set of large headphones. "Had my music on, which is why I never heard anything. I was planting seeds, and that's why I never saw anything."

"What about the men from Halfway? Know any of them?"

"No." She maintained eye contact. "Except Flint. Everyone knows him."

"They do. The armed robber at Cost Savers." He waited for a moment to catch her expression.

Blank.

"Okay, well, I'll be off then." He held the bags up. "Thanks for the veg."

"Hmm."

He walked out, across the garden, sensing her gaze boring into him. She'd seemed tetchy, wired, but that could just be her way. Then again, Val had said Olga wouldn't be off, she was kind, so maybe she just didn't like coppers.

Or maybe she had something to hide.

CONFESSION

I wasn't destined for this life, one where I'm selling veg like some elderly lady, acting older than my years. I was supposed to pass all my exams with flying colours, but it hadn't worked out that way. Anxiety played a big part, regarding the worry of getting caught for things I hadn't meant to do, and I'd flunked them good and proper. Now, I'm what they call a recluse, the mad widow who potters about in her greenhouse and rarely speaks unless she has to. There's a reason for that. If I start talking, the truth might come out, and then where would we be?

—Olga Scrivens

CHAPTER TWELVE

Olga shook from head to toe the moment Yeoman walked down the side of her house, out of sight. She rushed inside, through the kitchen and into the lounge, cursing herself for forgetting to take off her mucky Crocs. The cream carpet was filthy now.

At the window, she peered out. He walked towards Val's, the peachy streetlights playing on his dark hair and the shoulders of his black suit. The back of his white shirt collar appeared as a sinister, straight smile, and she shivered. Fanciful thinking, that was all it was, his visit giving her the collywobbles.

She should have known someone would have spotted her Saturday night caller. Those in Mulberry Lane were a load of nosy parkers. No one ever came round her place that late, the veg pickups mainly done during the day. Maybe Flint had seen the red car backing up closer to Halfway. He'd probably told the copper all about it, trying to get Olga in the shit. Get her back for seeing his accomplice.

Among other things.

The day of the robbery, a stout gust of wind had attacked her umbrella, tugging it inside out, revealing him exiting, and she'd watched him look back inside Cost Savers then shoot off to a waiting car. He'd got in the passenger side, and the vehicle had sped off. A white Fiat that could only belong to one of Phil's runners, and he was handy with a knife, so on the witness stand in court, she'd made out she hadn't had time to see the car, just a man in a balaclava, then she'd wrestled with her brolly, too interested in that to notice anything else.

I promise to tell the truth, the whole truth, and nothing but the truth had been a big fat lie.

There were so many things she couldn't tell the truth about.

She'd had warnings from the drug runner ever since. He sometimes stood over the road in front of her house and stared, the ominous bastard. Other times, he posted notes through her letterbox. Fifteen years this had been going on, and she hadn't said a word, and as for the other thing, she'd zipped her lips for a lot longer. Surely he'd believe by now that she wasn't going to say anything.

But no, he'd turned up Saturday night in a red car he'd been given by whoever, and bloody well pushed his way inside. He had a job for her, he'd said, and she wasn't to tell anyone about it. Once she'd done it, she was free.

She'd agreed, and what a stupid cow she was, because look what had happened. Delia was dead. Olga had lied, said she hadn't heard or seen anything, but she had.

God, she'd never forget it. The thud of Delia hitting the ground in the alley. A figure dragging her down the far end, away from Mulberry. Her bag left there, telling the story of abduction.

Olga shook the memories away and continued her perusal outside.

Yeoman knocked on Val's door, dropped off the bag of beans, then walked to Cheryl's house. What was he doing there? Olga twigged then. The red car. He thought it might have been Cheryl talking to Delia the other night.

Well, that suited the situation, but Cheryl would undoubtedly say it wasn't her, so there was an outstanding issue of another red car Yeoman needed to find.

Olga's heart missed a couple of beats, and it sent her squiffy. She lowered onto a chair, hand to her chest, and closed her eyes, leaning her head back. She trusted no one down here except for Val, and telling her what she'd been asked to do meant Yeoman would get wind of it. Val passed him information. She must have been the 'little bird' he'd mentioned.

Olga couldn't trust anyone now.

She sighed and opened her eyes.

He stood there, the man who owned the red car.

And in his hand? A knife.

CONFESSION

It's all working out nicely. Clockwork springs to mind. The payday will see me right. I'll be free once this is all over. And won't that be nice?

—Goat

CHAPTER THIRTEEN

This stupid bitch had come to the end of her veg-laden road. She'd had that copper here, must have told him what she'd seen and heard, ignoring the warnings.

Seemed she didn't value her life.

"All right, Olga?" Goat smiled.

She stared up at him, fearful, going by her expression, her features stretched, eyes wide, the red-veined whites on show. "W-what do you w-want?"

"Came for a little chat. I saw you had a visitor. Good job I was in the area really. Was about to leave you another little note and saw Yeoman on the patch. I parked out of the way. No sense in letting him see me, is there. I stood in the alley and watched through the hedge. Couldn't hear anything once you went into the greenhouse, though."

She clutched the chair arms, her nails dirty from all that mud she fucked about with. "I didn't tell him anything."

"Is that right. Well, I've decided I can't trust you, like I couldn't trust Delia." He held the knife up and inspected it. "Pretty, this. Got a nice glint to it."

"Please." She got up, sidling to the window, wary.

As she should be. Goat and a blade only meant one thing, everyone knew that. He was paid to use it. He hadn't been the one in the alley Saturday night, he'd just sat in his car and sent Delia down there, making out someone else would be along in a second to have a quick shag against the wall. It wasn't like he could make out it was him needing a service, Delia wouldn't go with him, although Val did on occasion. Once the other person had come into view at the far end down the side of Halfway, giving him a signal, he'd driven off.

Job done, money in his back pocket.

He'd bought a few pairs of Calvin Klein pants with it. Bloody comfy they were an' all. Oh, and a set of new knives. They were Japanese efforts, so sharp they'd slice through most things.

Like Olga's neck.

She tried to scoot past him, but her ankle turned in her stupid Crocs.

He should stab her just for wearing them.

"Where d'you think you're going?"

"I-I need a drink. My mouth's gone dry." She wrung her podgy hands.

Christ, she's put on the beef. Must be all that comfort eating since her old man carked it.

She trembled. "Can I just . . . ?" She indicated the space beside him: "Can I go past, please?"

"Go on then. Make mine a tea while you're at it."

She bounded off, and he followed her into the kitchen, closing then locking the back door, his gloves preventing any fingerprints. While she put the kettle on, he drew down the blind over the glass and did the same to the one up at her window. Neighbours, they were nosy fuckers, weren't they, the ones behind in Elderflower Mead no different to those in Mulberry and Regency. The streets on this estate were prongs on a comb, regimented lines, and everyone seemed to know everyone else.

Olga's hand shook, and she spilled the sugar she'd spooned from the canister.

"Three for me, because I'm not sweet enough," he said. "*If* you can manage to get them in the bloody cup." He sat at the table and watched her, just to ramp the tension up a bit.

Not that he needed to. She was already shitting bricks.

He liked the idea of that, always did when on a job.

"So, what did the pig want if he wasn't here to ask about Delia?" he asked. "You live right where she was taken from. Stands to reason you'd be questioned." He drummed his fingers on the table beside the knife he'd placed there.

She turned her back to him, lifting the kettle.

Smart move. He couldn't see her face to tell if she lied.

"Believe it or not, he nipped here for some veg. For him, plus he had a bag of runner beans for Val."

He nodded. Yeoman *had* carried a bag, he'd give her that. " Rightio. He was here for a while. Seven minutes and fifteen seconds. Long time just to get a few carrots or whatever."

"Was he?" The tinkle of a spoon against china told him she stirred the tea.

"He was. Those carrots, by the way. Nice." He'd had them with lamb chops and roast potatoes, a splosh of gravy on them.

His wife was a good chef. She had to be, as he couldn't abide shit food. He'd sent her on a cooking course, and it seemed she had a knack for it. Tonight he was having spaghetti carbonara to go with the red wine he'd stolen from someone's cellar after he'd knocked the rat bastard out cold for fun.

Olga faced him, a cup in each hand, one still with the spoon in it.

Maybe she planned to burn his skin with the back of it. The shock he'd get would buy her some time, but not enough. He'd still grab the knife and whip it into her before she'd had the nous to take a step back. Stupid cow. She had no idea how much training he'd had. Years of it.

A killer for hire, a man employed to scare people, had wicked reflexes. He might not look like he had ninja capabilities, and some might mistake him for an accountant or something, but appearances were deceptive.

Olga came closer. Made it to the table. She popped the drinks on the shiny surface, and he puffed out a quiet breath, adrenaline flouncing though his system. He'd anticipated her throwing the boiling tea at him then running through the lounge for the front door, seeing as unlocking the back one meant she was still too close to him, and she'd fumble in her fear, upping her chances of him getting up, despite the searing burn, and stabbing the hell out of her from behind. The thing was, more than one or two stabs meant you cared, that it was personal.

He tended to stick with one.

She sat opposite, staring at the knife.

He picked it up. Admired it again so she got the message. "These cost fifty quid apiece."

"Nice if you can afford them." Her voice had wobbled. "I got mine in a wooden block, twenty pounds for six in Argos."

"Bet they're not as sharp as mine."

"They do the job."

He knew what she'd really said. She had knives close by so could stab him back.

Not if her neck gaped in a scarlet smile and she was on the floor dying, though.

She probably hadn't thought of that.

He sipped some tea. "Tasty brew."

She ignored hers, the one with the spoon. Twiddled her thumbs. Darted her eyes here, there, and every-bloody-where. "Is there something else you need me to do, is that it? I thought with me keeping quiet that was all you wanted. That's what you said, wasn't it? What we all said?"

"Providing you did as I asked, yeah. I don't know if you reneged on our agreement, though, do I? I mean, that piece of filth you just entertained could come to my door, arrest me later while I'm enjoying my carbonara, and I don't like my meals interrupted by people with the stench of bacon about them. Funny, because my missus, she puts bacon lardons in carbonara, so you'd think I'd avoid eating it, wouldn't you."

She gaped at him as if the bacon ref had gone over her head, then seemed to get what he'd meant. Yeoman equalled pig.

She blinked. "Did he rush out of here? Did he look like he was running off in a hurry to arrest you?"

He'd give her that one an' all. No, Yeoman had ambled, that was the word for it.

"Fair enough." He sipped again.

"So, what *do* you want?" She stared at him. "We agreed never to speak again, yet here you are, back in my life."

A bit bold for his liking, that stare and what she'd said, how she'd said it. Rude.

"Just checking in on you." He put his cup down. This table would get ruined if she didn't use coasters. He insisted his missus bought them. No point in buying nice things if you intended to wreck them. "So I've got nothing to worry about, eh?"

"I don't know. He mentioned the robbery." She blushed, as though blurting that hadn't been on her agenda. Her mouth had run away with her after all.

No wonder he hadn't ever trusted her. Under pressure, she fucked up.

"Now why would he do that?" His blood heated.

"I have no idea."

"Are you sure?" He got up and walked behind her. Held the knife to her quivering neck with its two chins. "I'd keep really still if I were you. One slip . . ."

"I'm not a grass," she ground out.

"That's nice to know, saves my arse, but you're going to have to grass to me if you don't want to feel this steel biting your throat."

"Oh God, oh God . . ."

"He doesn't help anyone, Scrivens, you should know that. Look at how your old man met his end after the robbery. One minute that husband of yours was on his ladder washing that tart's windows for a living while she was in London shopping in Harrods, and the next . . ."

She gasped. Shook. Let out a pathetic whimper. A tear spilt. "It was *you*?"

He laughed, a full-on throaty bugger. "What, did you think he slipped like old Gammy Leg did, darlin'? Nah. That was the verdict, accidental death, but he had a helping hand."

God, he hadn't thought of Gammy Leg for ages, some bloke who lived in Elderflower, a man they'd taken the piss out of as kids every time they'd seen him.

"Oh shit . . ." She sucked in a big breath. "Why?"

"Because you living alone was easier. You might have been tempted to confide in your husband about certain things if he'd stuck around." He gripped her hair in a tight fist. "With him gone, there's no one else here to tell me to sod off if I came to make sure you kept quiet about me and Flint at Wasti's, among *other* things, and you know what I'm talking about."

"But I've never told anyone about you *or* about what we did. All this time . . . Oh God. I didn't say a word."

"Hmm." He licked his lips. "Problem is, I don't believe you anymore, and it doesn't matter whether I do or don't, because someone else wants you gone."

The slice was quick, the blood a rich burgundy sliding in a sheet down her throat onto her white T-shirt, obscuring the flowers on her stupid apron.

All in a night's work, but it wasn't over yet.

CHAPTER FOURTEEN

Morgan drove towards home, frustrated Cheryl had been at bingo Saturday night and had gone in her car. He'd got Amanda Cartwright to check CCTV outside Bustin's Bingo. She'd rung him back after tracing the owner of the car. He didn't bother telling her he'd already found out who it was. Cheryl was clean, had never been in trouble with the police, and to be honest, after he'd spoken to her, it was obvious she hadn't killed Delia. Gutted, that was one way of describing her, someone unable to believe her neighbour was gone.

It'd take her a while to come to terms with it.

He sighed at the sight of his home in the distance. It stood in its own grounds behind a wrought-iron security gate, tall, thick hedges either side, pruned to within an inch of their leafy lives. There was a smaller gate to come and go on foot. His wife, Lydia, had insisted on the security, although it was hardly that when the side gate didn't have a padlock. He'd mentioned having one, but she'd brushed it off, which was suss if she was worried about intruders. Some said she had ideas above her station, that she was nouveau riche so her airs and graces didn't match who she really was underneath.

Morgan had to agree with that. She acted vulgar at times, thought Daddy's money, which he'd acquired through the sale of his company, granted her the right to do and say whatever she pleased. She reckoned being loaded meant being a haughty bitch.

A lot of the time, Morgan wished she'd never been given such a vast amount of cash. It had changed her into someone he barely knew. He preferred the old Lydia, who'd shopped on the sale racks in Primark instead of having clothing made to order.

Morgan still went to Primark, Burton if he was feeling generous.

He clicked the fob to open the main gates, and they swung back slowly. Useless bloody things if you wanted them to shut fast because of someone following you. She'd had them installed last year. A Peeping Tom had apparently copped an eyeful of her tits while she'd stood at the window in full view after a shower. Who did that? The old version of his wife wouldn't have exposed herself, but the new one, well, she said Morgan worked too much, didn't pay her any attention these days, so she had to get it from somewhere.

Yeah, vulgar.

He drove through and pressed the fob again. The driveway had old-fashioned Victorian lampposts along it, the light from them glinting on the windowpanes of the three-storey house, ivy creeping up to curl around the frames. He shuddered at the memory of the man who'd come to clean them fifteen years ago, falling off the ladder from the top floor and breaking his neck. Morgan had come home from a gruelling shift and found him, his body in an unnatural pose on the mint-green pea gravel. Lydia? At Harrods, and she'd rung to stay she was staying over in London for a couple of days until he'd arranged for someone to replace the gravel that had been 'tainted by that perverted man'.

Apparently, the window cleaner was the Peeping Tom.

And Olga Scrivens' husband.

Morgan hadn't interviewed her, seeing as the death had occurred at his house and was, for want of a better term, too close to home. Hence him not knowing her personality type when he'd visited her earlier. He'd been surprised, when he'd introduced himself, that she hadn't mentioned her husband dying on his property because she'd have been told the owner's name.

Morgan parked in front of the garage, taking a moment to brace himself. God knew what mood Lydia would be in. He was late back because of seeing Val, Olga and Cheryl, so Lydia would have something to say about it, no doubt.

Nothing new there then.

A deep breath, and he was in the house, the white-tiled foyer a bit like Phil Flint's, who might have modelled his place on this one, seeing as he'd come here before. Lydia had told him when she'd . . . well, when her mouth had run away with her that time. He'd gone round to Flint's, told him if he ever sold sniff to Lydia again, he'd have him.

"Can't prove it," Phil had said. "And anyway, I don't deal in drugs, I deal in cars."

Fucking bullshitting knob.

"Is that a masked man or my husband coming in?" Lydia called. "Only, if you're my husband, I might not recognise you anyway because you're not here often." She trilled out laughter.

Shit, she was high again.

He closed the door and leant back on it. Shut his eyes for a moment to gather his thoughts, his mettle. It was going to be one of *those* evenings, because she'd scored from somewhere, despite Morgan warning them all off. Flint's runners had agreed to steer clear, or so they'd said. Then there was Phil, who could be coming here anyway, unafraid of Morgan, the brazen twazzock.

Morgan didn't need this shit, not on top of a murder, and not in general.

"Your husband," he said and walked through the doorway to the right.

Oh. Her friend, Alice, sat beside Lydia on one of the cream sofas, the pair of them in pyjamas, pink silk, costing an arm and a leg, although like she'd told him, her spending was none of his business. It was her money, nothing to do with him.

Fine. He preferred to live off his wages anyway. Even paid her rent, half the bills, since she'd bought the house outright. Funny how when it had just been him earning, she'd been happy to ponce off him.

"Nice that you have company." He got ready to scoot into the kitchen and leave them to it.

"Well, I hardly ever have yours, which is why Alice is here so often, but then you wouldn't know, as you're always at work." Lydia tittered.

"Stop it." Alice nudged Lydia's arm.

"Dinner's in the dog." Lydia stared at him. Dared him to say something.

Her blonde hair had been done at the salon today — she'd said she was going. Acrylic nails with shiny, pearlescent gel polish shone beneath the light of the chandelier, something just as fake as his wife and the tits she'd purchased.

"Right." Morgan gave Alice a tight smile and walked out, down the foyer and into the kitchen with its marble this and that, its 'fabulous' fridge, and 'wonderful' built-in oven, and its 'beautiful' gleaming floor.

He hated all of it. Preferred a normal house with things a bit worn, lived-in.

"All right, boy?" Morgan clicked his fingers at his German Shepherd, Rochester, named by Lydia, even though she'd bought him as a birthday present for Morgan and it should have been his choice.

Good job the name suited him.

The hound padded over from his posh crushed-velvet bed in the corner and sat, paw up. Morgan fussed him, crouching to let the dog rest his head on his shoulder. Rochester was the only one giving him love in this house, and Morgan took whatever was offered.

"Fancy a walk to the Chinese?"

Rochester barked.

"Come on then, sunshine."

Morgan got the lead, attached it to the collar, and left via the rear door. He skirted the building, Rochester padding beside him, and plodded down the drive, weary of his private life, unsure what to do about it. He opened the small gate and jogged down the street, thinking of why, if Lydia was so bothered about perverts, she'd refused to have CCTV installed. She'd said they didn't need it.

Lying, that was what she did best since she'd taken up snorting shit up her nose. Hiding things. If they had CCTV, he'd see her dealer on it.

At the end of the street, he turned right, the row of shops lit up in the not-too-far distance. Outside the Chinese, he tied Rochester to a post and entered, planning to order a large spring roll and a chicken fried rice with curry sauce. He'd eat it out there on the bench.

"Hey, Mr Yeoman," Li Wei said, his eyes bright. His white chef's hat had a splodge of something on it, maybe soy sauce. "The usual?"

"Just mine."

"That's what I meant. The usual. You're always here for just yours."

Morgan hadn't realised it was that apparent.

Li Wei shouted in his first language through the open hatch, and one of the cooks raised his hand in acknowledgement. Morgan sat on the long seat beside the fruit machine with its flashing lights, legs spread, hands dangling between them. He stared at the floor, wondering how much more he could take of Lydia's behaviour — and why she behaved that way, meaning the money and drugs. After he'd questioned her that time, when she'd slept her coke binge off, and asked if she remembered telling him Phil supplied her drugs, she'd said, "Phil who?"

He had no proof, and the uniforms who kept an eye on the man hadn't reported seeing him coming to Morgan's place. Then again, they weren't on permanent surveillance, so their form of keeping an eye meant Phil slunk around unobserved for the most part.

It'd be loud at home later. Lydia loved music, especially the eighties, and she'd turn the volume up, encouraging Alice to dance, to get off her tits with her by snorting lines off the glass-topped coffee table once Morgan had gone to bed. Where she kept her stash he didn't know — he'd searched from top to bottom — and knowing it was in his home, enough for Lydia to get right in the shit over if she was caught in possession, and him questioned by the DCI, got on his last fucking nerve.

"Here you go, Mr Policeman," Li Wei called.

Morgan paid and left the takeaway, checking the bag. Li Wei had put a fork in there. Another one of Morgan's 'usuals' he'd been unaware of.

Fuck's sake.

Rochester didn't bother getting excited about walking again. He sat patiently while Morgan parked his arse on the bench beside the post. Seemed even the dog knew his habits.

He ate. He thought. He came up blank once more.

Maybe he'd talk to Shaz tomorrow if they got a quiet moment. She'd know what to do. He'd told her about the state of his marriage before, and she'd given him her usual answer, where she saw things in black and white.

"If you're unhappy, leave." She'd sighed. "If you don't want to spend the rest of your married life shackled to a . . . well, I don't know what she is. Alky? You said she's always off her face."

He hadn't told her it was from drugs, not vodka or wine or any number of alcoholic drinks Lydia could have chosen over the white powder.

Rubbish in the bin, he untied the lead from the post and walked round the back of the shops to the field. Torch in hand, he unclipped Rochester and let him have a run. Morgan's street butted against the field to the right, Lydia's house just about visible through the tall pines at the bottom of her garden.

Yeah, Lydia's house, Lydia's garden, and best he didn't forget it.

He walked one length of the field and back, mind half on Lydia, half on Delia.

Faint screams rang out, and his heart thumped. He stood with his head cocked to determine where they were coming from. His street. A whistle to Rochester, and he ran, the dog catching up and keeping pace beside him, no need for the lead. He made a left into his road, running, running, running so fucking hard his chest hurt and his food formed a boulder in his gut.

No more screams.

A car's brake lights came on ahead, the engine rumbled, then the slam of a door cut through the noise of his breathing sawing in and out. The vehicle sped off, and Morgan slowed at the small gate, then swung round holding the frame it was attached to, lunging through onto the drive. Rochester overtook him, gravel spraying, and bounded into the house through the door.

The open *front door.*

Fuck. Fuck!

Morgan pelted inside.

Blood spots on the white floor tiles, some scuffed from the dog's paws.

He rushed into the living room, stopping short in the doorway.

Lydia stood in front of the vast fireplace, gripping her no-longer-perfect hair with one hand, shaking, staring at the cream carpet.

Morgan shifted his gaze.

Alice. Sprawled out on the floor. Her throat slit with one slice.

"Lydia." Morgan swallowed.

She ignored him.

"*Lydia.*"

She turned her gaze to him.

"Go and get your stash." He stared at her, hard. "And flush it down the toilet. *Now.*"

CHAPTER FIFTEEN

Goat sped down the streets until he was far enough away to slow. He'd memorised where the CCTV was in Pinstone over the years until it was stuck in his brain. He wouldn't be spotted.

Two slices in one night with his Japanese knife. It wasn't a record, far from it, but he hadn't done two for ages, and the thrill was like nothing else. Fucking brilliant.

It was a warning, doing that bird at the pig's place instead of her own. A warning to Lydia, who'd been told by a neighbour years ago that he'd toppled the Scrivens bloke off that ladder, and he'd kept her in coke ever since, so she was reliant on him and wouldn't drop him in it — on top of that other thing she knew about. And a warning to Yeoman, not that he'd know it was one, that if he kept poking into that fucking Wasti robbery after all this time, his wife might well be next to land on the floor with a second smile.

The tittle-tattle neighbour had just happened to wind up dead.

Christ, he was hungry. Still, the spaghetti carbonara would fill a hole. Maybe he'd have some of that lemon cheesecake for pudding. His missus was brilliant at making those. She baked them in the oven, all proper, like, and the house smelling of good food always calmed him. He'd gone hungry as a nipper, his parents skint as arseholes, and had vowed when he grew older, he'd never have a rumbling stomach again.

It rumbled now.

Best he get home then, eh?

CHAPTER SIXTEEN

Morgan sent Rochester to his bed, ordered Lydia not to move, and cleaned the ghostly remnants of coke lines off the coffee table. He washed the wine glasses, shut the dog in the kitchen, and rang Amanda on the front desk, giving her details while he paced the part of the foyer that had no blood drips.

Deceased, Alice Baines, thirty-five.

Slice to the front of the neck.

Pulse checked; negative.

Intruder drove off in a vehicle, most likely a car or small van, unclear.

"Officers and SOCO en route," she said.

He ended the call and slid the phone in his pocket, moving to stand at the living room doorway. Lydia screamed then, maybe on cue, maybe because what had happened had only just caught up with her, or perhaps Morgan reappearing had shit her up. The sudden piercing noise was a jolt to his system, and he suspected it was wailed out for effect. Then she silenced, staring at Alice again like she had when he'd first come in.

Blood coated Lydia's fingers and the back of one hand.

Shit.

"Lydia."

No response.

"*Lydia*, step over to me, making sure you don't tread in any blood. That's it, nice and steady."

She came to him, hands up at her throat, as though she imagined her own had been cut and she wanted to hold the spliced flesh together. He visually scoured her for blood elsewhere. Some had drenched one cuff of her pyjama sleeve, but otherwise, the material was clean.

Had she been involved more than she should have been? That cuff being dirty meant some had dribbled down her right hand, the hand she'd use if she'd—

"What did you do?" He gripped the tops of her arms.

"He . . . he . . . made me do it."

"Jesus fucking Christ." Morgan let go of her and stepped towards the kitchen, spinning in his panic, whirling to face her. "Who?"

She walked to him, teeth chattering. "Can't . . . can't tell you."

"You fucking well can."

"I can't. I *really* can't." Her lips had lost a lot of colour.

"What did he make you do?" His heart hammered wildly.

"He . . . he told me to slice her throat from behind." She lowered her hand and stared at the blood. "Oh God, oh my God . . ."

"Why the hell did you do that?"

"If I didn't, he said he'd kill *me*."

"What was it, a robbery?" He scraped a palm over his head. What the hell had gone on here? From what he could tell, nothing was missing. No furniture had been knocked over, no knick-knacks littered the floor, no struggle.

And he could guess why she wouldn't tell him who it was. It'd be that ponce, Phil Bastard Flint. Why did she insist on protecting him? If she'd just admit he sold drugs to her, Morgan could haul his arse into the station. He'd get a warrant, search his house and the car showroom, have him bang to rights with the proof of his dodgy dealings.

"No." She shuddered. "He wasn't supposed to come tonight — he'd already been earlier to drop off my . . . he'd been earlier. But he turned up, right after you took the dog for a walk. Said he'd watched you leave — he thought you were still at work so was surprised to see you taking . . . taking Rochester out. Something about you looking into a red car?"

So whoever it is knows I'm gunning for Delia's killer. A local then? "Why was he here?"

"A warning."

"About what?"

"He just said it was a warning."

"How come Alice's body is there" — he pointed — "and not on the sofa where she was sitting the last time I saw her?"

"She got up when he came in, scared. Tried to back away when he started shouting."

"Shouting what?"

"Things . . ."

He wasn't going to get much out of her tonight. Her vagueness drove him mental.

"You stupid bloody woman." He shook his head, mind twisting with scenarios, latching on to whatever it conjured because she wouldn't give the real picture. "You've committed murder, do you realise that?"

A tear fell. Just one, and probably from self-pity. "I was forced. He—"

"Shut up a minute and let me *think*." One second. Two. Three. *Bollocks*. "Get that fucking pyjama top off." He'd said it now, had taken that first step in covering up for her.

She did as he'd asked. He snatched it out of her outstretched hand.

"And the bottoms." He took those from her, too, then stared at her. "Go upstairs and get your hands and neck washed. *Don't* touch anything on the way. When you've finished, clean the sink and taps. No one will take much notice up there if you tell them he only went into the living room. Do *not* use bleach, they'll smell it. Use that disinfectant with no scent, then dry the sink after. Put the wet towel in the wash bin — you can say you had a shower earlier. Do it. *Now.*"

She scuttled up the stairs, naked, and Morgan stared at the clothing in his hand. Taking a carrier bag from the kitchen, Rochester whining with worry, Morgan stuffed the pyjamas into it then went outside, checking through the wrought-iron gates for anyone watching from the house opposite.

No one. Why wasn't anybody out after hearing the screams?

He put the evidence in his boot. Where he'd dump it after that he didn't know, but for the moment, he had his wife to deal with, not to mention the coppers who'd be here any minute. SOCOs swarming the house. Uniforms up and down the street doing door-to-door, flies on the shit Lydia had created.

Back inside, he ran upstairs. Lydia cried while on her hands and knees, drying the shower tray in their en suite. She must have had one, although she'd been sensible and hadn't got her hair wet. Her pretty style from earlier was now a scrunched-up, messy bun. He studied it for signs of blood, but no scarlet marred the platinum blonde.

"Get new pyjamas on, quick," he said. "Coppers will be here in a minute, so listen carefully. This is how it went. You opened the front door, thinking it was me coming back with the dog, and he burst in — wearing a balaclava, understand? That way you won't be asked to describe his face."

She nodded. Sniffed. Wiped the bottom of the shower stall door.

"He went *only* through the foyer and into the living room, nowhere else. He told you to stay out of it, that he was there for Alice." That would send the police in another direction, poking around for who disliked her enough to kill her. "Then he slit Alice's throat, saying it was payback for something she'd done. It's important you say that bit. Are you listening, taking all this in?"

"Yes!"

"That was the only things he said, got it? He left, taking his knife with him, and drove away. I walked in. That's it, right?"

She got up, brushed past him into the bedroom, and took clean pyjamas out of a drawer. "This means I have something on you." She laughed, maybe from nerves, maybe from coming down from her high and the shock.

Morgan didn't find anything funny.

"No, love, I have something on you."

"What?" She paused in buttoning her top.

"Your other pyjamas. The blood on them tells a little story, and that story is you killed your best mate — you have blood on the sleeve. And the killer has something on you as well, because I can't see you running off to the kitchen to get your pink Marigolds before you took hold of that knife. Fingerprints."

She paled. "Oh God. You wouldn't tell . . ."

No, he wouldn't, but who knew what the intruder would do. "Don't push me hard enough to find out, and you'd better hope whoever that bloke was that he'll clean that knife in a dishwasher."

Footsteps tapped downstairs. "Hello? Morg?"

"On my way down," he shouted and stared at his wife. "That's Shaz. Get in bed. We'll say I just made you go there because you're in a state. Someone will come and speak to you, hopefully Shaz. I'll tell her what happened, the coverup version. *Don't* balls this up, Lyd. If you do, we're both fucked."

She climbed into bed, a lost child beneath the duvet.

His chest tightened, and it surprised him. Despite how he'd been feeling since she came into money, how he'd grown to dislike her, he must still care about her a little.

Fuck.

He left her and joined Shaz in the foyer. Thankfully, she had booties on and had placed evidence markers beside the line of blood spots while he'd been upstairs. He imagined the claret dripping from the knife as the man had walked through.

"What the fuck went on here?" she asked quietly.

Morgan told the story, and Shaz wrote it down as his statement. Like anyone was going to question him too closely anyway. He'd been at the Chinese, Li Wei could vouch for him, plus CCTV outside the row of shops would put him sitting on that bench. And Lydia had never done anything wrong before, so they wouldn't suspect her.

Then again, would the camera spot him going to the field? The time it'd taken him to walk up and down it with the dog, he could have gone into the house via the back garden, killed Alice, then left, running back through the field to go home the street way.

But there's no blood on my clothes. Don't panic.

"So she's in bed," he finished. "Will probably need to be sedated." *Plus, that'll keep her from opening her mouth.*

"Have you rung the doctor?" Shaz asked.

"No, she's got sleeping tablets." He turned to the stairs and shouted, "Lydia? Take a pill."

"Okay." Reedy voice, distant.

He beckoned Shaz to the living room doorway. "As you can see from the blood spatter arcs and castoff, the throat was slit from behind. Killer and victim facing the front of the house. Curtains closed, so no neighbours would have seen anything. Killer let her fall to the right. Lydia was standing by the fireplace, away from any mess."

"Hellooo! Anyone home?" Cameron Quinton, lead SOCO, said from the front door.

"All right, mate." Morgan managed a smile. "You'll need some evidence steps in here. Fair bit of blood."

"Rightio."

Morgan walked off to the kitchen to let Cameron and SOCO get on with it. Lisa would arrive shortly to do her pathologist thing, and she'd get a time of death, although that could be dubious as Alice was most probably still warm. Dead about twenty minutes, *he* could tell Lisa that.

Rochester whined again, and Morgan let him out the back so he could cock his leg.

Shaz came in. "So he didn't go anywhere but the hallway and the living room?"

"Nope."

"Stick the kettle on then, seeing as we won't poke about in here. I'll just nip up and verify things with Lydia, then it should be a case of filling out the paperwork and nosing about to see who would have wanted Alice dead."

"I can't do it." He flicked the kettle switch. "Too close. Same for you. Lydia's known to you in a personal way. You've had enough dinners over here to class you two as friends."

"I know. I'll phone Tracy Collier, shall I?"

Morgan nodded. The head of Serious Crimes in this area lived fifty miles away. He was supposed to report to her in all matters regarding any murder inquiries . . . but rarely did. She didn't like him contacting her, unless it was for a brief update, saying she had enough on her plate as it was. Which begged the question, why was she running the squads in the region? The woman was arsey, more often than not, and shirked her responsibilities in her role as far as he was concerned, but none of the higher-ups seemed to care so long as the crimes got solved. Still, she was stuck with this one, although he didn't particularly want her on his patch while he was working Delia's murder. Tracy might step on his toes, and he didn't like that.

Especially with this shite here, now.

Shaz walked out, going upstairs, and Morgan made them a drink, plus a few for the officers in the other room, who he'd spotted entering the house, SOCO in their protectives, their gloves and masks. Lisa had also turned up with her medical bag, raising her hand in welcome then vanishing into the living room.

Shaz came back a few minutes later. "She said what you told me."

Good. "Right."

"She's going to sleep. Took a pill."

"Okay."

"Tracy's on her way. Said she'd be here in a couple of hours."

He nodded and wandered out to the foyer and stood in front of the living room door. "Coffees are out here if anyone wants one."

Various "Cheers" and "Thanks" came.

Lisa knelt on an evidence step beside Alice. She held up her temperature gadget. "Within the hour."

"Yep." Morgan sighed. Of course it was within the sodding hour.

"This slice, the way it is . . ." Lisa's eyes narrowed over her face mask. "Familiar."

Morgan's guts rolled. "What do you mean?" Fuck, his chest hurt.

"This is about the tenth unsolved we've had where this particular flick is made at the end of the slice."

Morgan peered at the gaping wound. Shit. He hadn't noticed the shape of it until now, the lower edge the short, downwards line of a tick. Like Lisa had said, all unsolved murders, put down to some gang or other dishing out their form of retribution to rivals. If the bloke who'd been here was something to do with Phil . . . Phil would know Lydia killed Alice if his lackey reported back. Morgan couldn't go after him for this on the sly. Phil wouldn't know Morgan already knew what his wife had done, and Phil would relish telling him, then watch Morgan to see what he did about it.

See if he dobbed his missus in.

He hoped Tracy Collier didn't succeed in apprehending the killer, although her solve rate was top-notch, so Morgan had no hope of keeping a lid on this.

"This'll probably go unsolved as well then," he said, his tone even.

"Different knife this time, though." Lisa leant forward to scrutinise Alice's neck. "Sharper blade, I'd say. A much cleaner swipe."

His phone rang. Amanda's name flashed on the screen.

"Yep?" He cuffed his sweating forehead.

"I know you're deep in it at your place, but you're needed elsewhere."

"Why?"

"Olga Scrivens has been found dead."

"*What?*" His nerves gained serrated edges on top of the ones that were already there. "Who by?"

"Emma Ingles from Halfway House discovered her."

"What was *she* doing there?"

"She was down the side of the building putting rubbish out and noticed Olga's front door open."

"So she went *in*?"

"Yep. Found her in the dining area of the kitchen. Slit throat."

His legs jolted, weakening. "Blimey. Right. On our way." He stuffed his phone in his pocket. "I have to go. Lisa, Cameron, we've got another body."

They both stared at him, eyebrows high.

"I'll go there with Shaz now, secure the scene," he said. "Collier's coming here to this one."

Cameron nodded. "Right, I'll get Henry over to you. He can head my second team until I'm finished here, although this is pretty cut-and-dried. The blood speaks for itself."

Thank the Lord.

Lisa stood from her perch on the evidence step. "I'm happy for this body to be collected whenever it's released from this scene. There's nothing I can see here that points to anything other than what went on." She looked to Cameron. "Just give me a bell when you lot have finished, and I'll send the van over."

Cameron bobbed his head. "Will do." He took his phone out. "I'll give Henry a buzz now. What's the address?"

"One Mulberry Lane," Morgan said. "Do you want the clothes I've got on? I need to change out of them anyway — cross contamination and all that."

"Yeah, just sling them in an evidence bag. Get your wife's, too."

Morgan's pulse accelerated at that. "Yep."

He ran upstairs into their bedroom and closed the door. Lydia must have hidden her head under the quilt. He walked to the side of the bed and peeled the cover back.

"Go away," she mumbled.

"I need your pyjamas."

She rolled over, her face blotchy in the light of the lamp on the bedside cabinet. "What?"

"Standard procedure. Evidence."

"But there's no bloo—"

"Shh. I know. That's the fucking point." He tugged her arm until she stood beside him. "They'll need my clothes an' all."

"Where are my other ones?"

"You don't need to know." He undressed, folded his things, and put clean stuff on.

Lydia held her pyjamas out then took a nightie out of the drawer. "This is so horrible."

"Prison is worse, so stick to the story." He'd kept his voice low. "Go to sleep. No one will bother you, unless the murder squad boss turns up and wakes you, but if you've taken a pill, she might not be able to. Say the same to her as what you told me and Shaz. *Don't* slip up."

She put her nightie on and climbed into bed, huffing. "You're bossing me about."

"Better that than me saying goodbye if they cart your arse down to the station, isn't it?"

"I suppose."

"I have to go back to work."

"Why?" She'd wailed it.

And it pissed him off. She was such a brat these days.

"Someone else had their throat slit."

She covered her ears. "I don't want to hear it."

No, she wouldn't. Her nasty little habit had brought them here, to this point, and he'd bet all she thought of now was how her evening of fun had been ruined. No dancing with Alice. No sniffing. That was how far she'd sunk, only thinking about herself. Maybe once the coke was out of her system, she'd have some compassion for Alice.

He walked out, taking the clothes, his shoes, and his phone with him, putting the stuff in evidence bags passed to him by a SOCO, who wrote on the labels with a black, thin-tipped Sharpie, capital letters: LYDIA YEOMAN. MORGAN YEOMAN.

"Bollocks . . ." He waved to get Cameron's attention. "I've got to let the dog in, but I'll put his lead on and tie it to the table leg by his bed. He doesn't bite. Soft as shit."

"Shame. If he did bite, he could've ripped the killer's arm off if he'd been here instead of being with you." Cameron rubbed his forehead with the back of his gloved hand. "Still, can't have it all our own way, can we."

Morgan gave a tight smile, took some shoes out of the hallway cupboard, and joined Shaz in the kitchen. He let Rochester inside, tied him up, and the dog flopped onto his bed, groaning, tail wagging at Shaz coming towards him.

She crouched and gave his ears a fuss. "You're a bloody lush dog, you are."

"Hands off. He's mine." Morgan put his phone in his pocket and slipped his shoes on. "Come on. Let's go and see what mess awaits us."

They signed out of the log at the front door, the PC there stamping his feet. It'd got a bit cold. In the car, Morgan blew out a long breath and rested his head back. Uniforms stood at the neighbours' front doors. *Did you see anything, sir? Did you spot the make of the car driving away?*

Guilt flooded him that bloody pyjamas sat in the boot, Shaz without a clue, but it was too late now, he'd concealed evidence, had lied to save Lydia's arse.

Now all he had to do was live with it.

CHAPTER SEVENTEEN

Something was wrong.

Delia got up out of bed and crept to her door. Had she really heard Mum walking about, or was it her overactive imagination? Since receiving the notes, four of them now, the last two menacing, threatening her with death if she told anyone who she'd seen in Wasti's, she'd been on the edge of terror. More than that, ready to topple over.

Her heart hammered, and her pulse throbbed so hard in her neck it hurt. The air seemed to hold its breath along with her, and she reached out to grab the door handle, waiting for the exhale that never came. The air was still rigid.

There it was again, a noise, although this time it wasn't footsteps padding down the stairs but a bang. The same bang the back door made when it closed. It was heavy on its hinges and tended to slam no matter how much she tried to stop it.

She twisted the handle and rushed out onto the landing, then sped down the steps, two of them creaking, an ominous soundtrack to her ragged breathing. Mum shouldn't be going out, not at three in the bloody morning. Lately, she'd taken to wandering, and that had nothing to do with her heart issues and everything to do with the dementia the doctor had suspected was well on the way to devouring her.

Delia missed the last step in the darkness and tripped, lunging forward. She held her hands out to brace herself on the wall beside the front door, but her palms met with the coat stand instead. It fell sideways, and she swung herself around to run down the hallway and into the kitchen.

The door stood ajar. It must have bounced back open.

Delia pelted over there and pulled it wide, switching the garden security light on. The grass lit up, and a hedgehog shuffled across it, desperate to get out of sight.

No Mum.

Delia searched the garden, even inside the shed, then she had no choice but to go out into the lane. She jogged down the side of the house and out into the front garden, drawing the wooden gate towards her and slipping through.

Pavement bit into her soles, and she cursed herself for not putting slippers or shoes on. A car driving off gave her pause, a moment of thinking: What if Mum's in it with some bastard or other? *She chased it, hobbling over loose pieces tarmac, but it sped away, disappearing into the T at the end of the road, up by Wasti's and The Tractor's.*

She panicked, unsure what to do now, and went back inside to call the police. Mum must have been abducted, someone spotting her wandering about. What else could it be but that? She shook her head, barrelling upstairs to check all the rooms in case she made a fool of herself with the police. Officer, my mother's in someone's car, except she isn't, she's in bed, and we must have forgotten to lock up and the wind slammed the door.

There wasn't any wind, though.

She switched the landing light on and opened Mum's bedroom door.

Oh God, there she was, and she was fine, fast asleep beneath the duvet. Delia walked in, to check it was really her perhaps, and the illumination from the landing wrenched her attention to Mum's heart medication on the bedside table. Every tablet had been taken out, the plastic of the blister packets indented, wonky. A piece of paper, writing on it, Mum's.

I CAN'T DO THIS ANYMORE, DEL. SO SORRY. LOVE YOU, MUM.

What? Mum couldn't do it anymore? And those tablets, did they mean . . . ?

An empty bottle of water stood beside the alarm clock, the glow from the green numbers colouring the white label. A drop of liquid, maybe where Mum had spilled it?

Delia threw the quilt back, and it was warm to the touch beneath. Mum can't have long taken the tablets. She checked for sounds of breathing, her ear close to Mum's mouth, and nothing came out, nothing at all. Heart twisted in all directions, Delia tried CPR, but Mum remined impassive, staring at the ceiling, the life and soul gone out of her.

Delia screamed.

CHAPTER EIGHTEEN

Olga's cream carpet was the proud owner of several muddy footprints. Morgan stared at their path — she must have come in from the back garden, as a line of them pointed towards the living room window, where they'd stopped, as if she'd looked out onto Mulberry. Two sat in front of a chair, then fainter ones by the window again, and finally, extremely faint walking back into the kitchen.

Unusual, to wear muddy shoes on a light carpet, but maybe she'd rushed inside and forgot to remove them. Crocs, as he recalled. Pink.

He moved to the dining area of her kitchen. She sat at the table, a cup of something or other in front of her. Head back, as if on a hinge, what with the slice in the middle of her throat, crossways, that little tail end of a tick pointing downwards, ripped from the force of her head going back.

Fuck. This was all he needed. Another murder by the same bloke, and it had to be a bloke if Lydia had told the truth. Why was there a connection between Olga and Alice, though? Why leave here and go straight on to kill her?

If Alice hadn't been there, would Lydia have copped it?

Morgan shivered at that.

Shaz turned from the sink. "There's a cup on the draining board. Washed."

"Hmm." He'd noticed already while staring through from the back garden, chatting to Emma Ingles about what she'd done and seen.

The woman had been so distraught, he'd sent her back to Halfway and would go and speak to her shortly. SOCO hadn't arrived yet, but uniforms had. One stood at the back door now, in the garden, ready for officers needing to sign the log. No signature meant no entering or leaving the crime scene. Others were doing house-to-house, the usual.

"Maybe it's hers from earlier," he said. "She might use a new cup with each drink."

"Or someone else was here, having a brew." Shaz used the back of her gloved hand to touch the kettle. "Still got warmth in it so was boiled recently, although it isn't hot, so maybe an hour ago, possibly more?"

It fitted, the time. Morgan had left Olga's, dropped Val's runners off, and spoken to Cheryl. That would have taken about ten minutes. He'd gone home. Walked the dog. Ate his dinner. Plenty of spare minutes for whoever it was to leave here and kill Alice.

"Left to right slice," he said and nodded at Olga. "That small tick bit is done at the end of the wound on the right. A signature? Or doesn't he even realise he makes that pattern?" His head sweated beneath the hood of his protectives, as did his palms in the gloves.

Lydia had to have lied. She said *she'd* killed Alice, the blood on her pyjama sleeve was evidence of that, so unless she'd been here, and she'd been the one to create all the other ticks on the unsolved cases . . .

Why tell him she'd murdered her friend if she hadn't?

"You know this is connected to Alice, don't you?" Shaz sighed. "Collier's going to get her claws into that info pretty quick. Much as you don't want anyone in your space, it's going to happen."

"I know."

"Tracy might even take this scene over as well."

"She might, but what if it's connected to Delia?" He told her how Olga had acted when he'd visited her. "She was shifty, like she was hiding something. What if she's been killed because she *did* spot someone the night Delia was abducted from the lane?"

Shaz shrugged. "Who knows. Tracy may well tell you to get on with this one *and* Alice's murder. You know what she's like. Flouts the rules. She won't care you're involved. She'll expect you to just push your emotions aside and get on with it so she doesn't have to. I bet she's only coming out to your place to show her face, show she's willing, even though she isn't."

"How do you know?"

"From what she said on the phone."

"Which was?"

"Paraphrasing here, but: Fuck me, I was just sitting down to my dinner. Damon's poured the wine and everything."

Damon, her boyfriend and work partner, a DS. Morgan had liked the bloke right from when he'd first met him. Quiet compared to the volatile Tracy. Opposites attracted, so the saying went.

"Oh dear." Morgan let out a long breath. "So she'll be snarky once she gets to my house. Shame I can't escape her, but I have to go back sometime, unless we string it out here."

"I need some sleep, thanks. You'll just have to deal with her when you go home."

"Fab." Deadpan, not amused.

Henry appeared at the back door in his white get-up, the elastic of the hood biting into his face, a mask dangling by his chin. "All right, Morg?"

"Not too bad, considering."

"I heard about the goings-on at yours. Nice." Henry placed the mask over his mouth and signed the log. "Bit of a shock, eh?"

"Something like that."

'Bit of a shock' wasn't what he'd call it, but he wouldn't argue the toss. It wasn't Henry's fault Lydia was mixed up with God knew who.

Henry stepped inside. SOCO gathered around the PC in the garden, white ghosts in the darkness.

"Oh, bloody hell." Henry stared at Olga. "I've seen that slice before."

"Yeah, Lisa said that at the other scene."

'The other scene' — saved him fully admitting he had coppers all over his house, his wife hopefully out for the count now, unable to open her runaway mouth, although it hadn't run away as much as he'd have liked earlier, what with her keeping the bloke's identity to herself.

"What, two in one night by the same person?" Henry's eyebrows shot up.

"Seems so."

"Busy fella," Shaz said.

What Morgan didn't get, though, was why Delia had been strangled with the blue snake. Why hadn't she been sliced, too? And what did the snake even mean? How come the killer wasn't normal and didn't use rope or twine? A necktie, a belt? Why such a distinctive object?

It was all a bit much, this. Too many things going on at once. Delia on Saturday, Olga and Alice today, and a fucked-up wife full of herself who was a danger to have around at the moment. Once Tracy had spoken to her — if Lydia woke up, that was; it depended which strength of sleeping pill she'd taken — he'd send the missus away. To Bora Bora, a place she loved. She'd be out of immediate reach there, shacked up in a posh hotel, although she wouldn't have any coke to hand.

She'd lose her septum before long. One gaping nostril instead of two would tell Daddy exactly what she did with her time nowadays.

Just why did Morgan hang around again? Why was he still with her? They stood poles apart, him stuck firmly in his roots, Lydia cutting hers away and running headlong into a new flower patch, one that had a few prickly and hurtful thorns in the form of her dealer and whoever else she wasted her time with.

SOCO filled the room, must have come in while he was stuck in his head, and he shook it to loosen the worries that had dug their heels in, standing there waiting to tear him down if he didn't get a grip.

He checked the rest of the place with Shaz, then they went into the greenhouse, memories of his time in there with Olga coming to the fore. What was it she'd said?

'*And to answer your next query, I don't know who'd* want *to kill her either.*'

Was it like he'd thought and she knew who it was? Had they come here to shut her up?

Then another thought, frightening in its intensity and the way it slammed into his brain: *Does Lydia know something about Delia's murder?*

"Blimey, talk about a lot of veg," Shaz said. "Shame no one's here to tend to it now."

"I bought a bag off her. Forgot to take it inside." It was on the back seat of his car. And shit, he still had the pyjamas to get rid of.

His stomach gurgled.

"Dinner not agreeing with you?" Shaz asked.

"Probably the curry sauce." He nosed around the greenhouse, but nothing appeared any different to when he'd last seen it. The headphones were plugged into a mobile. "That'll need to be bagged. She might have had a call after I left."

Shaz picked it up and pressed a button on the side. There wasn't a PIN request, so she accessed the call log — it had a screen that didn't balk at gloves. The last one Olga received was this morning, from a woman called Nadine. Ten seconds, so a short convo. Shaz went to the messages next, and all of them were about buying vegetables.

Back to the call log, and Shaz rang Nadine on her own phone. "Hi, I'm DS Sharon Tanner, Pinstone police. I just need to know why you rang Olga Scrivens this morning."

"Oh, is something wrong?"

"Nothing I can talk about at the moment. Can you answer my question, please?"

"It was to tell her I was outside her house. I had some seedlings for her. Couldn't get out of the car because I had to shoot straight off to work."

Morgan spied some small black pots with green sprouts reaching out of the soil. He pointed to them, and Shaz nodded.

"Okay, thank you. How well do you know Olga?" Shaz rubbed the end of her nose with the back of her hand.

"I met her a few years ago when we worked in the library, before her husband died. Why?"

"Can I have your address? I'll need to send some officers round to speak with you. Are you in at the moment?"

"Yes." She gave Shaz the details — number sixteen Elderflower Mead. "Only just, though. Been to Sainsbury's for about three bloody hours. I tell you, their café just sucks me in. Once I sit down, I don't want to get the shopping."

Morgan bit the inside of his cheek. Was the woman creating an alibi? Did she have anything to do with Olga's death?

"Okay, well, someone will be there soon. Thanks for speaking to me." Shaz ended the call. "Want me to organise the visit?"

Morgan nodded. Shaz was a good sort, the best partner. She'd know his head was all over the place at the minute, otherwise she wouldn't be butting in.

He wandered out into the garden and stared at the moon. Its cheesy grin pissed him off, as did the stars, twinkling as though nothing was wrong and everything was normal. Well, it wasn't fucking normal, was it, and wasn't likely to be for a while yet.

He sighed. Forced himself to get his head in the game and not on Lydia.

Shaz finished her phone call. "Sorted. Now, to Emma Ingles'?"

"Yeah. We need to get a proper statement off her — and speak to the lags. It could have been one of them, leaving the door on the latch so they didn't have to use their codes to get out."

"Emma didn't say the front door was open at Halfway, did she?"

"No, but they could have locked it again, gone to their bedsit, then she came out to dump the rubbish."

It was a long shot, especially as the killer was the same one who'd done Alice. Grasping at straws was the order of the evening and all he could be bothered doing.

Thinking about the truth hurt too much.

CONFESSION

I've been safe here for a while now, doing my job and minding my own business, but this murder, it's thrown me for a loop. It'll be in all the papers, and what if journalists turn up here and take pictures? What if they catch sight of me through the living room window and snap a shot? He'll know where I am. Then I won't be safe.

—Emma Ingles

CHAPTER NINETEEN

Emma Ingles shook from head to foot after DI Yeoman and DS Tanner left. All this was a weight on her shoulders and, not for the first time, she asked herself why she'd taken this job. The answer was obvious, even all these years later. She'd been a probation officer in a former life, married to Derek, a man who'd beat her senseless once too often, someone she'd needed to get away from but didn't have the balls to do it.

Until she'd seen the job advertised on the bulletin board in the work canteen.

HALFWAY HOUSE MANAGER NEEDED. PINSTONE. APPLY INTERNALLY.

Pinstone. It was over two hundred miles north from where she'd lived in Buckinghamshire, far enough to feel free, close enough to sneak back and visit family and friends, although she recalled thinking they might not want anything to do with her. Derek had distanced her from them in his clever, insidious way, so stealthily she hadn't noticed until things had got bad and she'd needed someone to talk to.

And no one was there at the end of the line. No one picked up her many desperate calls. She'd let him allow her to shoot herself in the foot, cutting herself off at his silent command, almost without notice until it was too late.

She'd applied and got the job, and leaving him had been easy yet fraught with terror. She'd admitted to her boss at the time what had been happening, how her life had turned into her being afraid of her husband, a man who packed a punch and blackened her eyes.

"So *that's* why you said you bumped into the cupboard door," her boss had said. "I should have picked up on it, seen the signs."

Emma had hidden them well, though. Too well.

The terror had come from getting out of the house with only a holdall containing a few clothes and her most precious items, cards and presents she'd been given from those who'd loved her long before Derek came on the scene. She'd convinced herself he'd cottoned on to her acting jumpy the night before, that he'd waited round the corner in his car instead of going to work, and he'd catch her driving away, following her to Pinstone.

Of course, that hadn't happened.

She'd arrived, safe and sound, and changed her name by Deed Poll, all existence of her as Fiona Denham erased with the help of her old and new bosses and colleagues, coming together to create Emma Ingles, this alien woman she was still getting to know who'd been afraid of her second life at first, yet oddly inspired by the fresh start.

No more bruises.

No more broken toes where he'd stamped on them.

No more Derek.

And she hadn't gathered the courage to return down south since, leaving everyone she'd known behind, closing that book of a different life, never to open it again by choice. Various scenes from the pages seeped into her dreams, though, and the nightmares: Derek tripping her over so she banged her temple on the hearth and blacked out; Derek adding her depression medication to her tea to keep her drowsy, subservient; Derek being an arsehole, coming at her with a broken wine glass, ready to jam it into her cheek, stopping at the last minute because he'd known, he'd fucking *known* questions would be asked about *that.* There was no explaining torn skin away, was there, unless she said she'd cut it by accident. Silly, clumsy Fiona.

She blinked the memories out of her head, focusing on what she'd seen earlier. The residents had all left their black bags of rubbish at the bottom of the foyer stairs, per the rules, a once-a-week collection on her part, and she'd taken them out one by one. With the final bag in hand, she'd paused at a rustling and glanced over at Olga's, her sight fuzzing while she breathed deep to calm her racing heart. It wasn't Derek, it was just a cat or something. Her vision had cleared, and she'd clapped eyes on Olga's open door, and wasn't that just odd?

Olga always spoke to people out on the path or in her back garden. It was rare the woman let anyone inside, and she never left the door wide like that. Emma had double-locked Halfway House using her fob from the outside so the residents couldn't leave while she was gone, then she'd walked over to Olga's.

It was the silence that did it, enticed her inside, and the muddy footprints in the living room had seemed peculiar and not like Olga at all. She'd told Emma once that her house was a 'socked-feet zone', but someone had ignored that and clomped through with dirty shoes on.

The dining room scene had scared her shitless, more than Derek ever had, and she'd stared, silently screaming, at the woman's throat, at how her head hung back, only attached by what had seemed a patch of skin and muscle and whatever else held a neck together. And the blood, so much of it, a sheet down her front, soaking into her apron, her white T-shirt, the edge of the red a ragged coastline. And, oh, Emma had wished she was by the sea, in a hot place, far away from there.

But she wasn't. She sodding wasn't.

She'd run, out of that house to Halfway's front garden, and phoned the police.

She'd spoken to Yeoman at Olga's back door at first, told him as much as her jumbled mind could remember, then just now, in her flat at the back of Halfway. They'd taken their protectives off on the doorstep, putting them in a carrier bag she'd given them. Yeoman and Tanner had gone to see the residents as well, then left, Emma trying to think if she'd missed anything out. Yeoman had asked her to contact him if something else popped into her head, and she would, of course she would, because she wanted this person caught.

A decision — she needed to make one. While the computerised log hadn't shown any residents leaving, she had the urge to ask them just the same, put her mind at rest that her house was all in order. She'd dedicated herself to this job, but some aspects of it left a sour taste in her mouth and dread oozing into her bones.

Maybe she should move on again if things weren't to her liking here, but what would she do, where would she go? To an office job, away from ex-prisoners, who'd been the mainstay of her career so far? In a new direction entirely?

Something to ponder.

She left her flat, entering Halfway through the door that led to the big kitchen. From there, she walked into the foyer, with its bare grey walls, the keypad by the front door, the doors to the lower bedsits, and the rickety stairs that required new treads, which lurked beneath a worn carpet that needed replacing.

She'd start at the top of the house and work her way down, mainly so she could get Oliver Elford out of the way first, him in number twelve. He gave her the creeps with his beady eyes and skin coated in sweat, as if he suffered from going cold turkey all the time, although what that cold turkey might be she couldn't fathom. Some of them got to her, these men, in a way Derek never had, the hairs on her neck rising in their presence.

On the second-floor landing, she paused at the hum of voices. It wasn't unheard of for residents to go into each other's bedsits, especially if they were diehard criminals who got to know fellow offenders while in Rushford time and again. A familiar face was a familiar face, no matter where you'd met, and perhaps they took comfort from that while being reintroduced into society.

But one of the voices she didn't recognise, and that was strange. Residents weren't permitted outside visitors, unless it was probation officers, the police, or someone from the social to talk about their benefits. All meetings of that sort had to be conducted in the main living room anyway, a place they could gather and mingle if the four walls of their bedsits crowded them too much, an unnerving reminder of being in the nick.

Maybe the resident in that room had his phone on speaker.

Yes, that must be it, because, she reminded herself, the log hadn't shown anyone opening the front door. No one other than her anyway.

She held her breath and listened.

"So you got our man to go over there and sort L out?"

The stranger's voice, and it was tinny from where it filtered out of the phone, although that phone must be close to the door — Emma made it out clearly enough. She envisioned the inside of the room. A chest of drawers was to the right of the door, so perhaps the phone was on that.

"Not her, no, but it sorts her just the same." The resident, not his usual cocky self. He'd sounded wary, waiting for a bollocking.

"So what happened?" Unknown said.

"Her mate was there, so as a warning to her — not the mate, but L — he um, he got her to do the business for him, although he stood behind her, his hand over hers, because she wasn't in any fit state to do it without guidance."

"Why do the mate? I didn't ask for that. What I did ask for was for *L* to be dealt with tonight. Our mutual friend told her things he shouldn't have while they were both coked up last week, the stupid bastard. We can't have her remembering and telling her husband. Plus, she knows about what went on in the past, which is the main reason for killing her."

"The contact said the mate was in hysterics, probably going for her phone. He thought he may as well do her there and then. Because it was A."

"A was there? I got told they all avoided each other now. A was being dealt with anyway, later, but it happening in L's house, it's created a bit of a mess, hasn't it. I need to go. Think about this. It's a fuckup, and I don't need it. They were meant to be two separate kills, not L waltzing around free. She has to pay like everyone else. Let's meet in the usual place. Talking face to face is better. Go there now."

What are they on about?

The resident clearly hadn't done the deed of 'warning' someone himself, but he knew who had. Was he a middleman? He spoke to a bloke who'd ordered it, from what she could gather, which meant the occupant of this bedsit had already veered off the straight and narrow track he'd promised her he'd take when he'd first moved in here.

The problem was, the resident wasn't someone she was prepared to cross, no matter that she'd signed an agreement that if there was anything nefarious, she'd report it, God's honest truth. His past deeds weren't nice, and he wouldn't think twice about hurting her. He'd been in Rushford more than he'd been outside.

Strains of emotions from her time with Derek seeped in. She shivered, a fist of fear punching her in the belly. She was back *there*, as Fiona Denham, a scared and insecure woman who didn't know where to turn. Despite being the more determined and confident Emma Ingles now, she couldn't rock her new boat. Couldn't allow its hull to smash against the rocks and sink, taking her down with it.

The resident's rap sheet was long and terrifying and wicked.

If she told on him, she wouldn't get a warning, she'd be dead, like poor Delia and Olga.

She stepped away, onto a groaning floorboard, and the resident's door swung open. He stood there staring at her, a scowl in place, his wallet in hand. He was clearly going out past curfew.

She let out a pathetic "Oh!"

"Did you want something?" he all but growled.

"Sorry it's late, but I just want your bedding, please." How she managed to sound calm she had no idea. "I know it's a day early, but the sun is due again tomorrow, so I can get them all out on the lines." She had a few strung up down the length of the garden, enough for all the sheets. "I'll just get the fresh set for you."

She moved to the door between his and another man's, opening it to reveal the airing cupboard. His gaze seemed to pierce her cheek, burning it, but she selected a flat white sheet, a duvet cover, and a pillowcase as if he didn't stare. As if she hadn't just heard him on the phone.

Whose wife did they mean? And who is their mutual friend? And the wife's mate? Who is L?

"Here you go." She held the pile out to him, the fabric free of wrinkles from where she'd placed them in the industrial heat press.

He took them, his fingers brushing hers, the skin so smooth and soft. Like Derek's. Penpusher hands. A bully's hands.

"If you can just strip your bed and leave the dirty linens outside your door, I'll collect them in a bit."

To hide her deception, she took another set from the airing cupboard and knocked on next door, continuing her charade. So it didn't seem suspicious, she got on with delivering to the rest of the men, climbing the stairs then coming back down to the second floor.

The eerie resident had left his things on the landing, like she'd asked. She swept them and next door's into her arms, carrying the bundle down to the kitchen along with those from upstairs and the bottom hallway, where she entered the utility room and dropped it all on the floor, ready for her to bung in the laundrette-sized washing machine tomorrow.

Emma swore there were footsteps then someone breathing heavily behind her. She spun round, but no one was there. The click of the front door . . . She rushed to her office computer to see who'd gone out, but nothing was logged. How could that even happen? At the side window in the hallway, she looked out, up the lane. There he was, walking towards the pub end, hands in pockets, head bent.

She should report him for leaving, for managing to outsmart the log system, but he was too scary, had done some terrible things prior to being in Rushford.

This job, these people . . . It was, she admitted, as bad as living with Derek.

She fled to the kitchen door and locked it so no occupants could come in and raid the cupboards. Then she entered her flat, her chest sore from being so tight, and stared at Yeoman's card beneath a small magnet on her fridge door.

She should ring him, tell him what she'd heard.

But she wouldn't.

CHAPTER TWENTY

Door-to-door in Mulberry had once again yielded nothing. No one so far had seen anyone arriving at, or leaving, Olga's house. Everyone had either been busy cooking their dinner or eating it.

While Shaz spoke to the rest of the neighbours to help the uniforms out, Morgan went to Val's. He knocked on her side door, wondering whether she had a punter in there if Karl was out. His appearance would cause problems. Tough shit really, but he liked her, and giving her aggro wasn't something he wanted to do.

Karl opened it, and his expression changed from curious to downright afraid once he registered it was Morgan on the step. Now was the chance to speak to the lad about his behaviour. Might as well kill two birds and all that.

"Yes?" Karl managed get out between tight gulps.

"I need to come in."

Karl stepped back and closed the internal kitchen door. "I didn't want to do it, but they said I had to."

Morgan walked in and shut the side door. What was Karl on about? He'd better not have anything to do with Olga and Alice . . .

"Do what?" Morgan asked.

"I stole a bottle of wine, all right? From Wasti's. That's why you're here, isn't it? I saw all the police cars and thought they were here because Wasti had seen me run down the lane."

"No, that's not why they're here and not why I'm here. What time did you do it?"

"About fifteen minutes ago."

So he hadn't killed Olga. "Where's the wine?"

"In my bag upstairs."

"Go and get it."

Karl left the room and returned clutching a cheap red. He closed the door and leant on it, holding the wine out. "I had to video myself pinching it. That's what they said to do, to prove I did it."

"Who's 'they'?"

"Just some kids I hang around with."

Morgan grabbed the bottle. "I'll take it back to Wasti in a minute. *Don't* do anything like that again. We've had our eye on your lot for a while. Walk away from them before you get dragged into the nick."

Karl nodded. "Okay. Okay."

"Where's your mum?"

"Oh fuck, you're not going to tell her, are you?"

"Why would I want her to feel disappointment in you?" Morgan paused. "Why would *you*? She's been a good mum and doesn't deserve any trouble you might bring to her doorstep. That kid you doss around with, the main one, Boggin or whatever the fuck he calls himself, he's shit walking around inside skin, masquerading as a human being. Keep yourself clean, right?"

Karl nodded again. "I will."

Morgan opened the side door, put the plonk on the step, then closed up again. "Right. In the living room, is she?"

"Yeah, watching telly."

"Surprised she let you open the side door."

"Me, too. I know what she does. Boggin told me."

"Thought he might, but it was to put food on the table. Don't judge. And she's giving it up anyway, so no need to let her know you're aware."

Karl kicked at an invisible stone on the floor. "I wouldn't judge. I get it, what she does."

Morgan bobbed his head once at the lad then went to find Val. She sat curled on one end of the sofa, a velvet blanket over her lap, lower legs folded beneath it. She gave an absent smile at first, as though she thought Karl had come in, then gasped upon focusing on Morgan.

He shut the door.

"What are you doing here?" She shifted so she sat straight.

"It's Olga."

"What about her?"

"She's been murdered, love."

Val shot to her feet, the blanket pooling on the floor at her ankles, and barked out a sob, hands to her face to hide the signs of ugly crying. He could do with a bit of that himself, a good old blart, but now wasn't the time, and he doubted there would ever be a time where he'd let all the tension out that way.

No, he'd duff someone up instead, forcing info from them — once he got his hands on whoever knew something about this mess.

"What . . . ?" Val wiped her eyes. "How . . . ?"

"They went in after I left the lane. Probably waited if they saw me. She had her throat cut. Did you see anything?"

She shook her head and went to the window, parted the curtain, as though she might find the information he needed out there. "No, I went straight into the kitchen after you'd dropped the runner beans off. I cooked them, and we ate at the table. Karl had closed the curtains in here before I came in once I'd done the washing up, so . . . Then I watched telly — Karl nipped out. Oh God, it wouldn't have been him . . ." She staggered backwards and landed on the sofa.

"No, I've just spoken to Karl. He only popped to the shop."

It was as if Val hadn't heard him. "Who'd do that to Olga? That's two people now who were something to do with Wasti's robbery. Why has it come back to haunt us after all those years?"

"I thought the same. Listen, I'm going to tell you something for your ears only, you got that?"

"Christ, what is it now?"

He told her about a man barging into his house and killing Alice. "The slices on the necks are the same, so you can understand why I need to find this fucker. He might come back for my wife, but I'll be sending her away. Keep your ears open, d'you hear me? I'll pay you triple. Listen carefully to what the neighbours say. Someone round here knows something."

She released a strangled whine. "You think one of my *neighbours* did it?"

"I don't know, but it won't hurt for you to do a bit of poking about. Listen, I need to go. Hear anything, ring me."

He walked out, waved at Karl sitting at the kitchen table, and left the house. Wine in hand, he jogged up to Wasti's and looked inside. Interior lights shone either side of the many posters tacked to the windows offering bargain-priced this or that. A few customers perused the shelves, and Wasti himself stood in his usual spot behind the till.

Morgan went inside and put the bottle on the counter. "This is yours."

Wasti frowned. "It is?"

"Yep, stolen earlier. When are you going to get CCTV?"

Wasti shrugged. "Too expensive."

"Notice any strangers in tonight, people who don't normally come in?"

"There are always strangers, people from other estates or folks dropping in on the way through Pinstone. Why?"

"Olga's copped it."

Wasti's mouth hung open. "Pardon me, Mr Yeoman, sir, but what did you say?"

"Someone murdered Olga tonight."

"Olga *and* Delia?" He patted his chest over his heart. "This is not good. Someone is very upset to be doing this terrible thing."

"Yep, and I'm upset that they have. If you hear anything, give me a buzz, will you?"

"I most certainly will." He took the wine and rounded the counter, heading for the shelf it belonged on. "This wine, who took it?"

"I'm just giving it back. You don't need to know who it was."

"I see. You are a good man."

"Yeah, so some say. Night, Wasti." He held up a hand in goodbye and walked back down Mulberry, taking in the sight of the bottom end like a civilian would. Police cars, lots of activity, slices of light coming out from doorways, front doors open, neighbours talking to coppers. It was all normal to him, part of everyday life, but to view it from here, it had to put the shits up people, especially if they'd been here earlier, murdering.

He joined Shaz on the pavement outside number one, and they took some fresh protectives out of the SOCO van, putting them on in Olga's back garden. Log signed again, they stepped into the house.

Lisa was there, inspecting Olga, and she dipped her head in acknowledgement. "Same slicer as at your place, Morg."

"I saw that." He was glad most of his face was hidden by the hood and mask, although eyes, they said more than you liked at times, didn't they, and he forced himself to keep his expression blank, his emotions hidden.

"Already done the temp," she said. "Estimated time of death, two hours ago, give or take."

"I was here at about six, and she was alive then."

"That narrows it down a bit." Lisa studied Olga's neck. "This went so far back. The blade, I mean. I know I said it was sharper at Alice's, but this is mental. A knife that can go so deep has got to be a specialist type. Say, a proper chef's one."

Shaz wrote that down. "Something to look into."

"He stood behind her, the same as with Alice." Lisa stood upright. "Her hair's scrunched, so maybe he gripped it."

Morgan hadn't noticed that previously. "Right."

He imagined a man holding her hair in his fist while placing the knife at her throat with the other hand. Olga sitting there, scared witless, not daring to move in case he carved her up. With that cup drying on the drainer, he had a feeling she knew who'd done this to her — she'd made him a fucking cuppa, and they'd sat here, talking. Olga's cup was full, though, so she hadn't had the chance to drink it. The killer had maybe got arsey quickly, deciding to kill her sooner. Or she'd said something to set him off.

Something about Lydia? Was that why he'd gone straight from here to Morgan's?

Supposition got him nowhere, but it *did* give him a chance to work out what had gone on, what he should do next. He needed to ask Lydia if she knew Delia and Olga. Maybe back in the day before Morgan had met her. Lydia had lived here all her life, could have gone to school with them. If so, why hadn't she said anything when he'd told her Delia had been murdered, that he was working the case?

He'd believed her brief story of who she was prior to them becoming an item, just some boring girl with nothing to tell. Why wouldn't he? Probing into a past she clearly hadn't wanted to discuss wasn't something he'd chosen to do. Fuck, he'd had shit happen while younger that he hadn't told her either, like his dad beating him up on a Saturday night after he'd rolled in from the pub, Mum standing there saying nothing, like it was *normal* to wallop ten bells of shit out of your kid.

There were some things he wanted to forget, and Lydia might, too.

But she'd *have* to remember if it was relevant to these murders. She had no choice. He'd get it out of her before he sent her away on her little holiday.

With nothing much they could do in Olga's house now, Morgan suggested to Shaz that she went home. Nigel or Jane could investigate sharp knives tomorrow, and street CCTV. He said goodbye to Shaz at the car after they'd taken their protectives off, and he drove home, greeted with a similar sight to that at Mulberry. Police. Neighbours out. Patrol vehicles parked at the kerb.

Sighing, he left his car on the road instead of the drive and got out, taking yet more protectives from the back of Cameron's van, and putting them on by the front door. He signed the log and walked into the house, going straight to the kitchen, where someone laughed and called Rochester a daft dog who didn't need any more treats, you greedy bugger.

He stepped in there to find Tracy Collier on her back, laughing, and it was a shock to see her amenable, human. Rochester stood over her and licked her face and protective hood. Damon watched her, love written all over his face, and Morgan asked himself when he'd last looked at Lydia like that.

Years ago, before the money, before things had gone to shit and coke had become Lydia's best friend instead of him.

"All right," Morgan said.

Tracy turned her head to gawp his way. "Your bloody dog! He has no manners. Look at him."

Morgan smiled, and Rochester made to bound over but was stopped by the lead tied to the table leg. "Bed."

The dog slunk off and settled down, moaning all the while.

Tracy stood and brushed hairs off her forensic suit. "What a bloody shitshow to happen in your own home." Some of her ginger hair escaped the hood.

"Tell me about it."

"And your wife's about as useful as a nun in a brothel. She wouldn't wake up when I nipped into your room and gave her a nudge. I dig your built-in wardrobes by the way. Where did you get them from?"

"IKEA."

"Christ." Damon groaned. "Please don't make me go there."

"We'll have a gander online, buy them that way." Tracy grinned. "They'd be nice down that long wall in our room."

She sighed. "Anyway, nice as it was to play with your pup for a bit, I'm glad you're here. How well did you know Alice?"

Morgan shrugged. "I didn't really. More of a 'hello, nice to see you' kind of relationship. She was my wife's friend, came here whenever I worked late. She was here tonight to give Lydia some company."

"You should have a missus you work with," Tracy said. "That way, she'll understand the pressure you're under and not bust your bollocks about the hours you do, plus, you get to see her at work like me and Damon do."

"Maybe I will." *Chance would be a fine thing. I'm married, and Shaz wouldn't be interested in me.* That thought gave him pause. Shaz?

"Trouble in paradise?" Tracy canted her head.

"Been on the skids for years. Just haven't got round to leaving her, and I won't now, not until this shite's been cleared up anyway."

"About this shite . . ." Tracy moved closer. "The reason I asked how well you knew Alice . . ."

Morgan laughed wryly. "I know what you're going to say. As I'm not emotionally involved other than making sure my wife's okay, I can deal with this case."

"Wow, how did you know?" Her eyes twinkled.

"Because that's you all over, Tracy."

"You're a clever man, Morg. You know it makes sense."

He nodded. "It does, because there's been another murder. Same knife slash. I think they're related to the murder I told you about on Saturday." *And with three murders, it gets Lydia off the suspicion radar.*

"Ooh, the plot thickens, even more reason for me to fuck off. Right . . ." She slapped her thighs. "Time for us two to skedaddle. We'll go and inform Alice's next of kin for you, but after that, you get on with it. Have fun."

"Fun isn't the word I'd use."

"Oh, lighten up. You know what I mean. Tarra."

She flounced out, and Damon followed her.

Morgan stared at their backs as they signed the log and left the house. Thank fuck she'd handed this scene back to him. He could cover things up nicely, have a handle on everything that was going on. He'd save Lydia's backside, wait for the dust to settle, then tell her it was over between them.

He went upstairs to the bedroom and stared down at her. She snored quietly, the proper kind, not the fake ones she adopted whenever he came in well late and she thought he might want to have sex with her. That ship had sailed an' all, all the desire for her gone once her new persona had appeared.

He'd stayed celibate for years. Maybe it was about time he did what Tracy had said and find himself a woman on the force.

Birds of a feather flocked together.

CHAPTER TWENTY-ONE

Val hadn't slept much last night. Yeoman bringing that horrible news . . . it had got to her, two friends dead, and their murders *had* to be related. Delia had told Val a secret years ago, about Olga, who'd seen someone waiting in a getaway car. Olga wouldn't tell the police, though, not when it had happened and not when Delia had given in and confessed everything to Yeoman.

Delia had blurted the lot to Val in a moment of desperation, the need that comes when everything is too much and you itch to spread the load. A problem shared is a problem halved, and it was for Delia, although taking that burden from her had cost Val. She'd carried it around with her for years, silently.

Olga's secret was hers to keep, Val hadn't betrayed Delia by telling Yeoman, although she *had* asked him whether the robber had run off on foot or had used a vehicle, just to put the thought in his head.

She'd felt mean for it afterwards, seeing as both Delia and Olga were being threatened at the time, nasty notes, although Olga didn't know Val was aware of them. Her saying what she had could have endangered Olga, and maybe her murder was because of it. Yes, time had passed, fifteen years of it, but with Flint out of Rushford . . .

It had to be something to do with him, didn't it?

But what about Yeoman's wife's friend? Why had she been killed, too?

And there was another problem she'd been wrestling with. Gary Flint was Phil's brother. She'd fancied Phil for years and always looked forward to him coming round. Their shared moments were never like work, more of a proper relationship, albeit only for an hour, but once a week, she got to taste 'normal'. Normal with Karl's dad was him off down The Tractor's each night, eyeing up every bit of skirt to walk past him, and even those who didn't. He'd ogle them from across the bar, it didn't matter to him. Then there were the affairs, the trust broken, and the moment came for them to part ways.

Who knew where he was now. He'd stomped from the house, caught out in his many strings of lies that created a tapestry of grief, and she hadn't seen him since. No child support, nothing, so she'd gone on the game after a conversation with Delia, whose mother had died. Delia had been left with bearing the cost of paying the bills all by herself, as had Val.

She smiled, thinking of the conversation they'd had about it. God, time had gone by so fast, and now her friends were gone. It was difficult to get her head around it, to convince herself she'd never see them again.

She'd made a decision, though, and that meant going to see Phil.

Coat on, she left the house and walked down the lane towards Wasti's, ignoring the SOCO van still outside Olga's behind her, not wanting to fully acknowledge it, because it would mean facing the proper truth, that death had touched the lane again. She knew it had, but the full brunt of it hadn't hit her yet.

She nipped into Cost Savers to get some biscuits. Phil liked those with his cuppa before they had sex, and maybe they'd have sex today, who knew. It would be weird doing it in his bed, but perhaps that was a better idea, all things considered. Hers was related to work, her bedroom, too, and this wasn't work.

She placed some chocolate Hobnobs on the counter along with a box of PG Tips. She only drank that, and Phil might well use a different brand.

"Terrible business down the lane," Wasti said.

"It is." A lump formed in her throat. "I still can't believe it."

"They were around for the robbery, those two women." He keyed in the prices on the till. "It isn't that rocket science business; it's obvious what is going on. They were killed because they knew things. Gary Flint had the brass neck to come in here last week on his way to moving into Halfway." He shuddered. "He bought a filthy magazine, from the top shelf. Naked ladies."

Val shivered, too. "I suppose it's difficult to find a woman when you first come out of Rushford."

"Yes, but Delia was available, on the corner, right outside his window. That's three pounds fifty-two, my dear."

She handed him a fiver. "She wouldn't have gone with *him*."

"Maybe that was the problem . . ." He opened the till and sorted her change, popping it into her outstretched hand.

"What do you mean?"

"She would not go with him, so he killed her. He was annoyed at being rejected."

"But there was a red car. Flint doesn't have a red one."

"What if he called to her from his window, asked her for the sex, and she said no? Then he rang a nasty friend, who came in the red car, took her away, and killed her in Queen's Wood."

Val had thought the same thing, of course she had, but with information from Yeoman, she knew this wasn't the case. She couldn't tell Wasti, though. Yeoman had told her to keep it under her hat. The red car did have something to do with Delia's murder, but the DI didn't know who owned it. Yet.

"Maybe." She put the tea and biscuits in her big handbag. "Well, whatever happened, it was horrible."

"There's word that Olga had her throat cut."

"Hmm."

"Not the same as Delia with the snake." He nodded sagely. "This is why I think it is two killers. Different approaches to murder. Red Car Man is the slicer, the other is the snake."

"You might be onto something there." She ought to keep him talking. Yeoman expected it of her. "So if your theory is right and Flint got someone to kill Delia, did Flint kill Olga? Did Olga see him trying to chat Delia up on the corner?"

The bell tinkled, and oh fuck, Gary Flint himself walked in. He stared at Val, his eyes piercing, then dipped his head and walked down the aisle with the fridge in it.

Wasti widened his eyes. Val did the same, a blush creeping onto her cheeks.

"So the offer for the bin bags starts next week, does it?" Val said.

"Yes." Wasti tidied his stack of lottery slips. "Three for two."

Flint came up behind Val, his breath hot on her neck. She shuddered, despite trying to hold it back, and stepped aside. He placed a meal deal on the counter — a chicken and mayo sandwich, a packet of salt and vinegar Walkers, and an apple juice. Wasti served him, and it was clear he was uncomfortable about having Flint in the shop at all. Fancy coming into a place you'd robbed, rubbing salt into a wound that had never healed.

"Coppers are in the lane," Flint said. "I hear Olga got murdered."

Val swallowed. Should she talk to him like she would any other resident? Ignoring him probably wasn't wise if he had killing in his blood. "She did. All very sad."

"It is. The Lord above must be disappointed." Flint paid for his lunch.

The Lord? Fucking hell, had Flint found God in the nick?

"Yes, the Lord would be disappointed in many people." Wasti glared at Flint. "Those who take what isn't theirs, be it money, cigarettes, or a life."

"Scum, pure and simple." Flint grabbed his things. "*And* He would be upset that I was wrongfully incarcerated."

Flint's still saying he didn't do the robbery? That Delia lied about seeing him?

Val bristled at that. Whether he'd turned to religion or not, what he'd done in the past was wrong. You didn't just walk into a shop with a gun, did you, and expect not to have to do time for it. He was in denial, always had been, and she reckoned no amount of being presented with the truth would change his mind. In his head he was innocent, and that was that. How odd to go around thinking that way, believing your own lies.

"Those who commit crimes should take the punishment," she said.

"Then you should, too." Flint stared at her. "Women of the night are wrong in what they do."

"I'm not a woman of the night." She flushed hotter.

"Given it up, have you?"

"As a matter of fact, I have, not that it's any of your business."

"Phil won't like that. He won't like not being able to come and see you." He frowned, probably wondering if he should let his brother know he couldn't get his end away with her anymore.

"I think you'll find he'll be pleased — again, not that it's any of your business." She was desperate to leave the shop, flounce out after her announcement, but that meant Flint would be alone with Wasti, and she wasn't prepared to put the shop owner through that.

"We'll see." Flint narrowed his eyes at her and walked out, pulling the door to deliberately slam it.

"So much for finding God, closing the door like that. Not very Christian." She turned to Wasti. "Are you okay?"

He nodded. "I suppose I should get used to seeing him in here."

"You could ban him."

Wasti laughed, but it wasn't the funny kind. "And have me on his naughty people list? Someone he can punish? No, I will serve him. I will take his money, because he owes it to me, as well as all those cigarettes."

So Wasti still wasn't over the robbery, and who could blame him? He must carry the violation with him.

"Sorry you're going through this." She patted his arm. "I need to go. Speak to Phil before his brother does."

"Phil will just have to accept it if you're giving up your job."

She smiled. Bless him, he had no idea.

"Yep." She waved and left the shop, pausing on the pavement to check where Flint was.

Down the lane, heading to Halfway. Good.

She rushed to the T road running along the top of the streets and bolted into Regency. A couple of police officers stood at doors, probably asking if anyone had seen or heard anything regarding Olga. It was like she lived in a movie she didn't want any part of, all these coppers around and too much death. Delia, Olga, that Alice woman. She remembered she hadn't finished her conversation with Wasti about the two methods of murder. It was probably something and nothing anyway.

She stopped at Phil's door and rolled her shoulders. This was it, her chance for a better life. The money Phil had offered was going to change everything. She could save some for Karl if he wanted to go to uni, or pop some away for a deposit on a house — imagine that, her with an actual mortgage, a proper grown-up.

Bloody hell!

She knocked, her stomach doing somersaults, and waited for him to open up. It was early, must be just past half eight by now, so she'd probably get him out of bed. He appeared on the threshold in a sharp grey suit, white shirt, and a burgundy tie held in place with a gold pin.

Bugger. He's off somewhere important.

Phil only ever put a suit on if he was playing at being a car salesman or visiting someone about money. He was more your jeans and T-shirt type, muscles on show, probably bulked up from his home gym.

"All right, Val? What brings you here?" His smile lit up his lovely face.

"I came to give you my answer."

"What, at the arse crack of dawn? Blimey, you're keen." He paused. "Keen to get rid of me or keen to agree, that's the question."

"Can I come in then? I mean, standing on the doorstep to tell you isn't exactly romantic, is it."

"Romantic, eh? Am I about to be on cloud nine?"

"Let me in and you'll find out, won't you."

He stepped back, and she walked into the 'foyer' as he called it, and that was the truth. A hallway it wasn't, not anymore. He'd done it up nicely, all posh, and she had the sensation coming over her that she was 'less than', lower class, and didn't fit in here. There was having nice things then there was standing in the presence of someone who only bought the best. Did that mean she didn't fit with Phil, too, even though he had similar lower-class roots? No, he was the same blagger he'd always been, rough and ready but kind, to her anyway. She knew how he used to be with others, those who'd crossed him, but nowadays, he had someone else to do that sort of dirty work. Was she comfortable with that, though? Knowing what he did for a living?

Drugs sold to kids who didn't know any better.

People addicted to his wares, ruining their lives.

Stealing stuff in order to sell it on so they had enough money for sniff or weed.

Had she thought this through properly? No, she hadn't. All she'd seen in her head while deciding was the real Phil, the one who held her tenderly, who cared about her. The promise of a good relationship. But she'd be taking wages, money from desperate people who'd paid it to Phil. She'd be part of the cycle.

"Something wrong?" He closed the door.

"Um . . . no. It's fine."

"Where are you telling me the news then? Kitchen, living room, or bedroom?" He winked.

"The kitchen. I've got some PG and Hobnobs."

His face smoothed, wreathed in something she couldn't work out. Love? The realisation that the biscuits had meant something to her, too, all this time?

"Fucking hell," he muttered. "Hobnobs."

"I know. We're going places."

She laughed and followed him to the kitchen with its mod cons and obvious cost outlay, a coffee maker on the side that looked more complicated than just pressing a button. She dug the teabags and biccies out of her bag, putting them on the white marble worktop, and sat while he made the tea. What would it be like to live here? Would they see each other at his place or hers? Probably better here. Karl discovering she was seeing Phil properly, albeit getting paid for it, well, it didn't give a good impression, did it? Not only was she a prostitute but a drug dealer's girlfriend. Hardly a leading example.

But there was love involved, so didn't that make it different?

Phil put the cups on coasters on the table and sat opposite. "Come on then. What's it to be?"

She felt cornered, rushed. "Are you short for time or something? Do you need to be somewhere?"

"I'd planned to nip to the car showroom, what with the coppers sniffing around. Thought I'd play the game, pretend to be going to work. But I don't have to, I can stay here."

"Right." *Just say it.* "Well, the answer is yes, I'll take your offer."

He didn't jump up, didn't do anything except give her a massive smile, but she knew him, knew he was hiding how he really felt, that he was pleased as punch.

He got up and grabbed the Hobnobs, shifting from foot to foot. "That deserves us eating the whole packet, I reckon."

It did, and she wondered whether, after they'd eaten them, they'd go to bed, like always, only this time, it wasn't pretend.

CONFESSION

It's hard to explain who I am. Selfish little bitch? Someone who enjoys danger, thrives on it? I thought I'd marry someone else, not Morgan, but life has a habit of snatching your imagined path away from you at the last minute. The man I was supposed to get hitched to went with someone else, and I'd been left on the shelf. Until I'd spotted the PC apprehending someone for shoplifting, a crime I'd witnessed but had decided to ignore until I'd seen him. I shouldn't have gone anywhere near him, should have stayed away, but like I said, I enjoy danger, and being joined in holy matrimony to a copper is about as dangerous as I can get. It didn't bring a happy ending, though. For either of us.

—Lydia Yeoman

CHAPTER TWENTY-TWO

Lydia woke to a note on Morgan's pillow.

GONE TO WORK. PACK A SUITCASE, YOU'RE GOING ON HOLIDAY. EXPLAIN LATER.

She could do with a holiday after what she'd been through, but what about the coke? She didn't know where to buy it abroad, and it wasn't like you could walk up to the scabbiest person on the street corner and ask them for a baggie. Each time she'd gone away with Morgan since she'd started sniffing had ended up a nightmare, her all jittery, needing a hit, him, at first, wondering what the hell her problem was, then later, after she'd opened her big mouth about getting drugs from Phil, staring at her, contempt clouding his eyes.

She was a fool, she knew that, getting herself into this mess. But being poor as a kid had given her a taste of wanting the good life, and she'd watched Dad build his business up, slaving away to earn money, then eventually selling, getting enough so him, Mum and Lydia, could live like a king and his queens. Morgan hadn't wanted any part of the money, saying he hadn't earned it so it wasn't his to spend or enjoy, and every holiday, he'd paid half out of his wages.

All the more for Lydia.

She stared at herself in the vanity mirror, despising what her life had become. She wasn't happy, hadn't been for years, although she still had a nugget of love for Morgan in there somewhere, and he must have that same nugget. Him covering for her showed that. The problem was, she'd shagged Phil one coked-up night, thinking something new was on the horizon with him, and free drugs along the way for that matter, but he'd come round the next day and told her it'd been a mistake, could never happen again, he'd only wanted to try out her fake tits.

And someone else would deliver her drugs.

The man in the red car. Goat.

He was a bastard, a total pig who always touched her up whenever he handed the gear over. A quick brush of his thumb on her boob. A sneaky feel of her thigh. Like she'd ever go with him when his hair was always so greasy. He was gross. She was supposed to be keeping away from him, they'd made a pact as kids, but he had what she craved, so whatever had gone on in the past didn't matter now. What she wanted, she got, but him turning up last night had been a massive shock, seeing as he'd already been round earlier in the day. She shuddered at the memory.

* * *

"What are you doing here?" she whispered at the front door. "Morgan's just taken the dog for a walk."

"I know, I saw him. Let me in."

"What? You can't come in here! He'll be back soon."

"What needs doing won't take long."

She stepped back, and he barged in, closing the door with a gloved hand. He always had them on, probably so his prints weren't on any baggies.

"Olga's dead," he told her. Blunt. Straight to the point.

Oh shit. Shit! Not Olga, too . . .

"Why?" She staggered to lean against the wall, splaying her hands on it for balance. The last thing she needed was to fall over, but she wanted to. Land on the floor, curl into a ball.

"You know why."

"But . . . but that was ages ago. How come her and Delia have been killed now? Why not back then?"

"To pin it on Flint. You're meant to be next. Now. Tonight."

She sank to the floor, the place she most wanted to be, the cold of the tiles seeping through her silk pyjamas. And God, Alice would be in the hall in a minute, asking what was going on. She'd see him, know who he was, and everything would go wrong. She was meant to stay away from Alice, too, but they'd been best friends for years, and no amount of threats would keep them apart.

"Me?" Lydia squeaked.

"Yeah, you. The lot of you are being taken out."

"But I didn't do anything, I just watched."

She thought of back then, what they'd done, her and her friends thinking they were funny, clever, when they really weren't. That was what youth did to you, gave you courage, the idea you were invincible, and until Delia had been strangled, she'd thought they were. A group of people never to be caught. Who had bided their time, though? Which one of them hated Flint so much they'd frame him at the same time as killing everyone involved? Flint had been there, too, part of the gang.

What a mess. A terrible, wicked mess.

"But you were there, and that's all that matters now." He grabbed her arm and hauled her upright, fingertips digging into the tender flesh. "Look, I agree, you didn't do anything, but he still wants you punished."

So it was a man then. And why didn't that man want Goat killed?

"Can't . . . can't you just tell them you roughed me up?" She hated her pleading tone.

"Hmm. It might fly. But only if you agree to something."

"I'll do anything, I swear."

"Anything?" He cocked his head, smiling that leery smile of his, the one that showed his manky teeth and let his rancid breath waft out.

She nodded, frantic. "Yes, just tell me what it is, and I'll do it."

"Shag me once a week. Kinky. Toys, cuffs, the works. And I'll whip you, every time, so you never forget what you were a part of."

Her gag reflex sprang into action. "Okay. Okay." But she wouldn't do it. She'd run away. Take her money and set up home somewhere else.

She didn't need Morgan, and he didn't love her like he should anymore, and her parents hadn't been the same with her since 'it' had happened, so what was the point in hanging around? "Yes, I'll do it. Whatever you want."

"Good girl." He licked her cheek.

Oh God. Fucking hell, no . . .

She resisted wiping the saliva off.

"What's going on?" Alice appeared in the living room doorway.

"Nothing," Lydia managed, conscious of the lick drying, tightening her skin. "It's all right, go back in there. I won't be a minute."

Alice frowned, staring at Goat. "Hey, aren't you—?"

"Fuck off in there like your good friend told you," he shouted.

Alice took a step forward. "No, you're G—"

He launched himself at Alice, pushing her backwards into the living room. Lydia chased after them, needing him out of there before Morgan came in. If he knew who she bought her drugs from . . . Alice reached for her phone on the coffee table, and Goat grabbed hold of her hair, placing her in front of him, a knife appearing in his hand, one he held up to her neck.

"Want to really make sure you're going to keep your mouth shut, Lyd?" he asked.

"Jesus Christ. Leave Alice out of this."

"I can't. She's a part of it, too, you know that."

Alice struggled to get away from him, but he raised the knife in front of her eyes, and she got the message: Stay still. Stay calm.

Goat leered. "Besides, this will let you know what it feels like, someone you know dying, you seeing it happen, like he imagined it happen, you lot acting like it meant nothing. You actually doing it this time instead of just standing there."

"No, please, no, don't make me do that. Not that . . ." She held her hands out as if it would stop him, her powers of persuasion unleashed via some kind of invisible force.

"Get round here and stand where I am," he ordered.

She obeyed, legs leaden, her heart a painful set of throbs, and all she had to do was scream and someone might hear, come running. But whoever that was would find her and *Alice dead, she was sure of it.*

Screaming meant he'd have to shut Lydia up, and maybe he'd lied about the kinky sex happening. Maybe he intended to kill her anyway.

Lydia found herself sandwiched between him and Alice, his hand over hers on the knife. When had he put it in her hand? And fingerprints, there'd be her fingerprints. Hers. He jerked her hand, and hot blood gushed on it. Goat dragged her back, and Alice slumped to the floor, the red stuff coating Lydia's beautiful carpet, and she was a bitch, a nasty cow for thinking of that, scarlet splashes mattering more than murder.

He grabbed the knife off Lydia and rushed out, calling back, "I'll be round on Wednesday, ten o'clock in the morning. Be naked."

Lydia screamed in anger, loud and long, took a breath and screamed again. Breathless, she ran to the window to peer out, using her clean hand to part the curtains. He'd gone through the side gate and stood in the street, casually lighting a cigarette, the brazen bastard. Was he waiting out there for Morgan? Was he going to kill him as another warning to Lydia?

Shit. Shit!

He must have stood there smoking a quarter of his fag by the time he got in his car and revved the engine. Then he was off, driving away, and Lydia let the curtain go and stood by the fireplace, away from Alice, whose blood oozed rather than pumped, spreading a hideous puddle that soaked deep into the fibres.

That carpet had cost a grand.

* * *

She rubbed her arms, bruised from where he'd gripped them. He'd be back here, Wednesday, but she wouldn't be around to let him whip her, cuff her, or whatever he meant by 'kinky'. And she wouldn't be packing a case to go on holiday, as per Morgan's suggestion. He couldn't know where she'd gone or he'd follow her, find her. She'd leave, go and stay somewhere, using cash from the jewellery box beneath their bed. If she used her cards, he'd know, do a search on her finances and pinpoint exactly where she'd spent money.

She should never have married a copper, not after what she'd witnessed back then, not after being part of the gang.

But it was too late, that aisle had been walked, complete with an evil-scent-riddled bouquet, and how she needed to extricate herself before she had *her* throat sliced.

She should never have continued to meet up with Alice. She'd broken the rule.

Delia's murder . . . she would've put it down to a hazard of Delia's job, but then Olga . . .

He was coming for them all, only he was using Goat to do it. She should leave a note, tell Morgan everything, who the killer was, but that meant confessing to the past, and she wasn't prepared to do that.

No, she'd be a coward, run away.

It was best for everyone.

But mainly herself.

CHAPTER TWENTY-THREE

Delia dealt with the paramedics, everything to do with a death at home, and now, with Mum gone these last few days, the house had an eerie feel, as if her spirit was still there, haunting the walls, the floors, the ceilings and Delia's dreams.

She sat on the sofa, staring out into the lane, and wondered whether this was a punishment for what she'd done all those years ago, what she'd been involved in. You couldn't just walk off from something like that, could you, and get away with it, but they had.

Delia, Alice, Olga, Lydia, Flint, Steve, and Goat, all of them had escaped punishment, although that was debatable. If guilt hounding you every day was punishment, she'd suffered enough.

But not as much as the victim, and not as much as the bloke who'd gone down for the crime instead of them.

God, it was awful, all of it, and there'd been many a time she'd wanted to step inside the police station and confess. Tell them everything, including her role, and take her chances. Do her time. Flint still being around the lane had prevented her from letting it all out, though, his presence a constant reminder of the promise they'd made. She'd seen him about, averted her gaze so she didn't have to make eye contact with him, get involved with him again, and had managed that.

Until the robbery.

She'd be a fool to grass him up, because Flint could grass her up in return. If he served time for the robbery, why not add a few more years for his part in the past? And everyone else could be dragged into it, too.

Val walked past the window, probably going to Olga's for her veg. Olga had taken to gardening to soothe her mind, so she'd said once, to forget not only what they'd done but her parents dying. She'd been just eighteen, a week after her birthday it'd happened, them drowning in some freak accident off the coast in Smaltern. Tending plants helped with that, as well as the tragic loss of her husband, and if Olga grew things for the residents, she was giving back, making amends in her own way. She gabbled on about the moon and the universe a lot, music healing her, and Delia wondered whether the years since 'it' happened had addled her brain.

When gossip had arrived that Lydia was marrying a copper, Delia had zoomed down Panic Street, that place they were all familiar with. What was Lydia playing at? Did she think if she married him, this lovely constable, she'd be safe, protected? Delia doubted Lydia would tell him anything. She was all about saving her own skin, although she still hung around with Alice on the sly.

Delia stood and peered outside. Val was at Olga's front door, them chatting, nodding, then they disappeared down the side of the house. So Val was *getting veg then. Probably to make her revolting husband a nice dinner. He perved on everyone, and Delia had told Val about the time he'd pinched her arse in The Tractor's, how he stared at women in the wrong way. Why was Val sticking with him when they had a little boy who'd learn from his father's example? Karl was in playschool now, bless him, and he deserved a better dad.*

Delia knew that more than anyone. She'd grown up with Steve, he'd been part of the gang. Steve, the one who'd instigated the incident. She'd never told Val this, what with the gang vowing to keep it to themselves, but God, she'd been sorely tempted on many occasions. Val should spend her life with someone better than him.

Opposite, a new neighbour bustled about in her front garden. She'd moved in last week and potted flowers in glazed blue urns, all very nice, too nice for the lane, and someone would nick them soon, probably tonight once darkness cloaked them. You had to be careful with your possessions around here, and the neighbour would learn that, given time.

Val came past, pausing for a second or two, as if she debated calling on Delia, probably to check if she was okay. They hadn't met up since Mum's funeral. Then she continued up the lane. Delia craned her neck to the right. Steve was in Val's garden with Karl, and it all looked domestic bliss, him steering Val indoors by holding the back of her neck, a possessive but caring gesture for those who didn't know any better.

But Delia knew better. She knew his penchants.

She sat, she sighed, she pondered what she was supposed to do now, no Mum to care for, no penance to serve by caring for her. She had to think of something else to replace it.

The letterbox clattered, and she jolted, remaining where she was, not wanting to see who'd delivered something. Not wanting the cold, hard truth of knowing who was threatening her if, indeed, it was another note.

She rose, going out into the hallway, and stared at the prickly mat with a piece of pink fluff anchored to a cluster of bristles. From Mum's slippers, most likely. The sight of it hurt, brought a lump to her throat, as did the familiar folded paper.

Shaking, she collected it and walked into the kitchen, sticking the kettle on and making a cuppa to delay the inevitable. She sat at the table, steam writhing from the cup in grey curls, and opened the paper.

DID YOU UNDERSTAND THE WARNING THIS TIME? YOUR MUM DIDN'T KILL HERSELF.

She flung the paper away, knocking her tea over, and allowed the liquid to drip off the table edge and burn her thighs. It was what she deserved, that pain. She'd basically signed her mother's death warrant. By being silent, she'd killed her.

She got up and wandered into the living room, a daze overtaking her. Absently, she reached for her phone and dialled a number she'd told herself she wouldn't. Lydia would definitely want to be left alone now she'd married Yeoman. It was better for her that way. But everyone needed to be made aware. These warnings might not just be about the robbery. Whoever it was might have got to Flint, made him send these letters, made him kill Mum.

"Hello?" Lydia said. She must have deleted Delia's number. Her voice was enquiring, with a lilt at the end: "Who is this?"

"It's me." Delia held her breath.

"You're not meant to contact me."

"I know, but . . ." And she told her what had been going on.

"What do you want me to do about it? I can't tell Morgan, for God's sake. He mustn't know about any of it."

"I'm just letting you know, in case they come for you."

"They? Wouldn't it be him? And how can he when he's in Rushford?"

"Maybe he's paid someone to scare us, to kill Mum. Maybe he's got to Flint, and I thought the notes were about the robbery when they weren't, they were about that. *Olga's had some, too, but she saw a get-away driver at Wasti's, so we assumed . . . Have* you *had any notes?"*

Lydia laughed. "Don't be silly."

"It's not funny, Lyd."

"No, it isn't, and neither is you ringing me. Don't do it again."

The line went dead, so Delia rang Steve. She explained everything.

"If this is something to do with that," he said, "I'm going to have to fuck off. I can't be doing with this, the past keep rearing up. He's in prison, and that should be the end of it."

"What, you'd leave Val and Karl?"

"What else can I do? Fuck, she's coming. I'm in the back garden. She's been sniping at me all morning about an affair. I came out here for some space."

"You're cheating on her?"

"Of course I bloody am, and it's the perfect excuse to scarper. Laters."

Delia stared at the phone, her stomach in knots. Steve was going to leave Val, probably use the affair argument as an excuse. More guilt for Delia to cope with. Bloody hell!

She phoned Olga then Alice, explaining the situation, warning them it might not be the robbery but what they'd done. Alice said she'd go round and talk to Lydia about it, tell her to be vigilant and not brush this off as a joke, and Olga, she'd barked at Delia, telling her she wished she'd never known them all, wished she'd never let it happen.

They were fucked, all of them.

Their chickens were coming home to roost.

CHAPTER TWENTY-FOUR

Morgan had left Shaz at the station looking into CCTV with Nigel. Jane Blessing, sour as anything earlier that morning, had declared she'd poke into Olga's background and find any family members. No next of kin had been discovered in Olga's documents at her house to inform them of her death — her parents and husband were deceased, and it didn't appear she had any other relations either. No neighbours in the lane knew if she had family. Val hadn't been in when he'd nipped there, so he'd wait for her to answer his text about that.

He hadn't set anyone tasks regarding Alice Baines. He'd deal with that, do the usual rooting around to make it seem like something was being done, but ultimately, he'd let it die a quiet death. He didn't need the shit.

With all three of his team busy, he'd told them he was going out to question the neighbours again. He needed privacy.

Billy Price had sent a coded text.

Morgan sat in a pub on the outskirts. Drinker's Rest cuddled the edge of Cobbs Moor, a damn creepy place at night, the expanse so big, the trees standing alone every so often, their naked branches a close resemblance to kinked spiders' legs. The pub was too remote for the likes of those lazy arses on the estate, too far away for them to want to travel to it, even by bus. Too pricy an' all.

He stared through the window nursing an orange juice, waiting for Billy to turn up. Someone walked a dog out there in the distance, the silhouettes of man and hound black against the blue-grey sky spotted with bulbous clouds threatening rain. Quite a hike, out on the moor, and not a jaunt Morgan would entertain no matter how much he loved Rochester.

His mind drifted.

This morning, seven o'clock, he'd left Lydia asleep, a note on the pillow. SOCO had buggered off around four a.m., Alice's body removed by someone in Lisa's team. There was a carpet to rip up and replace, but that could wait. He'd arrange it while Lydia was away. He'd have to bang it on a credit card.

He'd managed to grab a couple of hours in bed, the one in the spare room. Sharing with his wife wasn't something he could bring himself to do, not after she'd murdered someone. Not after he'd crossed the line, the real line, into illegal territory. He was shielding a killer, albeit one forced to commit murder — if her story *was* true — and would go down for a stretch himself if ever he was caught.

Billy's flatbed lorry trundled into the car park, whatever was in the back walloping the sides on a right turn. He parked up, scaffolding poking out, so he must be on the same job as he'd been before. The man got out and wandered over to the pub door, paint-splattered overalls needing a good wash, and pushed inside. He glanced around and nodded upon spotting Morgan. He ambled over.

Morgan had already bought him a tonic water, Billy's usual tipple during the day, and Billy sat, air puffing out of the leather seat on the low stool.

"What's the deal?" Morgan asked.

"This'll cost two hundred. It's big stuff."

Morgan shook his head. "I only have fifty on me."

Billy peered over his shoulder. "There's a cash machine there."

Morgan sighed, went over to it, and took out the notes. There was a scheme going on at the station, where he could get the money back out of expenses. Billy and Val were down as registered civilian grasses, their official title Covert Human Intelligence Sources, more commonly known as narks. Still, two hundred was pushing it, but he'd take the hit if it was deemed too high for the coffers to pay out. Billy had said it was something Morgan would want to keep quiet, so he'd pay for the info even if was five hundred.

He returned to the table and held the money in his closed hand. He'd give it to him once Billy had spilled the beans. "Come on then, out with it, and remember to keep your voice down."

"It's about Lydia."

Morgan's blood ran cold, and goosebumps erupted on his neck. That explained the fee. Billy needed it to keep his mouth closed even more than usual. A copper with a wife in trouble, if that was what it was, meant Morgan might be dragged into shit.

More shit than he was already in.

Did someone know what had gone down at his house last night? Did they know she'd killed Alice? Had whoever burst into his home run his mouth off, telling all and sundry Lydia's name?

"Okay." Morgan brought his poker face into play. Inside, his emotions raged. He wanted to punch Billy, hurt him, but that action was nothing more than a misplaced attack. It wasn't like Lydia was here for him to bawl out instead.

"Word has it she's a target." Billy sipped his water, bubbles popping and dispersing onto his nose.

Don't I fucking know it. "In what way?" *Calm. Collected. Act like you don't give a shit.*

"For something she did as a teenager." Billy shrugged, an *I don't fucking know what it's about, I'm just passing it on* gesture.

"Right . . . So she did something as a kid. Didn't we all? And?"

"That's about it in a nutshell."

"It isn't worth two hundred." That had slipped out. He was supposed to be scared, worried for his wife, not annoyed she was bringing extra crap into his life, extra dung for him to shovel up and hide. "I need more. You *know* more — I can tell. We've worked with each other for a long time. Your face gives you away. Little tic in your eyelid."

Billy sighed. "I just know those people I heard this off are bad, proper bad. Got a nasty feeling about it. Someone is after her for whatever it is. They just got out of Rushford and—"

"Flint?"

"No, he's not the one, although he *is* being framed for it. He's an easy scapegoat. He was in on whatever happened in the past, too."

Morgan's mind ticked over. "Delia? Olga?"

"You've got it. And some bird called Alice was involved as well."

Morgan swallowed. Straightened it all out in his mind.

One: Delia, Olga, Lydia, Alice, and Flint had done something as kids. It was coming back to bite them on their arses. With Delia, Olga, and Alice gone, Lydia and Flint had to be shitting themselves.

Two: Someone in prison, newly released, was coming for them, one by one by the look of it.

Three: Flint wasn't being killed because he'd be taking the rap.

Fuck me . . .

"Alice was popped last night," Billy said. "So I heard. At your house, of all places."

It was redundant answering that. "Anyone else involved?"

"Some bloke called Steve, you know, Val's ex-husband, and another fella, but they didn't say his name."

Morgan stood, slapped a hand to his head. Paced, his heart banging. "Christ. Right. And who did you hear this from?"

"That's the thing. I don't know. I was earwigging in The Tractor's last night, my back to whoever it was. After they started discussing it, I was fucked if I'd turn around. They sounded dangerous, know what I mean? It seemed the one in the red car—"

"You what? A red car?"

"Yeah, he's the one who did Olga and Alice. There's three men, from what I gathered. One: the killer; red car. Two: the one who gives instructions to the killer; chap just out of Rushford. And three: the main man who wants them dead, also just out of Rushford. The main man did Delia himself because she'd been gobby to him when 'it' had all happened, and he's carried that niggle around with him ever since, apparently. Red Car has also been in Rushford, by the way. Got talking to man number two, who introduced him to man number three. That's how they got together to do all this. Cooked up a little scheme on the inside."

So one and two might well be in Halfway House.

Billy rolled his shoulders. Glanced about to check if they were being overheard. "They were discussing your Lydia and what to do next. Red Car was supposed to kill her last night, and he said Alice being there was a bonus, because he was going to hers next. Oh, and Lydia promised to shag Red Car, just so you know."

Morgan's skin prickled. "Why would she do that?"

"So he doesn't kill her. That's what I got out of it anyway. Like, she didn't do anything back then except watch, she didn't participate as such, so she asked if she could just get roughed up."

"Roughed up."

"Red Car took it to mean in bed, so he offered her a kink deal."

"A kink deal." Morgan's jaw stiffened.

"Yeah, whips and chains and—"

"I fucking know, all right?"

Billy flushed. "Sorry, thought you needed clarification because you repeated it."

"I don't."

"I've gathered that now, haven't I." Billy cleared his throat then drank some tonic water. "So let's get this straight, because it's all a bloody jumble to me. The teenagers did something — what, we don't know."

Morgan nodded. "And someone wants to get back at them for it — let's say they need to pay for what they did."

"Right. Middleman met that someone in Rushford. I remember now, Red Car was in there on drug dealing charges for a few months last year, and he's friends with Flint still; he did a stint of threatening Olga and Delia about the Wasti robbery. That was a brag, let me tell you. Middleman said Red was pleased with himself about it."

"Sounds like a right prick."

"Hmm. So, Red carries out the neck slices, but Main Fella, he did Delia. Flint was part of the teenage gang, but he's not being bumped off because he's set to go down for killing all the others."

"Now there's Steve left to kill, plus the unknown bloke."

"Maybe Lydia if the kinky shit isn't enough to keep her quiet. Main Fella said he'd rather she be offed but that Red Car could have some fun with her first. Lull her into a false sense of security."

So whoever it was, they were a sick bastard.

But that depended on what had gone down when they were kids.

What the hell had Lydia done? What had all of them done to make one man want them dead? Morgan hadn't been aware Lydia even knew Delia et al. She hadn't batted an eyelid when he'd told her he was working the Delia Watson case when it had come on the news. He'd put that down to her being high or uninterested in his job, because that job had pushed the wedge between them, according to her. The least she heard about it the better, so she'd muttered.

And what about Val? Did she know Steve was a wrong 'un? Was that the real reason he'd walked out on her, because she'd found things out?

Again, what was so awful that they were being killed for it?

"Is that the lot?" Morgan asked, still pacing.

"Yeah."

"Right, you know the rules anyway, this kind of shit is kept to yourself, but this particular shit? Forget you ever heard it. None of this discussing it business during pillow talk with the missus."

"Teaching a grandmother . . ." Billy held his hand out.

Morgan made to shake it, transferring the cash. He walked out, nerves ragged, brain steaming, anger rising. In his car, he gunned the engine and sped from the parking area, working out which person to see first.

Flint was his best bet.

He pulled up outside Halfway House ten minutes later and pelted up the path.

Emma opened the door, clearly shocked to see him.

"I need a word with Flint," he said.

She frowned, as if confused, as though he was supposed to be there for someone else, and that got him thinking. Did she know something about Middleman?

"Everything all right, Emma?" He stepped into the hallway.

She closed the door — and her eyes, but only for a brief moment. "Yes, just finished cleaning the bedding. I hung them out. The weatherman promised sun, but looks like rain's on the way. They always get it wrong."

"So you're harassed from that, eh?"

She nodded. "Yes, just that."

'Just that.' It told him more than she probably thought. She was confirming 'just that' and nothing else, although there *was* something else, he'd lay a bet down on it.

"Any of the residents use a red car?" he asked. "Maybe you forgot to tell me when we discussed Delia's abduction."

She appeared genuinely confused by that. "None of them own cars, I told you that, and if they did and it was red, I'd have said so."

So he must have been loaned one, whoever it is. Where is it parked? Or does Main Fella have it dropped round each time Red needs it? "Got anyone in here who seems extra dodgy?"

She laughed, a nervous one. "As opposed to just normal dodgy?"

"Heard any chatter?"

"No." Said forcefully. Said: *Leave me alone. Don't make me tell you.*

"Are you sure?"

"Of course." She smiled. Tight. Fake.

He left her there, couldn't be arsed to argue at the minute, and went to Flint's bedsit. He knocked, loud, urgent, no messing about.

Flint opened up. "Aww, fuck me sideways. *Really*?"

"I need a word with you." Morgan shoved him in the chest.

Flint stumbled backwards. "I haven't done anything, I swear to fucking God."

"I know you haven't."

Flint's eyes popped wide. "What?"

Morgan entered and closed the door. "Now, we're going to talk quietly, because there's someone here who means to pin those murders on you, and we can't have him catching wind that I know, got it? He's been paid to use someone to do it."

Flint plunked into the chair and fiddled with the neckline of his white T-shirt, LORD HAVE MERCY across the front in red. "Here? As in, Halfway House?"

"Yeah. Apparently, you used the killer to frighten Delia and Olga years ago. About Wasti's robbery."

"I didn't!" But his face said otherwise. He knew exactly who it was, the lying little bastard.

"Let's pretend you did, just for this conversation." Morgan strode to the window, moved the nets, and peered out. No red cars. Like there would be. "Where would you know a man like that from? Childhood? Where would you know a man prepared to kill for someone else? A middleman at that, not even the real brains behind it. The brains is keeping well out of the way, apart from offing Delia. He wanted her for himself. Something about her being gobby. Do you know a man like that?"

Flint paled, his eyes seeming to mist through recollection. Was he seeing Delia mouthing off? Did he know exactly what and who Morgan had referred to?

Flint shook his head as if to remove the images from his mind. "Just for this conversation, yeah?"

"Yeah."

"We were in a gang. Not a bad one, not like the ones these days where you go round having wars and shanking people and shit, just a normal gang. A group of kids who hung about, smoking, maybe drinking, a bit of gin." He winced at the word 'gin'.

Morgan filed that away for later. "Right. Something went down involving that gang, and somehow, that fella who did the frightening, he's now been given the job of murdering everyone, bar you, for someone else. The middleman has been in Rushford recently, hence him now being in Halfway." *And he's employed the killer who's been selling my wife coke.* "Who might that be, d'you reckon?"

"Let's just say I know who you're on about regarding the killer. If the main man knew who the Halfway bloke had employed to do it, he'd be sick to his stomach."

Morgan pulled away from the window. "What do you mean? The killer met the main man in Rushford through the middleman."

Flint laughed. "The main man wouldn't have recognised him. For reasons. The killer was part of the gang an' all."

This was confusing as fuck. "Why would the brains be sick to his stomach?"

"Hypothetically speaking, like, we're making up a little story here, aren't we, and it isn't being taken as the truth, on record . . ."

"Not at the minute, no."

"Well, the brains must be something to do with the child who . . . who . . . had stuff done to him. The Incident, we call it. If the brains knew the bloke Middleman had employed was actually there, had seen it all, and was hiding in a fucking cupboard, he'd be raging." Flint laughed again, a bit too deliriously. "He's bloody paying someone already involved when he should be killing him. What a dick."

Patience thin, Morgan punched Flint in the nose. Flint's head snapped back, and he lifted his hands to his face, hiding the blood streaming from his nostrils.

"Ow. Bleedin' hell. *Ow.*" Flint's eyes watered, tears streaming.

"This might be a damn joke to you, but it concerns my sodding wife — yes, I now know she was in that gang, too. So, who is the man organising this? And who is the bloke in Halfway, the middleman? And who, for fucking hell's sake, is the killer?"

Flint lowered his hands and reached for a loo roll on the TV unit. He mopped up the blood. "Now that, I won't tell you; who the killer is, who any of them might be. I'd rather get framed for it all. The killer is a nutter — okay on the outside, but in his noggin? Fucked up. I don't fancy being offed with his usual style, thanks. Better to do time than that."

Morgan chuckled derisively. "So you do a stretch in Rushford, with the same bloke who's now got hits out on you all, someone who was in your gang, was once your mate, maybe still is. Priceless. You survived the main man having something done to you inside if he recognised you, you said you didn't even do the robbery, you said you turned over a new leaf, yet you'll take the blame for murdering your old friends?"

"Listen, I'll give you clues but I won't give names. My brother could get dragged into this, and I assure you, Phil's clean where this is concerned. Do you remember your last conversation with Oliver Elford upstairs, him from number twelve?" Flint sniffed some dribbling blood back up his nose. "He told me all about your chat when we had a cuppa together. Said he'd almost called you a—"

"Yep, I remember it."

"What did he say after that?" Flint gazed about, as if pondering it. "Hmm, let me think. Something about you being like the big black bastard who beat him up in the nick."

"Who's black? The organiser, Halfway, or the killer?"

"The organiser, the brains. He had a nice home to go back to, though, so no Halfway House for him. And the killer, he got to know him while he served time for drugs, clearly omitting he had any dealings with what our gang did. I was on a different wing to the organiser, thank God, but the grapevine's always alive inside, so he'd have known I was there. I kept under the radar. In our little tale, this fantasy we're discussing, the killer works for my brother, but then don't a lot of people who tread White-Powder Road around here. If you've got eyes on Phil, you'll work out who it is."

Morgan pegged it out of the bedsit and down the stairs. He rushed to his car, diving into the driver's seat, and grabbed the list out of the glove box, the one with all the residents of Halfway on it.

Who was it? Which one?

Movement flickered to his right. Emma coming out, heading towards him.

He wound the window down.

"Someone's bolted," she said. "I just went to check they were okay as I didn't . . . I had a funny feeling about them last night. No answer. The log said he was in his room, that he hasn't ever left since he came here, which is odd, but he has been outside, I know that. I went in, and all his stuff is gone, so he must have bypassed the system somehow."

"Who is it?"

"Martin Olbey."

"I'll deal with it." He made to drive off.

"Wait. I was too scared to phone this in last night . . . I'm sorry. I heard him talking. On the phone. I'm sure they were discussing a murder — once I thought about it all in bed, it was obvious. A woman has been killed, he called her A, and she's friends with someone beginning with L."

Alice and Lydia . . .

"And," she went on, "A was supposed to be killed after L, at A's house, but A was already at L's . . . The man on the phone still wants L killed, not left to 'waltz around', I think he said."

"Right. Did the log show Martin going out last night, after you heard him on the phone?"

"No. That's why it's odd. I'd collected all the bedding ready to wash today, and I just knew someone stood behind me in the utility room, but when I turned, no one was there. Then the front door clicked. I checked the log, and it didn't register an exit or entry. So I looked out, and Martin was walking up the road, towards The Tractor's."

That made sense. He'd gone up there to meet the black bloke, the organiser, and Billy had heard their discussion. Now all Morgan had to do was find out who drove the red car, then he'd have the killer. As for Martin, the middleman . . .

"Okay, I'll phone this in. You let his probation officer know he's gone AWOL. It might not be anything to worry about — he could have a new permanent address and just didn't tell you. Did he come back last night?"

"I didn't hear him, and again, the log detected nothing."

"Okay, so he could have left, come back to get his stuff while you slept, then scarpered. You act as normal. It's part of your job to say someone's absconded. Be more vigilant, though. If he returns, ring me direct."

He drove away and glanced in his rearview. Emma remained on the pavement, hands clenched together, watching him leave. Poor cow. But she knew what she'd stepped into when taking the job. You had to be thick if you didn't think there'd be any trouble while living with cons.

He parked outside Val's and knocked on her side door. No one answered, so he went round the front and peered through the living room window. He sighed and got back in his car, wishing he could have warned her in person, but a message would have to do.

He tapped out: *Watch yourself. Steve's involved in something. If he contacts you, get hold of me immediately — and don't let him in your place if he turns up. Explain later.*

He drove off, round the corner into Regency, and stopped at the kerb in front of Phil's. The man wasn't likely to give up the name of the bloke in the red car, admitting he employed a drug runner, but Morgan had to try.

He had something to do before he got out, though.

Speed dial one. Lydia.

Phone to his ear, he got agitated at the constant ringing. It clicked over to voicemail.

"Hi, it's Lydia, if you could just leave a message . . ."

"Ring me, Lyd. Something's up."

He cut the call. Waited for her to phone back. Shit, had something happened to her?

House phone. No answer.

Bollocks. He was going to have to go home.

CONFESSION

It blows fancying your work partner, knowing you've got no chance whatsoever, not only because he still seems stuck on a wife who treats him badly, but because you're just not his type.

—DS Sharon Tanner

CHAPTER TWENTY-FIVE

Shaz hated it when Morgan went off on one by himself. He'd been doing it more and more lately, and she dreaded to think what he was up to half the time. The bloke had a knack of exuding menace if the situation called for it, and she'd turned a blind eye on more than a few occasions. A little punch here, a grip of someone's shirt front there, all designed to get information they wouldn't receive by playing nice.

She'd do anything for him, even putting her career on the line. Keeping her gob shut wasn't a hardship. Well, unless he went too far, *then* she'd have to step in, but only for his sake. Why should a brilliant copper lose his career over bullying info out of creeps who ought to be in Rushford, the key thrown away?

The years they'd been together on the job had forged a bond, one she hadn't expected, where she wanted more than he could give, where she wanted what he wasn't even aware of. Fair enough, he was married, and there was no way she'd cross the line in *that* regard, wouldn't make a play until he was well away from Lydia. And Lydia . . . Wow, what a caustic bitch. She didn't even curb her tongue if Shaz was round there for dinner. Out the nastiness burbled, and Shaz would swear the woman was on something. Drugs, be it recreational, addictive, or prescription. She wasn't right, the way she blurted mean shit out like that.

'Morgan's rarely at home, so it's like being married to a ghost.'

'Morgan's so devoted to his wife, and it isn't me. No, his wife is the police force.'

'The only thing Morgan loves apart from work is that bloody dog. I should never have bought it for him.'

Shaz sighed, holding back her temper the memories had brought to the fore.

"You okay?" Nigel asked beside her.

She shrugged. "Yeah, just don't like being chained to a desk when my partner's out there having all the fun."

"Join the club." Nigel laughed. "Now you know how me and Jane feel, staying behind doing all the grunt work, although I must say, I enjoy it really."

Jane huffed and peered at them over her monitor. She'd changed her desk around a few months back, saying she liked the privacy. "Why would you want to be with *him*? You'll get yourself in trouble before long if you allow him to drag you into things he shouldn't."

"Jane?" Shaz smiled sweetly, although inside, she raged.

"Yes?"

"Fuck off."

CHAPTER TWENTY-SIX

Val sat on the closed toilet seat in Phil's little loo. She had a specific message tone for Yeoman and couldn't ignore the text. He rarely sent them, and when he did, it was usually important. She must have been in bed with Phil when the first one arrived: *Do you know Olga's next of kin?*

She stared at the words on the screen, the second message, blurry now she'd read it: *Watch yourself. Steve's involved in something. If he contacts you, get hold of me immediately — and don't let him in your place if he turns up. Explain later.*

What the hell did that mean? Steve had been gone for so long, she'd been allowed to divorce him after years of him not coming back. Why would he even turn up at her house anyway? And what could she possibly do to help him if he *was* involved in something?

The not knowing, the vagueness of the text, frustrated the hell out of her, but if she left now after promising to stay with Phil all day, he might ask questions.

How was she going to go back into that kitchen and act normal?

They'd had sex after the biscuits, and he'd confessed that his conscience had pricked him lately, regarding what he really did to earn the majority of his money. Something about a lad he knew, rolling up to the corner of Regency to buy drugs for his mates, a lad he didn't want walking down that dangerous road. He'd been tempted to ring the police on him but hadn't wanted the mother to be disappointed in her kid, so he'd kept his mouth shut, especially after he'd found out the lad ran with the wrong crowd.

She'd had the strange sensation he'd been talking about her Karl. Just something about the way he'd hugged her closer to him at the mention of the mother. And because Karl was weird last night after Yeoman had been round, coming into the living room and telling her he'd be a good son, someone she could be proud of, and he was sorry if he'd ever upset her.

Had Phil warned Karl to behave himself? Had Yeoman? There had been a gap in time between the side door being knocked and Yeoman talking to her, and at one point, Karl had clomped upstairs, come back down, and gone into the kitchen. Had he handed over drugs to Yeoman?

Karl was bound to run into weed or whatever at some point, being in college. They were rife around here, those men who peddled baggies for the man she cared for. But . . . well, she'd had higher hopes for Karl, and maybe, if he'd been spoken to, he'd get back on the right track.

If he'd even veered off it. Might just be her imagination.

She shuddered at the thought of Steve strutting back into her world. There was no way she'd be helping him, so phoning Yeoman wouldn't be a problem. She had a new life now, part three. Part one had been her days up until Steve walked out, two was the period of her bringing Karl up and selling her body, and three, that was now, Karl moving out to a flat and her being with Phil. She didn't need it tainted by her ex. He'd done enough of that in part one.

"Have you fallen down the shitter?" Phil called then laughed.

She jumped, deleted the messages, shoved her phone in her pocket, then flushed the loo. Hands washed to add to the charade, she joined him in the kitchen. He was her everything now, this man who'd promised her he'd be giving up the sale of drugs. He had enough money to last them the rest of their days, no scrimping either, and if she could just pretend he'd earned it legitimately, things would be peachy.

Yes, she could pretend. She'd done it with every customer, making out she enjoyed what they were doing to her. She was good at putting on a front.

Which she did now, smiling at Phil as though her insides weren't churning.

CHAPTER TWENTY-SEVEN

Delia had waited a couple of hours after Steve had stormed out of Val's, her backside numb from her perch on the living room windowsill. She'd wanted to give Val time to come to terms with him leaving her, if that was what had gone on. She didn't doubt Steve when he'd said he'd use the affair as an excuse to leg it. He'd always been a shyster, the bad seed of the group along with Flint and Goat. All them had run drugs for Phil since they were twelve, Steve giving it up once he'd met Val, Flint moving on to robbing and duffing people up, Goat remaining in Phil's service.

She sighed and, drawing the fronts of her cardigan together, left her house and walked to Val's. There was a selfish reason for going — to see if Steve had opened his mouth about The Incident and her role in it. She wouldn't put it past him if he needed extra leverage to leave. That man would do whatever to get what he wanted, just like Lydia.

A slight breeze ruffled Delia's greasy hair. She couldn't remember the last time she'd washed it. Grief was the culprit, stealing the days between Mum's murder and now. She shivered at thinking of murder, but that was what it amounted to. Someone had come in that night, breached her once safe sanctuary, and forced Mum to write that 'suicide' note and take those tablets. All the while, Delia had slept, only waking when they'd left, slamming the door. She often wondered how long the killer had been in the house. He must have waited for the tablets to take effect, ensuring Mum was dead before he'd walked out.

She hated herself for not waking sooner.

At Val's picket gate, Delia pushed through and trudged up the path, her shoulders heavy with so much weight — the past, the notes, Mum dying, the new note. She was desperate to offload it to Val, the one woman she trusted, but to burden her friend after Steve had fucked off was more than a bit rude. And besides, if she told, something might happen to her. They might creep in and slice her throat or strangle her while she slept.

She moved down the ginnel, her steps sluggish.

Florrie Dorchester flung her landing side window open and poked her head out. "Fair warning, there's been a row, Del."

Tell me something I don't know. *"Okay."*

"He was out in the garden on the phone to someone, then he storms inside and starts effing and jeffing, the noisy bark. I heard everything." She folded her arms on the sill and leant out farther. "Been having an affair, hasn't he. Someone up at The Tractor's by all accounts. Filthy sod. I've been up there many a time and seen him ogling the girls during quiz night when Heidi's asking the questions. I could have told her this was coming."

"Why didn't you then? I told her stuff. She deserved to know."

"Well, it's not my place, is it. I mean, I didn't have proof. He could tell her looking didn't hurt, so long as he didn't touch. Mind you, there was the time he pinched that girl's tit, made out he'd bumped into her by accident and just happened to squeeze. Hmmm, maybe I should have told her."

"Yes, you should." Delia shook her head and knocked on the door to the sound of Florrie slamming her window shut.

Val opened up, her eyes red-rimmed, Karl round her skirt, grabbing at the material, his chubby hands smeared with chocolate. Poor little mite. Had he witnessed them arguing and Val had given him a bag of chocolate buttons to make it all better?

"I heard he left," Delia said.

Val nodded and walked away, into the dining area. Delia entered, locked the door in case Steve had a mind to come back, and went straight to the kettle, sorting things for their cuppas.

They were going to need them.

Drinks done, she sat at the table opposite Val, who blurted everything, crying, snot dripping until she cuffed it with her cardi sleeve.

"And then he just walked out, no clothes in a bag or anything," she wailed. "As if our marriage meant nothing."

"I'm going to sound harsh, but what if it didn't mean anything? He was messing with other women, love, I warned you about it. You don't need the likes of him. I felt so bad when I first met you, after you married and moved in here with him. I wanted to tell you he was a git, a waste of space, but you seemed so happy."

"If you had, there'd be no Karl, so it was worth it to get him." Val smiled fondly at the lad playing at her feet with a train. "I wouldn't change that part of it for the world."

"What will you do? For work, I mean. Steve paid the bills, didn't he?"

Val nodded. "I don't know. Go on the game?"

They laughed at that, although a seed sprouted in Delia's mind. It was just sex, she could compartmentalise. She'd done enough of that to block out the past.

"I'm up for it if you are." She sipped her tea. "We could club together and get some business cards done, leave them in phone boxes and on message boards."

Val roared, probably thinking Delia was joking. "Ladies of the night, willing to service your needs."

"Why not? You could do it during the hours Karl's at playschool. I could do it at night so we're not taking each other's trade. Fuck it, I'll even stand on the corner outside Halfway. There's some business right there, lags who're desperate. I'll do them down the alley. They'd be so excited, they wouldn't last long." Could she, though? Could she really?

"But it's wrong." Val ran her fingertips around the rim of her cup. "And immoral."

"If it pays the bills . . . I need money because my wages aren't enough without Mum's social. You need money because, apart from Child Benefit, you have nothing coming in. Steve earned a lot, being an electrician, and he's not the type to hand over maintenance, so can you really see yourself going down skint street? The dole is crap, and you'd have to work all hours in the supermarket where you were before Steve came

along. Then there's paying for someone to watch Karl after playschool. You'd hardly see him except at bedtime. What sort of life is that for you both? He needs his mum around." Before he turns into someone like his deranged father.

"All fair points." Val sighed. "But can you seriously see yourself shagging strangers?"

"Shut your eyes and think of England."

"Oh God, you mean it, don't you?"

Delia nodded. "I do. I want to be in control for once, not the other way around."

"What do you mean by that?"

"Nothing."

"Yes, there is something. Tell me."

It spilled out then, everything about seeing Flint in Wasti's with the gun, Olga spotting a getaway driver, but please, please don't tell her I told you that. She didn't mention the past, it was too horrible, too mortifying to admit she'd been the kind of person to be involved in such things, when it wasn't funny like Steve had thought it was, it was awful. She never said about Mum being murdered either, just that she and Olga had been threatened with notes.

"Tell the police," Val said. "You can't live in fear like that, just because you know it was Flint. And what about Wasti? I bet Flint's been in that shop loads of times since. What if he decides to hurt him? Rob him again?"

Delia thought about Lydia and the copper she'd married. Should she contact him?

Val went on and on, beating Delia down, telling her she really should tell someone in authority or risk them hurting her.

Delia mentioned Morgan Yeoman. "I'd feel better talking to someone who's married to my friend. Okay, we haven't seen each other for years, but she's still a mate, and I don't know him from Adam, didn't get invited to the wedding, but . . ."

"Makes sense. Go on then, ring him."

"I don't know his number."

"Bloody hell. I'd say look it up online, but I don't have a computer. Here, let's fetch the Yellow Pages."

Delia frowned. "What? Can't we just ring the nick and ask for him?"

"Good idea. Want me to do it?"

Delia nodded.

It took ages for him to arrive after Val's call. So much so that Delia had stayed for dinner, the pair of them making it together, a nice bit of boiled gammon with Olga's potatoes and peas, covered with onion gravy.

Although telling Yeoman who'd robbed Wasti's was frightening, it brought a massive sense of relief. It was out there, in someone else's hands, and Yeoman told her they could place her in a safe house until Flint was put away. She declined; she'd take her chances. If the note-writer chose to do something to her, so be it.

After all, it was what she deserved after The Incident, and if she got done for that should Flint open his big fat mouth, she'd go into custody quietly.

CHAPTER TWENTY-EIGHT

Morgan struggled to get the key in the front door, his hand shaking. He'd got wound up on the way home, convincing himself Lydia had endured that kinky shit with the killer, then he'd murdered her afterwards, adding her blood to the carpet in the living room. He'd imagined the sex and oddly hadn't experienced the pang of jealousy a spouse was supposed to have jabbing his heart and his gut. He'd imagined her throat being cut, that signature downwards flick at the end. And he'd imagined finding her, trying to bring her back to life and failing.

"Fuck's sake!" He paused, took a breath, and inserted the key without a problem. He flung the door wide and launched into the foyer, still with Alice's blood spots on it, dried black now.

The alarm didn't blare out, so she must be in.

"Lyd? Lydia?"

A quick look in the living room. Just the dark puddle on Lydia's expensive carpet, the shape of it showing where Alice's head had rested.

The kitchen. Nothing but her breakfast plate and a cup in the sink, plus all the mugs the coppers used last night on the worktop, ones he'd meant to put in the dishwasher before he'd left this morning, but he'd wanted to get out, away from the stench of death, away from *her* house and everything in it.

He ran upstairs to their bedroom, and all he needed to know was right there. Open wardrobe doors, clothes removed. The two big suitcases gone from the top. The quilt scuffed where she'd packed, a tube of mascara nestled between two hills of material. Drawer open on her bedside cabinet — she'd probably taken her passport. All her perfumes missing from her vanity.

The en suite — toothbrush gone.

He'd planned to send her away abroad, but she'd taken it upon herself to arrange it. Without telling him where she was going. There had been no note propped on the mantel, the usually dreaded Dear John, something he'd like to have seen in other circumstances, saving him the job of ending their marriage, cowardly bastard that he was.

What could he have said anyway? I'm leaving you because you're a fucking skanky druggie? I'm leaving you because you killed your mate? I'm leaving you because, fuck me, there's some nasty stuff in your past that you haven't told me and it's resulted in murder? But most of all, I'm leaving you because you've changed into someone unrecognisable, and it's changed me into a different person an' all.

Or had she always been this way and he'd been too blinkered by love to notice?

He phoned her father. "Hey, it's Morgan. Is Lydia with you?"

"No, we haven't spoken to her in over a month. Now why isn't that a surprise? She's all but cut us off since taking the money, barely gets hold of us. We have to ring her just to make sure she's still alive." A chuckle.

Morgan jolted. "You say it isn't a surprise. Did you *expect* her to take it and run then?"

"You could say we know our daughter well. She's a law unto herself, son. Lydia cares for no one but Lydia. What's going on? Have a row, did you?"

"No. She was supposed to be going away for a while, for a bit of a break. Alice was murdered here last night, and Lydia witnessed it."

"Alice? Alice Baines?"

"Afraid so."

"No wonder her mother blanked me this morning in the newsagent's shop, probably too caught up in grief. Good God, that's bloody awful. What on earth happened?"

"Random break-in. He shoved past Lydia then cut Alice's throat. Exited just as quickly as he'd come in." Sort of the truth. "I came home from walking the dog, found them in the living room. My lot have been here. Lydia went to bed with a sleeping pill, and last I saw her she was out for the count this morning. I rang her to check she was okay, no answer. I'm home now, and she's packed suitcases, taken her passport."

"You should know she bolts when she's frightened or wants to punish, even if it's just down to London for the weekend. There was this one time, God, she must have been about thirteen, when she ran away, you know, for over a week. Did she ever tell you about that?" He blustered on without giving Morgan a chance to reply. "Well, something had happened between her and the people in this little group she hung around with. I don't know, she probably argued the toss about something and they had a go at her. She wouldn't have liked being reprimanded, and she never did give us a reason for going missing, just that she 'needed space'. We have no idea where she went either. We had the police out looking for her, of course, and she also wouldn't admit to them where she'd been."

If Morgan had run a check on her when they'd met, he'd know this. He hadn't wanted to, instead taking her as the truthful person she'd presented.

"Can you remember exactly when that was?" he asked.

"Not off the top of my head, no, but around about the same time, that lad got murdered. I remember worrying in case the killer had got to her, too, and the police were very good, worrying along with us."

What? "Who was it?"

"Blimey, what's his name . . . ? Um . . ." The crackle of the phone touching something on the other end of the line. "Love, what was that boy called, the one who got tortured and killed when Lyd was younger?"

Tortured?

"Jacob Everson," the mother-in-law said.

"Did you hear that?" Father-in-law.

"I did. Cheers. Well, I've got to go. If Lyd rings you, can you let me know?"

"Will do, but don't hold your breath. She'll be in the Big Smoke, fucking about in Harrods. Tarra."

Morgan stared at the phone screen, trying to take it all in. A kid, tortured, murdered. It had to be what the gang had been involved in. A big coincidence if it wasn't.

He went downstairs and checked the laptop. The dozy cow had left her search history up, and she'd visited a site for airline tickets. He checked to see where she'd got them from, but without digi forensics, he wouldn't be able to find out anything more unless he contacted the website direct.

He moved to the fridge to get a bottle of water, his attention drawn to a ripped-off sheet of notepaper, Lydia's scrawl all over it. Her 'high' scrawl. She must have sniffed some cocaine before scarpering, which meant she hadn't flushed it down the loo like he'd asked.

GONE ON THAT HOLIDAY. WILL MAYBE SEE YOU SOMETIME, BUT DON'T BANK ON IT. THANKS FOR NOTHING.

Ah, the Dear John, albeit brief and bitchy.

It was bloody vague, no mention of her return date, and it had the air of finality about it. She'd left, run like her father had said, for good, and Morgan sighed in relief. She wasn't dead — unless someone had forced her to write the note and had packed her cases to make it look like she'd fucked off. She knew who was after her and why, knew kinky sex wasn't all she'd suffer through. And if she'd been involved with torturing someone, she didn't deserve to be sunning it anywhere.

But how is killing her mate any different? Why should she walk free from that, too?

Billy had said Lydia hadn't participated, just watched. So why were they after her? Because she hadn't put a stop to it?

Probably.

Morgan let Rochester out for a wee, set the alarm for everywhere except the kitchen so the dog didn't set it off, and drove back to the station. He walked through the incident room waving the team off so they didn't bother him. Slammed into his office. He locked the door — didn't need Shaz coming in and seeing what he was up to. At his desk, he took out a pad and pen. Computer booted up, he accessed Google and typed in a name: Jacob Everson.

Shitloads of headlines came up.

Murder! Child Suffers Prior to Violent Death!

Flats Cordoned Off. Body Discovered!

Justice for Jacob After Harrowing Torture.

Morgan's guts rolled. He hadn't lived here at the time this had happened, moving to Pinstone on a transfer a year or so prior to meeting Lydia, so this was all news to him. He scrolled to the one that would give him the name he needed, an article in *The Pinstone Star.*

MAN ARRESTED FOR
JACOB EVERSON SLAYING

Katie Violet — Lead Crime Journalist

A man has been arrested this morning on suspicion of torturing and murdering Jacob Everson, a thirteen-year-old boy from Elderflower Mead, Pinstone. Jacob's body had been found in a derelict block of flats in a squat on the second storey, Vicar's Gate. He'd been beaten and stabbed to death.

The man in question is forty-one-year-old David Ives, who has been in Rushford for assault and battery in the past.

Ives' vomit and fingerprints were discovered at the scene, the fingerprints lifted from Jacob's satchel, which was lying beside him in the squat. Ives declares he's innocent, but a police source said:

"The evidence against David Ives means we are going ahead with prosecution. CCTV footage also shows the accused coming from the derelict street and running farther onto the estate. Sadly, there is no footage of the walkways outside each flat, but with enhancement on the film we do have, we are certain, along with the fingerprints and vomit, that Ives is our man."

Here at The Pinstone Star, we once again offer our condolences to the Everson family for the senseless killing of a studious boy who was kind and an asset to Pinstone Secondary, where teachers and schoolchildren alike mourn his loss.

Rest in peace, Jacob. Justice will be done.

David Ives . . . Morgan tapped that into the police database, staring at what came up on the screen. A photo. It was that fucking man from The Tractor's, the one who'd stared when Morgan and Shaz had gone to pick up the CCTV from Terry. The man from Nigel's screen.

Morgan looked up Ives' details.

Release date from Rushford was last week.

Current address: Three Elderflower Mead.

What the fuck? He lives in the same street as the kid?

Morgan did a search for the files relating to the case and brought up info on Jacob's parents. They no longer lived in Elderflower, had moved to Shadwell soon after the trial, probably unable to stand the association with what had happened — and that the killer lived just down the road, four doors away. How had they stood that? How had they coped knowing a killer's family, maybe people they knew, were friendly with, resided a stone's throw from their front door?

He lost himself in the rabbit hole that was Jacob's case and, sickened to his stomach, emerged an hour later, stunned and destroyed.

If Lydia had watched that and done nothing, she was a revolting human being. Kid or not, to stand by and allow such things to happen to someone from her school and not step in to stop it . . .

He hated her, hoped she never came back from wherever the hell she'd gone.

But he hated himself more for covering her arse. She'd killed Alice just so she didn't get her neck sliced as well.

What kind of monster had he married?

CHAPTER TWENTY-NINE

Goat's dinner from last night kept repeating on him. Must be the garlic in the carbonara. Or the cream. His IBS had never accepted it. Lydia would most likely want to vom when he breathed on her.

He sat in a grey car, having told Martin Olbey to arrange something else, seeing as Goat had used the other one for Delia, Olga and Alice. With coppers snooping around, it didn't do for him to get caught in the red one, and with the car switch, that detective bastard would be chasing a ghost vehicle. Martin said it'd been crushed at the scrappy.

The main man didn't play about, did he? All angles covered.

Goat stared over the road at Yeoman's. He had to go inside there in a few to drop Lydia some more gear off. She'd have snorted the stuff from yesterday already, he'd bet, what with Alice being there, and anyway, he needed a word with her, remind her about the kink.

Maybe he'd get her on that job today instead of Wednesday. He'd originally said midweek so she had time to stew, to hate the thought of him touching her, like she'd done all those years ago. She'd been drunk that night, off her fucking tits on a mix of gin, vodka and cocaine, their first time trying the powder. He'd gone to deliver the baggie to some old fucker who had it on the regular, but when he'd got there, an ambulance arrived, lights flashing bright blue in the darkness, a couple of women standing on the path gawping, Old Man Cossack being carried out on a stretcher.

"Heart attack, I bet," another neighbour had muttered from a garden beyond the tree he hid behind.

"Not surprising," her friend said.

Then one of the women on the path had outright asked what was wrong, and yes, it *had* been a heart attack.

Goat had waited for the neighbours to go in and the ambulance to move off, then he took the key out from under the stone in the back garden, the shiny one with white veins running through it. Marble, Cossack had told him once. He'd entered the house, nicked the money for the coke from a jam jar in the bedroom, and walked out, locking up behind him. Money dropped off with Phil, there was the little matter of having enough coke for several thin lines in his pocket.

What to do with it? If he sold it again, Phil would know. That man had eyes and ears everywhere. The extra cash would come in handy, though . . . Goat had always wanted to try coke, properly like, not just a little taste on Phil's fingertip when he shoved it at him, rubbing it into his gums and laughing, saying a kid on a bender was the funniest fucking thing.

Or dangerous.

Goat had walked off to Wasti's, bought some sweets, then he was off to meet his mates, who'd promised to wait for him in the squat. What a night that had turned out to be, them all legging it, a couple of them covered in Jacob's blood, the rest just high as kites, drunk as skunks. If he recalled right, when Delia had been caught running by David Ives, she'd shouted at him, thinking he was some kind of demon she'd conjured up. She'd said blue snakes had writhed from his head, but Christ, it was just his dreads. She must have been hallucinating.

A bit of a mess, all of it, the drugs and alcohol lending spiteful hands, pushing them to do stuff they wouldn't normally. Who'd suggested they muck about with Jacob? He never could remember. Blurry memories skewed the retelling afterwards, so it'd got confusing as to what had actually occurred. They each had a different version of events.

Fuck this, he was going over to Lydia's now. *She* was stupid like Cossack and left a key under a rock, too, except this one was beneath that bush in front of the living room window, the ball-shaped one.

He got out of the car and looked around. No one seemed to be poking their hooters into his presence there, and it didn't matter if they did. He was a regular, a man Lydia had told her neighbours was a finance fella, there to chat about all that money she'd been given, sorting her investments. He didn't turn up in a suit, just smart casual. No need to look like a drug dealer, was there.

He opened the side gate and walked through, the gravel scrunching beneath his expensive shoes. He crouched to collect the key, let himself in, and turned off the alarm. Easy to get the code from a woman under the influence.

She'd said so many things she shouldn't. Especially that night.

'Come on, let's get off with each other . . .'

He'd been shocked his crush had wanted him, too.

'There's a condom in my back pocket, Goat . . .'

He'd wanted her to use his real name, to care enough to use it.

'No, stop it, I don't want to now . . .'

She'd switched off, just like that.

'It isn't funny. Get off!'

'I'm trying to get off,' he said, hoping to lighten her darkened mood, 'but you're running hot and cold.'

He wished he'd been the one to kill her just for that.

Well, he'd get some kink now, wouldn't he. All good things came to those who waited, and blimey, he'd waited.

Phil had given her a good poking, so he'd said, around the time she'd started buying drugs off him. He'd dumped her the next day.

Maybe she was shit in bed.

Goat shut the door, his usual gloves on, no worry about fingerprints then, and touching a woman while you had leather on your hands, well, that was a massive turn-on. His wife and all his other women thought it was weird and wouldn't allow it, but Lydia would have no choice. He called out to her, waited for her to shout back that she was coming — massive LOL — but silence replied, the air prickly with it.

A mooch around the downstairs told him a few things. No one had cleaned the blood off the carpet. No one had washed up all the mugs — what, had the coppers had a fucking tea party in here last night or what? The big dog wasn't afraid of him, galloping over for a big old fuss. And Lydia had buggered off. A note was on the kitchen worktop, a bit scarce with information but enough to get him in arsey mode.

He'd have to tell Martin.

Great. Martin would pass it on, and David was going to go mad.

Even madder if he found out who he'd employed to kill everyone.

Goat swiped an apple from the fruit bowl, laughing at how he'd got away with not being seen by David years ago. David didn't have a clue he'd been there, and everyone else had kept their gobs shut. They'd all agreed to forget about it, pretend it hadn't happened. For years David had sat in his cell for something he hadn't done, and now he expected those who'd killed Jacob to pay.

Best I keep my mouth shut for a bit longer then, eh?

Once the others were all dead, it'd be plain sailing.

He burped. Damn carbonara. Maybe it was pasta that didn't agree with him anymore.

He set the alarm, locked up, and slid the key in his pocket.

Who knew when he'd need it next.

CHAPTER THIRTY

Phil was cock-a-hoop. Everything had changed in the bedroom after Val accepted his offer, as though they'd both been holding back their true feelings, and now they were together as a couple, they'd moved on to the next stage. All right, all right, he was paying her, but he could pretend he wasn't, same as he'd pretended before with the biscuits.

She'd been a bit funny, though, once she'd come out of the loo, and he told himself she'd probably had a text from Karl. Always something up with teenagers, wasn't there. He remembered his brother as a lad. He'd gone well weird around the time Jacob Everson was murdered, but Phil had put it down to association when something occurred to another near your age: *It could have been me.*

Especially as Gary had tended to go to that squat often to dick about. Not after the murder, though, but that wasn't surprising. Who the fuck would want to sit drinking booze where someone had been killed, and by that David Ives fella an' all? Anyway, the windows had been blocked with steel plates instead of wood a week later, so no one could get in.

Ives had always given Phil the creeps, the way he'd stared at him once Phil had made it clear to everyone on the estate that he was the one to get drugs from, not David, who'd been wiry and slender with long dreads and easily manipulated. Carefully, like, Phil had whispered to buyers that his gear was the best, and cheaper, too. Ives had fancied himself *the* dealer, getting his shit from someone in Shadwell. He probably didn't like an up-and-coming squirt like Phil on the scene, although Phil was well into his twenties when he'd fully taken over Pinstone and could handle the likes of Ives.

Turned out he hadn't needed to for long.

He'd used Gary and Steve as runners, plus that horrible little shit of a kid, Goat — Phil employed him now to visit the high-end clients along with a couple of others who'd learned how to conduct themselves with toffs. Those original three had hung out with the girls, Delia, Alice, Lydia and Olga, a right bunch of buggers, discovering drink, spending time in the squat, and, come to think of it, they hadn't really got together after Jacob died.

Odd. Why hadn't he taken much notice of that before? Probably too caught up in his own life, his own self-importance. Phil hadn't been the most pleasant chap back then, treading on toes, punching people's lights out, ego the size of a planet. *He* was the only one in these parts to offer drugs, the only one folks needed, and anyone else even thinking of doing the same thing would be dealt with, quietly, behind the scenes, Phil appearing innocent on the outside, when really, he was the one instigating shit.

He ought to be ashamed of himself.

He thought about Delia's murder — and Olga's. Strange for two friends to go one after the other. *And* Alice — Val had said something about that earlier, Alice being murdered at Lydia's, but she'd sworn him to secrecy. Yeoman had asked her to keep it to herself, so she should have really, but Phil wasn't about to tell anyone. Yesterday, she'd mentioned Delia getting weird notes around the time of Gary robbing Wasti's, and it had got him thinking. There was Gary, out of Rushford and likely to get the blame for Delia, yet Phil's memory had been jogged. Goat in a red car outside Olga's the night Delia had been killed. Phil had been coming round the corner after speaking to a teenager and had seen it all.

Why had Goat spoken to her through the open car window — to ask what her fee was? Granted, he'd driven off and she'd walked down the alley, but he could have gone round the back into Elderflower and picked her up from the other end.

Like Phil had said to himself, Yeoman needed to concentrate on Mulberry. Shame he hadn't stationed a copper there. Olga might not have been killed then.

Hindsight.

"Off in your head?" Val pushed his cup of coffee towards him.

"Yeah, mulling things over." He told her about his runner but didn't mention it was Goat. "Thing is, while he's a bloody weirdo, I've never had any problems with him. Okay, he was away in Rushford for a bit, but he never grassed me up as the supplier. Took all the blame, probably so he had job to come back to after. Why was he at Olga's?"

Val looked uncomfortable, as if the information swam around inside her head and she didn't know what to do with it. Oh, Phil knew all about her telling Yeoman shit, her being a proper nark, and it was okay for her to tell the copper what he'd said, except . . .

"You can tell Yeoman." Phil sipped some coffee. "Just not that you got it from me. I don't want him asking me questions, especially when I'm all about giving up the business. A clean pathway, that's what it needs, so I can sell my patch to someone else."

"Right."

The doorbell rang, and Phil rose.

"Probably him now," he joked.

He didn't expect to see Yeoman at the door really, but there he was. For a moment, he thought it was David Ives. He was out of Rushford for Jacob's murder, and Phil wouldn't put it past him to come round here and start trouble. Heh, maybe he could offer Ives the patch back, not that he'd have enough money to buy it, but it'd be funny to watch his face fall when Phil mentioned the price tag.

"I need a word." Yeoman held his ID up, the twat. What was the point of that?

Phil shrugged. "Your nark's in the kitchen." He stepped back to allow the copper inside.

"I'll speak to her after." Yeoman entered and closed the door. "Now, Gary . . ."

"What about him?"

"I know you're older than him and were moving in . . . different circles when he was a teenager, although word has it he was one of your first runners, but what do you remember of him back then?"

Phil laughed. "He got drunk, he pissed about. What else do teenagers do?"

"What about his behaviour after Jacob Everson got murdered?"

And there was Phil only thinking about that earlier. What was going on? "Everyone was shocked. It was a kid on our estate, for fuck's sake. You don't get over something like that lightly."

"I've been to see Gary. Warned him he's being framed for the murders. Were you aware of that?"

"He might have said he was worried about it."

"A little bird tells me the real killer works for you on White-Powder Road, so he's selling to the more affluent of Pinstone. That's what you call it, isn't it? White-Powder Road is for the rich, Cut Street is for those with less money, the drugs lower quality. One of the customers is my wife, but then you knew that, didn't you."

Shite. Did he know Phil had shagged her an' all? Was he keeping off Phil's back lately so his missus didn't get in trouble for buying cocaine? After all, she usually bought enough to be classed as possession with an intent to sell. A copper with that much in his house — wouldn't go down well.

So Yeoman was a bent copper, prepared to ignore the rules. Interesting.

"I wasn't aware I had a killer working for me," Phil lied.

"Hmm. Fella in a red car, although he didn't kill Delia, just Olga and Alice Baines."

"Who *did* kill Delia, do you know?"

"I have an idea, although I can't talk about it."

"Thought as much. I'll have to check which of my employees owns a red car. What's in it for me if I give you the name?"

"Same fee as Val gets, not that you need it." Yeoman pointedly stared around the foyer. "Nice gaff."

Phil got uncomfortable. It was an obvious dig at how Phil made most of his money. "Is that all you wanted to ask? Why do you need to know about Gary as a teenager?"

"Ask your brother, although hopefully he'll keep his mouth shut for now. I'd be grateful if you did an' all. I don't need the killer or his . . . acquaintances getting wind of me knowing who they are."

Acquaintances? What's Goat got himself into? Why's he killed Olga and Alice but not Delia? Who killed Delia? And why?

Not knowing was going to dog him off.

"I'll keep my ear to the ground." Phil offered a smile to show he meant it, because shit, he was going to do some detecting of his own. "As I said, Val's in the kitchen."

Yeoman nodded. "You have her coming round here for your stint now then?"

Stint? It was more than that. It was love.

"It's her call as to whether she tells you anything about her private life." Phil walked off into the living room and waited for the clop of Yeoman's footsteps on the tiled foyer floor. Then he went back out there and padded to the kitchen. Pressed his ear to the closed door.

"Shit, I got your message," Val said. "What the hell's going on? The last thing I need his *him* coming back."

Him?

"Did he ever confide in you about his teenage years?" Yeoman asked.

What the fuck's all this teenage crap about?

"Only that he was a bit of a sod, drinking, smoking."

"You know he hung around with Delia, Olga, Alice, Lydia, Flint, and some other kid, don't you?"

"Yes, Delia mentioned it."

"With Delia, Olga, and Alice dead, Flint not giving me the other kid's name, Lydia God knows where, and Steve off the scene, I have no one to ask who that kid might be. That kid . . . I need to speak to him. Flint's being framed for their murders. They all saw or did something years ago. A child got tortured then killed."

"Oh no, not Jacob Everson . . ."

"Yes."

What the hell?

"That was awful," Val said. "Everyone was upset about that. But David Ives got put away for it, so what does that have to do with them?"

What, indeed. Something I want to know as well. If Gary's got something to do with that lad's murder, I'll fucking kill him.

Yeoman coughed. "Because *they* may have killed the lad, and David got the blame. Listen, I shouldn't be telling you any of this, but I've been through the file. David's fingerprints were on the satchel. His vomit was in the squat. A jogger saw him at the scene, twice — once on the bench out the front, then again on the balcony outside the squat. His fingerprints were also on Heineken cans left on that bench — Wasti is down as saying David bought them from him. He was seen on CCTV leaving the derelict street. Now listen to this: his statement mentioned some kids had been in the flat, but he didn't give names. He claimed they'd done it and he'd gone up there after they'd run off."

"Why wouldn't he give names?"

"Who knows. Because they were kids? Because Flint was there and Phil would go after David if he dropped his brother in it? Back then, I heard Phil was a bastard, not the calmer man you know today. Look at him funny, you got beaten up. Grass his brother to the police, you got killed."

Phil's face heated with shame. It was true, all of it.

"But David was put away for *years*," Val said. "He's still in there — think he's due out next year, isn't he?"

"No, he's already out, Val, living in Elderflower with his mother. And people have been murdered. He could have learned a lot in Rushford, how to kill, how to organise so many being murdered, and he's built like a brick shithouse. Phil would do well not to cross the man now. I'd say it'd be the other way around — mess with David and *you* get killed."

Phil's blood chilled. Fuck, David was the brains behind the murders? He'd killed Delia? Why just Delia? Why delegate the other murders to Goat? Did Phil want to mess with this and go after Goat, make him disappear? If David was as menacing as Yeoman reckoned, if he found out Phil had interfered . . .

Phil couldn't risk Val or Karl being brought into this. He'd keep his mouth shut — but he would be having a word with his dear brother. Gary had some explaining to do.

"Why didn't I hear about David being back in Elderflower?" Val said. "One of my old customers lives there. He'd normally have told me."

"*Old* customers? So you gave it up then, the job?"

"I have."

"Well, it's no secret David's out. I saw him in The Tractor's."

A phone rang.

"Shit, that's Shaz." Yeoman coughed again. "She'll be wanting to know where I am. Right, I'll be going, need to ring her back. So, if Steve returns, let me know."

Steve? Now there was a man Phil wouldn't mind hurting. The things Val had said about that bloke was enough to curl your toes. Philandering, bullying, a bit of a psycho.

He went into the living room and sat on the sofa. Yeoman walked past the doorway, hand held up in a wave.

"I know you were listening," the copper called. "Thing is, mate, I won't know whether your employee killed Steve or you did it. Just remember to do the tick."

"The tick?"

Christ, Yeoman was more bent that Phil had imagined. He'd basically just told him he could kill Steve.

Phil got up and poked his head around the doorframe.

Yeoman made a motion across his neck. "Like that."

Phil nodded. "Right."

"And wear gloves. Other than that, keep your nose clean." Yeoman opened the door. "Things will be hotting up around here. You need to look after Val, make her your priority."

Phil understood what Yeoman hadn't said — that Phil could get caught at last for the drugs because of David, Goat and the murders.

"Oh . . ." Yeoman paused on the threshold. "If you happen to see a man called Martin Olbey, let Val know for me, won't you."

"What's he got to do with anything?"

"He's the middleman, the one going between David and the killer. He needs stopping."

Phil nodded. "Got it."

"I hope you do. Clean your shit up — before you get caught." Yeoman walked out.

Bloody hell . . .

Phil went into the kitchen, scratching his temple.

Val sat there, shaking. "He might come back. Steve. Oh God."

"I know. I heard everything. Move in here. I'll get Karl set up in one of my flats." Phil hadn't told her he'd bought a few last week as investments. He planned to rent them out. "I've got a nice one that'll suit him. He can get a couple of mates in there with him. I'll deal with the rent and bills."

Tears fell down her cheeks. "What did I do to deserve you?"

He smiled. "You gave me biscuits."

CHAPTER THIRTY-ONE

The week of Flint's release, Delia stood beneath the streetlight on the corner, mulling over a snipe she'd overheard earlier in Wasti's. She was well aware of what people called her. The Woman on Mulberry Lane. It was better than 'prosser' or 'slag', but still, the title spoke of what she did, how immoral she was, just in a less obvious way. Most of those in the lane and in the other streets on the estate were kind to her, though, same as they were with Val, who'd opted to conduct her job in the daytime in her house, like they'd discussed. It was the rare few who looked down their noses at them, and the muttered "Dirty bitch!" in Wasti's proved not everyone liked her taking up the corner every night.

"With kids on the lane an' all. Pure filth."

This from the man who'd turned up on her doorstep after Mum had died, saying he was her dad, asking for any money Mum had left. Upon first hearing his claim, Delia had wanted to laugh in his face — him, her father? — then experienced her heart fluttering with hope. Had he come to see her, make sure she was okay, be her parent now her other one was gone?

But no, it was for money.

She'd seen him around all her life, thought of him as the 'bloke with the limp', the gang all taking the piss out of him as kids tended to do. A difference in others meant you attacked. But he was supposedly her father, and that had shocked her silly. He'd admitted to living in Elderflower Mead all this time, the street behind Mulberry, but she already knew that, and a twist of anger had curdled her gut because Mum must have known and never said. Delia could have skipped round there a few times a week to see him, but that wouldn't have worked. Mum had said he hadn't wanted to know before he'd walked out, let alone afterwards. He was a waster, a loser, and Delia was better off without him.

And she was, she supposed, considering what Gammy Leg had done to earn such a nickname. Word had it he was a chancer, a burglar, and had fallen from a top-floor window one night, the resident catching him climbing in and pushing him off the ledge.

Creepy how Olga's husband had a similar fate, except he'd died and Gammy hadn't.

Delia had sent her father away with a flea in his ear and moved on, avoiding his gaze whenever she saw him afterwards.

Then the court case had come and gone, Flint going down for fifteen years. He'd have been out a damn sight sooner had he not come into Wasti's with a gun. A raid on his house after his arrest provided information that the gun was fake, purchased from Tim's Tip-Top Toys in town, but the intent to menace with it had been there, so he'd been sentenced as if the gun were real.

The notes had continued for years, and as nothing had happened to her, it was almost like they were just something to be endured, read, then put in a file ready for Yeoman to collect. Delia had always handed them over to Val for safekeeping, and she'd passed them on.

To earn extra money, Val had become one of those paid grasses, and Yeoman's weekly presence in the street was a comfort. If whoever sent the notes watched Delia, he'd never know when the copper would turn up as it was random. Yeoman had said he'd done that on purpose. Nice to know her safety was important.

Thirteen years later, the notes stopped coming, and she wondered whether the sender had decided, at long last, that she wasn't a threat, and Olga wasn't a threat — her *notes had stopped, too. Or perhaps he'd moved away. Then again, he could have been in Rushford. People like him, prepared to drive a getaway car, to force a woman to overdose in her bed, and to send nasty letters, was bound to end up in the nick in the end.*

She'd hoped he stayed there forever.

Finally, Delia relaxed, although that wasn't strictly true. She'd always have the far past in her head, and sometimes, David Ives appeared in her dreams, turning them into nightmares, his dreadlocks shifting into blue snakes that wiggled, coiling around one another in some mad dance to silent music. Of course, by the day after The Incident, when they'd all met up at the park and huddled beneath the slide's metal awning, sheltered from the tipping rain, she'd realised the cocaine had sent her silly. No one else had seen the snakes, but then again, they'd been too busy running from what they'd done, leaving her behind.

The newest member of the group had laughed, cattle-like, at her retelling of what she thought she'd seen. She'd always steered clear of chatting with Goat much — his eyes were too close together, and that bothered her a lot — and him hiding in the cupboard once the bad stuff had kicked off . . . She wished she'd gone in there with him, despite how he gave her the willies. She also wished she hadn't kicked Jacob in the head with her pointed shoe like Steve said she had to.

God, that cocktail of drink and drugs had sent them wild, no better than rabid animals, eager to hurt, to maim. She was ashamed of her part in it, should have just watched like Lydia, or better yet, walked out as soon as Steve suggested picking on Jacob when they'd seen him coming along the street. They'd gone out onto the balcony to play dares, Steve once again the instigator, their leader. Lydia had a secret thing for him, and Delia had never understood it. Steve was a pig, a thug.

He'd said, after they'd gulped neat vodka and gin, and had all sniffed a thin line of cocaine off the dusty windowsill in the squat, that they should hang off the walkway railings for as long as they could. For a laugh. Whoever had the most seconds didn't have to chip in to buy the sweets and alcohol for next weekend.

But Steve had spotted Jacob in his flat cap, carrying his tan leather satchel that everyone took the piss out of at school, and he'd whispered, "Let's fuck that little dick up."

Delia hadn't remembered what Steve had said after that, she'd zoned out, but at first, it had apparently been agreed to push Jacob around for a bit, scare the kid, see what he carried in that bloody satchel, but Steve's instructions on what they had to do next . . . She'd known it was wrong, but a part of her, addled with booze and coke, had wanted to fit in so badly, to be 'someone', that she'd obeyed him. Lydia had stood back, pressed against the wall, just watching, then there was Goat going in the cupboard, out of the way. Everyone else had done something bad to Jacob, but Steve, he'd been the worst.

She'd always thought he'd killed the boy just for suggesting they fuck him up.

Delia shuddered. She might go to a hypnotherapist to get her mind clean now she had a fair bit of money behind her and could afford a few sessions. She wouldn't have to suffer the reminders then, the memories that drifted in quietly, then exploded into Technicolour that wasn't glorious at all. Her life was governed by The Incident, and every time she saw someone from the gang, her mind conjured images, even if only for a brief moment, and shame filled her.

She deserved everything bad that had happened to her.

"Stop it," she muttered. "Stop reliving it all the time."

It was hard not to now Flint was out, and living in her street, no less. His release had dredged the memories up, all of them, not just snippets, of Jacob and the robbery.

Delia hugged herself. Glanced up and down the lane. A red car had parked outside Olga's while she'd been stuck inside her head, the driver nowhere to be seen. She shrugged — it was none of her business who Olga had in her place, but it was weird for the woman to have anyone inside. Olga rarely let people in. The Incident had scarred her, and she'd pulled back from being friendly, from attachments that could get her into trouble. The driver might even be in another house, leaving the car there and walking up the street.

The hairs on the back of Delia's neck stood at attention, and she squirmed from how uncomfortable it was. Over the years, she'd gained more than a sixth sense while out on the corner and conducting business down the alley, and it alerted her now to someone watching her. She knew who it'd be. The weird feeling came from Halfway House behind her, the kind that said someone stood there, staring two holes into her back, holes of hatred.

She turned, and there was Flint in his bedsit window, giving her a mad glare. She maintained eye contact, buggered if she'd look away first. Despite them being mates before, in the same gang, what he'd done at

Wasti's, pointing the gun at her . . . Their connection had died then and there. He'd been intent on getting money, his sole aim to line his pockets, and her presence in the shop hadn't made a difference. She'd thought, perhaps stupidly, that what they'd done to Jacob tied them forever in some secret link, one nobody but the gang members knew about, except his action in raising that gun had said more than he ever could.

She wasn't important to him, like she wasn't important to her dad. So what did it say that Flint hadn't shot her? Did she matter just a bit after all? Had the secret tether flared inside him and he'd chosen to let her live?

Delia refused to think about it. Bottom line, she'd grassed up her old friend, probably because of his dismissal of her, a childish thing to do on her part that harked back to her feelings regarding her father abandoning her, but even then, Flint hadn't opened his mouth about Jacob.

She was a sneak, he wasn't. At least that was what his stare told her.

He shook his head as if she were shit on his shoe, his silhouette eerie in that square of window, yellow light behind him and to either side. The nets swung closed, and the curtains snapped shut. His way of saying she meant nothing to him now? Oddly, it bothered her. She wanted to apologise, yet at the same time, why should she?

God, life was so bloody complicated.

She closed her eyes for a few moments, picked up footsteps then the slamming of a car door. The rumble of an engine forced her to open her eyes and spin round to face the road. The red car reversed up to the kerb in front of her, the windows tinted illegally, too dark, too obscuring. She didn't like not seeing customers before they spoke, she preferred to assess them, see if they looked funny or had the potential to hurt, a glint lurking in crazy eyes that took her in from head to toe, telling her that although she was 'dirty' and a 'slapper', they wanted to do her anyway. A cheap shag.

She wondered whether her need for male attention in this job was also a link to her feelings about her father.

The soft snick of the lock engaging on the front door of Halfway House almost had her turning, but from the corner of her eye, she caught sight of a man walking up the lane. She wished he'd hang around in case the driver wanted trouble.

The window slowly moved down, a pair of eyes visible. Eyes too close together. Eyes she'd know anywhere. They were his, *and she staggered from the shock. Why was* Goat *here, wanting to use her, when they'd all agreed back then to steer clear of one another? Okay, Delia and Olga chatted every so often, they lived in the same street, for Pete's sake, but they kept their distance for the most part. How could you not speak to someone if you bought their veg?*

But . . . maybe he didn't want to have sex with her.

Could she even do that with him, though? He'd been pushy with Lydia in the squat, insistent that she get off with him, and changing her mind wasn't allowed. But then Steve must have noticed, suggesting they go outside, and the rest was history.

Wicked, terrible history.

"All right, Del?" Goat said.

She kept a shiver at bay. Hugged herself harder, her cream leather jacket squeaking from the pressure. "Yep. You?"

"Busy. Had a stint inside recently. Came out and got my old job back, plus another one. That'll pay well, providing I do it correct, like."

"Right . . ." She persuaded herself not to move from foot to foot. He'd know she was nervous and that he had an effect on her if she couldn't keep still. She clutched her bag strap tight with both hands, something to steady her, ground her. "We're not meant to talk. What do you want?"

"There's a punter who doesn't want to be seen in the lane." He lowered the window some more, revealing all of his face.

Christ. He looked madder than a closed box of wasps, and so old compared to her, like life hadn't been inclined to keep the proof of age at bay.

"And?" She cocked her hip, wanting him gone, to just piss off out of her face. She should go home, now, and cut her losses. Tonight was a slow one, no customers so far. Until he'd come along with this proposal.

"You're a cocky bitch." He sniffed. "I wouldn't be if I'd got notes posted through my door."

Delia's legs almost went out from under her. It was him*?* He'd *sent them? "Notes? I don't know what you're talking about."*

"Your mother didn't kill herself." He laughed, quietly, the spooky bastard.

And it made sense, why the notes had stopped. Goat had been put in Rushford for a while. Why hadn't she put two and two together?

She went to walk away but sensed movement to her right, as if someone had intended to come down the lane but stopped, out of sight, waiting for her to finish her conversation. Maybe it was the punter he'd mentioned. She was safe then, even if the person was hidden. If something happened to her, she'd have help at hand, unless he was a mean fucker as well.

"Look, this is all news to me," she said. "I'm going home."

"I wouldn't if I were you." He stared over at her house.

Was someone in there?

She had the urge to bolt to Olga's but doubted she'd let her in. Olga would tell her to go away if she wasn't buying veg, and especially if she knew Goat was out here. Val's then, she'd leg it there, get Yeoman to come round and check her place was safe to return to.

"This punter," Goat continued, "is willing to pay quite a bit to fuck you down the alley."

"Who is it?"

"Someone you're just better off shagging. Get it over and done with, take the money . . . else you might well get more notes, and I may follow up on them this time and hurt you, kill you . . ." He scrunched his eyebrows. "So, down the alley. Now."

He drove off, and she stared after the car, memorising the number plate. She'd learned to do that years ago in case someone attacked her. The thought of being killed by him churned her stomach, so she made the decision to go down the alley, do what he said. After all, she tuned out customers while with them, so this would be no different.

She tottered along the alley and waited at the halfway point, the darkness swamping her in shadows. A sound echoed from the far end, in Elderflower Mead, and she looked in that direction. A man stood there beneath the light of the streetlamp, the mouth of the alley filled with his bulk. A black man with a blue snake draped over his head.

She wasn't hallucinating this time. He honestly had a snake.

She parted her lips to scream, but he ran up the alley at top speed and was on her in seconds. He clamped his gloved palm over her mouth, and she struggled, her handbag strap slipping down her arm, the bag thunking on the path.

She had a moment of thinking Olga watched from her greenhouse, then, "Hello, Delia," he whispered close to her ear. "Fancy seeing you here."

CHAPTER THIRTY-TWO

Val let herself into her house, her day with Phil cut short. He wanted to go and see Flint, find out exactly what had happened to poor Jacob Everson. She didn't want to know the details. Those that had filtered through the years were enough, the older generation talking about it in hushed voices every anniversary. David Ives, the monster. David Ives who'd hurt the boy so bad, had he lived, he'd have suffered brain damage, a wheelchair his best friend.

Except David hadn't done anything.

She'd shaken from the shock of that, cross — no, *livid* — with Delia and Olga for never saying anything, for pretending to be people they weren't, *friends*, the type of women who wouldn't torture a schoolboy. Val had allowed them around *Karl*, for God's sake. She'd let murderers near her lad and she'd never forgive herself for it. What if he'd annoyed them with his incessant chatter or need for them to play with him and they'd snapped? Where had the violence in them stemmed from? And how had they suppressed it since? Surely if you'd been horrific once, you had it in you to do it again.

Everyone made mistakes. But this one? It was a good job Delia and Olga were dead, otherwise, Val would have a few choice words to say to them. She was hurt, betrayed, and not only did she mourn their death but also the loss of who she'd thought they were.

More confusing was her still seeing them as kind people, especially Delia, who Val knew better. That was all she'd known them as, kind, so to find out *they* were the monsters and not David . . .

A lot to get her head around.

She flicked the kettle on then checked the house in case Karl had come home early.

"Ah, you're in," she said at his bedroom door. Time to tell him what Phil had said she must. "I've found you a flat, and the deposit and rent are paid up for the next year."

Karl, sitting on his bed, textbooks spread out in front of him, gaped at her. "What? How did you afford *that*?"

Val shrugged rather than outright lie. Phil didn't want Karl knowing he'd sorted everything.

"Doesn't matter. There are three bedrooms, so choose your flatmates wisely."

Karl's face turned pink. "Um, about that . . . Some of the lads I started hanging out with at the beginning of college . . . I'm avoiding them now. Not good people."

"I see. Well, what about your old friends from school?"

"Hmm. Can't I live there on my own?"

Her stomach rolled over, but she had to feign nonchalance. Her son was eighteen, a budding man, and had to learn to look out for himself. She couldn't mollycoddle him forever, much as she'd like to be an invisible source of comfort and advice throughout his life when he wasn't with her. She had to trust that she'd brought him up well enough to be self-sufficient, content in his decisions.

"If you like." She tossed the keys over to him and passed along the address written on a neon-pink Post-it page. "Internet's already set up, and by tomorrow morning, after the furniture has been delivered by the owner, it's move-in ready."

Phil was a good man, suggesting that. "It'll save the lad trying to afford his own stuff," he'd said. "Studying and working . . . Let's just have him concentrate on his education, shall we? Make out you've paid up for a year so he hasn't got to worry about anything. So *you* haven't got to worry about anything."

"What about my place?" she'd asked. "*If* I move in with you, that is."

"I'll buy it off the council. You can have it in your name. Security for if we don't work out. Rent it out on a month-to-month basis. I care about you enough to not want you feeling stuck with nowhere to go. It's been years, Val, me and you dancing round one another. I've loved you all along."

And I thought Steve was the benchmark of how all men behaved.

"What do you think of that then?" she said to Karl. "Furnished, so all you have to do is take your bedding, towels, clothes."

"I love you, Mum."

"And I love you, kid." A lump flowered in her throat. She cleared it. "Now then, I've got something else to tell you."

"What's that?"

"I'm moving into Regency."

Karl nodded. "With Phil."

Her heart thudded hard. "How did you know?"

Karl laughed. "Anyone can see how he feels about you. So you're . . . you're not bothered how he makes his money?"

"He's sorting things so I won't have to be bothered."

"Right." He frowned, clearly not understanding.

"You'll get it soon. I can't say anything yet. He's a good man underneath."

"Yeah. Always been nice to me. Can I go and look at the flat?"

She nodded, although a string of chills gripped each vertebra, twisting around them and clutching tight. The flat was in the block that had been built on the site of the squat, Vicar's Gate no longer derelict now, of course, everything demolished, flattened to the ground after Jacob's murder, new buildings in their places, although she supposed they weren't so new now, not with all the time that had passed. Still, Vicar's Gate was a nice place, a couple of streets along on the comb from Regency, so they wouldn't be far away from each other should Karl need company or a hot meal he couldn't be bothered to cook himself.

"I'm going to be giving you three hundred and fifty a month to live off," she said. "That should be plenty for food and new clothes. All the bills are in with the rent, see."

"Bloody hell, Mum, have you come into money or something?" He stood, walked over and embraced her, then leant back to look in her eyes. "It's Phil, isn't it. He's paying you instead . . . instead of the other men."

Her heart thundered so violently she thought she might faint. She'd tried so hard to keep what she did from him, and it looked like she'd failed. But if he thought badly of her, he wouldn't be cuddling her, would he?

"It's all good," he said. "I've known for ages, and actually, I think you're fucking top-notch. You did what you had to — for me — and that's more than my sperm donor ever did."

Tears burned, and she swallowed at the mention of his father. Should she tell him the wanker might turn up here? But why *would* Steve come back? He'd distanced himself from the gang, was probably living elsewhere, a new life, a new identity, his disgusting past behind him. She wouldn't fuck that up if she were him.

"I hated doing it," she whispered.

"I know." He clumsily wiped her tears away. "Coming to the flat with me?"

She smiled, overwhelmed he wanted her there, so pleased with herself for bringing him up not to judge and to accept people's walks of life without sneering.

Maybe she should do the same. While killing Jacob was a monstrous act, Delia and Olga had so obviously tried to live good lives in adulthood.

Val nodded to herself. She'd remember her friends as she'd known them, not what they'd been before they'd met. Decent, lovely women who'd been killed for being murderers.

She might not be a detective, but even she knew David Ives had a bone to pick, several, and he wasn't going to rest until he'd snapped every bone in the skeleton made up of the gang members.

Maybe he'd track Steve down as well.

Funny how she felt no emotion whatsoever about that.

Perhaps she was a wicked person, too. Perhaps everyone had the capability to be cruel, deep down.

CHAPTER THIRTY-THREE

Lydia hung the last dress up in Hotel Santuario, meaning Sanctuary, one of the reasons she'd booked in here. Secluded, out of the way, and perfectly Spanish. She would have gone for Bora Bora, but not only was it thirty-one hours away, Morgan would know where she was. She'd always turned her nose up at any mention of a Spanish holiday, so of course, that was why her destination was 'perfectly' Spanish.

He'd never believe she'd come here. He'd never believe she'd thought of an old acquaintance, one who'd hide her, look after her, someone who'd always given her a rush, that element of danger.

While her financial advisor sorted her funds and new bank accounts — her real advisor, not that creep who peddled drugs — she had enough cash from the box beneath the bed to live here for a year. The hotel catered to permanent residents, so the acquaintance said, and they should know. She'd held her breath in customs outbound and inbound, waiting for them to discover her money haul, but thankfully, she'd breezed through both.

Maybe her Pamela Anderson look had distracted the male guards.

Morgan couldn't have put an alert out on her then. She wondered how he fared, cleaning up her mess, and whether he'd discover through his investigation who she really was. An observer to a child murder, a girl who'd stood there and watched instead of helping Jacob, because that was what she'd been told to do.

'If I know you're watching, it'll get me hard . . .'

Why had she messed around with Goat that night?

Because she'd wanted to make someone else jealous.

She asked herself if she should feel guilty about the murder. Why should she, though? She hadn't liked Jacob, hadn't cared what they were doing to him, and the only thing she'd carried with her from the moment they'd run out of the squat was the fear of being caught, put inside for it, her true self being discovered, that of a girl who'd always wanted her own way no matter the cost, and if her standing and watching meant Steve liked her more, then so be it. She'd buggered off for a week, wanting to stay away from any fallout. Turned out, when she'd gone back home after she'd seen the news, everyone had kept quiet as promised, David Ives arrested instead of them.

And he'd never said who they were.

Why?

That part had always bothered her, as had her getting coke from Goat. He was the only one apart from Alice she'd still had contact with, mainly because, since her first time sniffing on the night of the murder, she'd craved to do it again.

She brushed the thoughts away and changed into more fitting attire, a pink bikini beneath denim shorts and a white vest top, her fake boobs swelling nicely under the tight fabric. Morgan had never touched them. Their relationship had gone downhill in that department years ago. Her enhancing herself, adorning her body in pretty clothes, having her hair and nails done, all of it had been a bid to win him back, only because she didn't like him not wanting her, but he hadn't chomped at the bit. Her half an hour in the sack with Phil proved she still had it in the bedroom department, but even he'd brushed her off the next day.

She'd wanted to stay with Morgan for safety, for the security being married to a copper brought, the status, and he'd done exactly what she'd suspected he would, hiding who'd really killed Alice. At first she'd thought he still cared about her, but upon closer inspection of the facts, it was to save himself.

The phone call she'd received after Delia's murder had scared her at first, but then a plan had formed, and once Alice had died, the plan had grown stronger. She reckoned fate had pushed the person to ring her. They'd seen the news, even as far away as they were, and advised her to leave the country. With Delia dead, who knew what would happen next. Who knew whether another member of the gang would be killed.

And they'd been right.

Barefoot, Lydia took the lift down to the ground floor and walked through the lobby, the marble cool on her soles. She moved out onto the sunbathing area. Ahead, two turquoise pools, to the right a free-standing bar with a thatched roof, and to the left, loungers complete with tanned and toned bodies on them.

This was the place to be. Lydia had found home.

And maybe she'd also found a bed mate for life, judging by the stare of a trim man coming towards her, his smile devilish, his body to die for.

Who needed Pinstone? Who needed Morgan? Who needed to constantly sniff coke in order to get the same high she'd had during Jacob's murder?

Her high was right here, in front of her, an old high renewed.

"Well, hello there," she said, drawing him to her.

He smelled of sunshine and happiness.

With a hint of danger.

She stroked the backs of her fingers down his cheek. Yes, it was still there, that spark. "I've missed you, Steve."

CHAPTER THIRTY-FOUR

Phil didn't want to set foot inside Halfway House as it was a place for former criminals, people who were *still* criminals, the point between leaving Rushford and finding new digs outside the prison walls for those who didn't have a permanent residence yet. For Phil, it gave him reason to think about whether, if he'd got caught supplying, he'd have ended up in a bedsit after a stint in prison, his big house sold to pay for his legal fees, the majority of his cash seized as ill-gotten gains. All he'd have left was the legitimate dosh from the car lot.

A sobering thought.

Emma Ingles opened the main door, of nervous disposition, twitchy, a tic in her eyelid, her bottom lip quivering. Because of him? She must know who he was, word spread like manure on crop fields around here, and she'd lived in Halfway for long enough to get the measure of folks on the estate. But his days of threatening people were over, so she needn't fear him. Maybe his notoriety preceded him.

"Oh. Oh, I thought . . . I thought you were someone else."

Was that why she appeared to shit a brick?

"Nope, just Gary's brother. Is he in?" He smiled to reassure her he wasn't there for trouble or to peddle anything to the lags. Even turned out his front jeans pockets: *Look, nothing in there.*

"Yes, you can chat to him in the main living room." She moved back and held her arm out, gesturing for him to come in.

She was a well nervous sort, and he wondered why she was like it, why she'd been employed to look after the needs of dangerous men if she wasn't able to handle it without quaking in her boots. Or was her expectancy of him being someone else sending her into panic mode? She'd bolt any second, he was sure of it.

He ignored what she'd said about where he could talk to Gary. "Um, I need more privacy. What room is he in, love?" God, some brother he was, not knowing that, but you couldn't choose your family, and if he could, he wouldn't opt to have Gary in it. A bad apple, that one.

Life had been good with Gary on the inside. No fuckups to attend to, no calls from him saying he'd robbed this or that and could Phil find an out-of-town buyer. No *mess*. Gary equalled aggravation, a burden Phil had never wanted to carry once their parents had died and he'd spotted his sibling had no brains when it came to staying under the radar. The Wasti robbery said it all: Gary was inept, a bumbling prat.

Shame he hadn't been sent to Rushford for longer.

Despite that, here Phil was, in the foyer of Halfway House, Emma pointing to the stairs and telling him which bedsit was Gary's. He thanked her and went up, taking a deep breath in front of the door, about to hear something he didn't want to, he was sure, but needed to be aware of all the same.

He knocked, he waited, tapping his foot. A slice of Gary's pallid face appeared in the slim crack afforded by the gold safety chain, eyes wide, mouth downturned. His face blossomed with relief and perhaps happiness that Phil had deigned to enter this fucking crook-shielding house, here for the brotherly visit Phil had said would never happen.

The chain rattled, the door swung wide, the hinges faintly creaking, the whine of a balloon going down. And there stood

Phil's brother in a pink T-shirt, a black cross over the chest, the words HE SHALL SAVE YOU beneath.

"What the fuck is that?" Phil flicked Gary's torso. "When you said you'd turned over a new leaf . . ."

"You can mock, but until you've spent years in confinement, you'll never understand. You have a lot of time to think, and demons from the past rear up, frightening the shit out of you."

Phil stepped in. Maybe he *sort* of got what Gary meant. Prisoners needed something to cling to, some focus, and why not God?

Because Gary's never been Christian. He's a dick.

Gary closed the door and double-locked it, putting the chain back on and sliding a top bolt across. A bit excessive, but maybe the security of being in a cell had remained a requirement in his life outside the walls of condemnation.

"What's that all about?" Phil indicated the door.

"Keep your bloody voice down, will you?"

"Why?"

"I'll have you know, I'm not paranoid after all. There's someone living here who's helping to frame me for the murders. Walls have ears." Gary darted his eyes in all directions, as if the bloody walls were, in fact, earwigging to their conversation, ready to pass on any pertinent information to the relevant party.

Phil's curiosity piqued. Did Gary know it was Martin Olbey? He tested it with, "Who?"

"Doesn't matter. Yeoman told me I was taking the rap, but he knows it wasn't me, so there's no rap to take."

There bloody well is. For murdering that lad!

Gary sat in the chair by the window and reached across to pull the nets aside. He looked out, nodded as though satisfied he wasn't being watched, then let the curtain fall back into place.

Phil stared at it, buying time. It shifted from side to side three times each way then came to a stop, uneven pleats, something Phil's cleaner couldn't abide.

Come on, no sense in holding off any longer.

"I've just had a visit from Yeoman myself." Phil took a perch on the bed. Firm mattress. "Something I don't need at the minute."

"Why just at the minute?" Gary picked his nose and inspected his findings. "You could do with *never* seeing Yeoman." He grabbed a loo roll off the TV cabinet and wiped his finger.

Phil didn't bother saying he wouldn't need to worry soon. Gary might spill the beans before the deal was complete, but if David was caught for organising the murders and killing Delia, Phil wouldn't be selling the patch to him. He'd have to put feelers out, find someone else.

"Look, I need to ask you a few questions." Phil inhaled, nice and deep. Stared at Gary so he knew he meant business. His 'big brother' glare. "What the *fuck* did you have to do with Jacob Everson?"

Gary paled even more than his usual vanilla ice cream skin tone. "P-p-pardon?"

"You may well stutter, you little bastard. Come on, I want to hear it from you, not someone else." Phil's chest spasmed from apprehension, and if he didn't watch himself, they'd end up in a scrap like when they were kids, rolling around on the floor, each trying to land the hardest punch.

"I don't know what you're on about." Gary gripped his knees, probably so Phil wouldn't see his hands shaking.

Too late.

"Is that why you found God? You think by talking to the big man you'll be forgiven? What a load of bollocks."

"I don't talk to Him, I listen, and He says we're forgiven for our sins so long as we confess."

"Who did you confess to?"

"Him and one of his followers, a man who promised he wouldn't repeat a confession."

"Oh right, so you don't have the balls to tell someone who might get you banged up again for it. Coward."

Gary eyed Phil as though impatient. "It was a long time ago. We were kids. We said we'd never grass each other up, we'd all say we were at the park instead of the squat." His knuckles whitened, the material from his trousers poking between his fingers.

So he was *there. He* did *have something to do with it.*

Phil didn't know how to feel, what to think, how to react. "Go on."

"I've made my peace with it." Gary sighed, an exhalation of irritation at having to explain himself. "And with being a bad lot. Shit went wrong once I became your runner. It's your fault my life went to pot. Mum and Dad snuffed it, leaving me with you, and what did you do? Shove me out on the street peddling weed."

"Oh, so you don't have a mind of your own then, where you could have said no to selling and killing a fucking schoolboy? I'm your brother, not a monster. If you'd said no to running, I'd have found someone else, but it was *you* who asked to join the business, *and* you suggested Steve and that other twazzock, and Jesus Christ, the latter is someone I wish I'd never met. Conveniently forget all that, did you? Confession rubbed out certain memories, has it? And as for Jacob, there's doing wrong, then there's absolutely annihilating any goodness you might have had inside you. I do bad shit, I supply, I push stuff that kills people, but it's *their* choice to buy. Just like people who pick up a cream cake every day in Greggs. Don't blame the baker if you get fat. Same with weed or coke — don't moan when you're hooked. But there's a massive difference. Jacob Everson didn't *have* a choice." He paused. "Did he?"

"We were drunk. High."

"So that excuses it, does it? High on what? My product?"

"Yeah."

"You *stole* from me?"

"No, What's His Face brought it along. Goat. He was supposed to sell to Old Man Cossack, but the silly bastard had a heart attack. Money was stolen, handed over to you, then we sniffed the drugs. No one was any the wiser."

"So what happened?"

"I can't go through it again. I confessed to God in the presence of the prison chaplain, made my peace with the mistakes I've made and—"

"Mistakes? Killing a kid is a *mistake*?"

"You know damn well what I mean."

Phil could hardly talk, he'd allowed his men to complete hits on people — bad people, but never kiddies. "All of your gang were there, yes?"

Gary nodded, at last loosening his hold on his knees.

"Who instigated it?"

"Steve."

"I should have known. He was always a loose cannon. So why didn't David Ives dob you lot in?"

"Probably scared of you. If he said I was involved, got me nicked . . ."

True. Back then, like Yeoman had told Val, Phil would have had Ives sorted. Nowadays, though, he'd let Gary take the punishment, serve time, like he had with the Wasti robbery. He hadn't lied to give Gary an alibi for that by saying he was with him all day, which Gary had asked him to do. Fuck that. "Yeoman knows you were there."

"Yep."

"And it's only a matter of time before you get pulled in. I reckon the reason you're sitting there, still free, is because he needs to concentrate on finding the pricks who're involved in the recent murders."

"I don't want to go back to Rushford."

"I don't suppose you do, but it's where you belong." *Hark at me, all honourable now I've shacked up with Val. But I don't want anything to taint it. This is a new start.*

Phil could definitely see how Gary wanted to forget the past and begin again. Phil had done things he was proud of at the time but was ashamed of now. What was right once wasn't right anymore, it was despicable, so wrong, but that was easy to say with a hefty bank balance and no worries. In the past, he'd done what he had to in order to get where he was today.

Still no excuse.

Maybe he ought to go to confession, too. Unlikely, but it was the thought that counted. What a pair they were. Two brothers born into a criminal family, both eager to make amends for sins committed in a different time, a different mindset.

"I get you," Phil said.

Gary frowned. "What?"

"I get the need to put it all behind you."

"Err, thanks?"

They sat in silence for a while, and the sad thing was, Phil could well see Gary hurting that boy, considering the type of teenager he'd been. The news article during the trial said Jacob was beaten, kicked, burnt with fags, left to die in a pool of his own blood. Gary had an evil streak, always had, but could that ever be erased? Phil could only hope so, especially regarding himself, because he wanted to be a good person now he had Val, the best person, someone she'd be proud to be with.

He stood. "I'm off then."

"You won't be back, will you." Gary rose and peered out of the window again.

What did he expect, for men to be out there watching?

"Nope. Good luck. You'd best hope God is still your mate when you go back inside." Phil unlocked the door and strode out, thinking not of his sibling but of what Yeoman had said. He'd given the green light for Phil to kill Steve without getting arrested for it, but what about Goat who regularly trotted down White-Powder Road? Surely he was included in that blind eye as well?

Phil had one more thing to do before he walked the straight and narrow. He'd take the signposted street to Murder City and get rid of the killer before Lydia and Gary reached their end. As for Steve, if Phil ever saw him again, there'd be no stopping the gun being pointed.

A real gun at that, not a toy like Gary's.

Fuck the tick slash.

CHAPTER THIRTY-FIVE

Goat whistled while walking up the garden path. The missus had texted to let him know dinner was imminent, homemade chicken pie, mash, peas, and her proper gravy. Comfort food, something he could do with at the moment. With Lydia gone, once he'd left her place he'd experienced an unusual sense of fragility, that perhaps the walls were crumbling or at least cracks were showing. If David found out she wasn't there to be bumped off, what would happen? Martin would come down on Goat, that was a certainty, but would David ask for a meetup, bawl him out for not killing Lydia when he should have done? Would he remember who Goat really was and recall he'd been in the gang?

Goat should never have thought with his dick, never have wanted the kink, should have just followed directions, but he'd never really been any good at that. If he did as he was told, he wouldn't have hidden in that cupboard. The demand had been that all of them except Lydia torture that brainbox kid, but the ferocity of their attack meant he'd sidled inside, out of the way while they were busy, watching through the gap where he hadn't closed the door properly.

He hadn't sniffed as much as the others, nor had he drunk as much, so his mind wasn't altered to the degree theirs was. They'd acted in a pack, converging on the boy, all but foaming at their smiling mouths. The fear on Jacob's face, the way he'd gripped the strap of his satchel . . .

Fuck this for a game of soldiers.

He hated the way the past crept in, a constant reminder, and he'd taken on the job of killing them all not only so his part in it would never be revealed but to punish them. They'd never really accepted him fully, him being the last member and late to the original group, their positions already established way before he'd come along, the pecking order firmly in place.

He shoved it all from his mind and entered his house, the smell of burnt pastry insulting his delicate nasal passages. Anger sizzled. He'd been looking forward to that fucking pie ever since she'd messaged about it, and now he was expected to eat tainted offerings?

Bleedin' woman.

He thundered into the living room, thinking she'd be there with a glass of wine, beating herself up for the dinner faux pas, but the trendy cream space stood empty. Next he checked the dining room, her maybe setting the table with all the pomp and ceremony she usually did, fancy glassware, a centrepiece of flowers she arranged herself, and all the fine china he'd let her buy. But no, a bare shiny table, not a polished knife or fork in sight. The kitchen then. She'd be in there, toiling over more pastry, hoping to get it right this time before he walked in and caught the fact she'd cocked up the first time around.

She was there, on the other side of the centre island, her platinum hair so like Lydia's, something he paid for so she resembled the girl he'd had a crush on, the woman he still fantasised about. He hadn't gone so far as to pay for new tits, but maybe he'd hand over the cash for them once he'd finished this job. Still, her originals were perky enough. But that'd change once a nipper came along and tugged on them.

The pie sat in its red dish on a wooden heat saver. The puff pastry had risen lovely, just that it had a hard, shiny black top. She stared at him, tears in her eyes, as well she might, not only for doing wrong, but her hormones were in overdrive at the moment.

"How the hell did that happen?" he barked. "You know manky food reminds me of being a kid. Only poor people have shit dinners. Where the chuff were you in the pastry lesson on the cooking course? Shagging one of the chefs?"

She didn't answer, just flicked her eyes downwards.

"Need the optician, do you? Is that why your peepers have gone all funny? Need goggles?" He stepped closer and inspected the room.

No potatoes bubbling on the hob. No peas. She'd intended to cook them, though, as a bag of petit pois was on the worktop, and spuds had been chopped, perfect small cubes on the glass chopping board. Peel rested in dirty curls on the drainer beside a knife. That was remiss of her not to put them in the bin.

She stared at him even harder, her eyes manic. Fucking Nora, she was going to have one of her recent meltdowns.

"How come you burnt the pie?"

"I . . . someone came round. I wasn't allowed to take it out of the oven until the smoke alarm went off."

"Wasn't allowed?"

"He—"

"*He*?" His stomach muscles contracted, jealousy searing his gut, bile racing up. It was all right for him to mess around, but she had to stay loyal. "Who was it?"

"I'm not meant to say." She winced. "Ow!"

"What's the *matter* with you?"

"Nothing, I just . . . I just stubbed my toe."

"What, on the island?" This was getting weirder by the second. How could she have stubbed her toe when she hadn't moved? She was pissing him off, winding him up, when all he wanted was his sodding dinner, and *that* would be a good half an hour, because the bastard potatoes hadn't even been boiled.

Give me strength . . .

He stomped over to the cupboard beside the cooker on the left and pulled out a saucepan. He'd cook it his damn self if she was playing silly buggers. Maybe she'd found a bag of his gear and had rubbed some into her gums. Coke got people like that sometimes, all weird and not with it, but if he found out that was the case, he'd lock her in the bedroom for a couple of hours to teach her a lesson. She wasn't meant to take drugs anymore.

He had his back to her, and that was a good thing at the minute. If he had to see her mad staring any longer, he was likely to snap. With no prospect of having kinky times with Lydia, he wasn't in the best of moods.

Oh God, the missus was coming up behind him. Her footsteps tapped on the fake wood lino.

Something pressed into the back of his neck.

"Love, you're really pressing my buttons," he said. "Go and act weird somewhere else. It's been a day, and I just want to have a chilled evening."

"It's been a day all right." A male voice.

He spun round, saucepan raised, and stared into the business end of a gun. Beyond it, someone's face, someone he hadn't expected to stand in his kitchen, the barrel coming closer, now pressing on his forehead. The bloke yanked the saucepan out of his hand and threw it into the hallway.

"You really ought to be more careful who you dick around with," the man said.

Urine trickled, a hot stream.

The trigger cocked, a life-threatening crack.

He glanced over at the wife, who remained rigid, eyes wide, then back to the intruder.

"Sort it out, mate," Goat joked. "No need for this, is there?"

"There's every need."

CHAPTER THIRTY-SIX

Phil stood behind a tree in Goat's back garden and peered around it, staring through the kitchen window. Shit, a gun to a forehead, and a menacing-looking man he hadn't expected to see wielded the weapon. A woman stood stock-still, her hair a flawless white-blonde sheet down her spine.

The back of the drug runner's head exploded, then the late retort of a gunshot had Phil jumping and gripping the rough trunk. No scream from the woman, just her husband slumping, falling, disappearing from view.

The shooter turned to her, his mouth moving, and she nodded. He walked to the back door, and Phil whipped his head to the side so he wouldn't be seen. He'd come here to kill that skanky piece of shit, but someone else had got there first.

The man left the house, strutting to the side gate and flinging it open. Phil ran across the garden, checking inside the kitchen. The woman remained where she was, probably too scared to move, to even look at her dead fella on the floor. At the gate, he peered down the drive, but the bloke had gone. A car engine grumbled as if annoyed it'd been switched on, and Phil walked out onto the lane, but the vehicle wasn't there. No neighbours came to investigate the gunshot. He ran up the road and got in his car, doing something he never thought he'd do — he phoned Yeoman.

"DI Morgan Yeoman."

"It's Phil."

"What have you got?"

"David Ives just shot Goat."

"What? Who the fuck is Goat?"

"The White-Powder Road fella. I went there to have a word, find out where Steve was . . ." Lie.

"And?"

"I was in the back garden, was going to get Goat's attention and gesture for him to come outside, you know, so his wife wasn't anything to do with it. Only David appeared from nowhere and shot Goat in the forehead. There's blood and brain all over the steel splashback on the wall behind the oven."

"Where's David now?"

"He fucked off."

"Where are you?"

"In Goat's street in my car."

"Piss off out of it. I don't need the extra paperwork of you being there. Keep your fucking mouth shut and your head down. Don't go looking for Steve. Only talk to him if he turns up. Got it?"

'Talk to him.' Which translated as 'murder'. Morgan must be within earshot of someone else. He could hardly say 'take him out' in that case, could he.

"Right," Phil said. "How will you say you found out about Goat?"

"None of your business. Now get lost."

Phil disconnected the call and shoved his phone in his pocket. He didn't gun the engine, couldn't give the neighbours any reason to look out of their windows and recognise him or his car. Flash BMWs tended to gain attention, as did Phil driving one. Yeoman might not have any control over who did door-to-door, therefore, no control over what was reported.

"Fuck it. I should have gone back to Val's instead of coming here."

He drove there, his mind churning with speculation. Had David found out Goat had been one of the gang? Or had he killed him for not murdering Lydia? Goat had been employed to off the gang, yet he'd allowed Lydia to live when it would have been just as easy to slit her throat then Alice's.

I need to get away from this sort of shit. Retire. Live a better life.

He drove along the comb top, his limbs shaking from what he'd witnessed. The way the back of Goat's head had exploded . . . How had Phil enjoyed seeing that in his youth? How could he have thought it was the right thing to do?

He was as twisted as Gary and no mistake.

A car came towards him on the other side of the road. Phil glanced over as they came almost level. Yeoman and the Tanner copper. Yeoman nodded imperceptibly, then the car passed, and Phil made eye contact with him in his rearview mirror, Yeoman staring into his as well.

Phil had a pig on his side, something he'd never thought possible.

How times had changed.

CHAPTER THIRTY-SEVEN

Lydia sat at the vanity table, shaking and more than a little out of sorts. She'd often thought about what it would be like in bed with Steve, but she'd never imagined what she'd just been through.

Steve liked to grip her throat, it seemed. Fingertip bruises marred her neck.

Maybe they'd fade soon. In the meantime, she'd wrap a chiffon scarf around them, pretend it didn't matter and she wasn't scared.

"So what's been going on in Blighty with the old gang then?" he asked.

She stared in the mirror at him in bed behind her. He scratched his nuts, and a flash of irritation went through her. She'd forgotten how crass he could be. Morgan would never behave that way in front of her.

She had a feeling she'd made a mistake, had romanticised the past, building the picture she wanted to see rather than what was really there.

"I haven't spoken to any of them, except Alice, then Delia a few years ago when Flint robbed Wasti's. Goat was the getaway driver, and apparently, Olga saw him waiting in his car outside. Delia received nasty notes through the door, threatening her to keep her mouth shut. Olga had them, too. Delia phoned to ask if I'd had any. I soon told her where to go."

"Best thing, that. Word has it my son's grown into a strapping lad."

"I wouldn't know."

"And my ex-wife — I assume she filed for a divorce after all this time — is a prosser. Never would have thought it. She was an ice block in bed. I only hung around because she cooked my dinners. Got my kicks elsewhere. Plenty of sexy sorts down The Tractor's. They used to come out in droves for quiz night."

"Hmm." Lydia didn't know his wife. They'd gone to different primary and secondary schools, although she had experienced a shitload of jealousy finding out Steve had got married — the cheeky sod had sent her an invitation to Mum and Dad's house. Like she'd ever go and see her crush marry someone else.

He was a sick bastard, something she'd liked as a teenager, but now . . . no, she didn't like it. She'd got too used to having a gentleman in her life, someone with respect for her.

Or was she romanticising Morgan as well?

Steve hawked phlegm, and she almost barked at him not to be so revolting, stopping herself in case he turned nasty on her.

"What about the others?" he asked. "All right, Delia's dead. That was a shocker to see it online, I can tell you."

"Olga's dead as well. And Alice, but then I told you this when I got in contact before I came here." How could he have forgotten? Or was he testing her, seeing if she repeated the same story?

"What were you doing while Goat was in your living room?"

"That's the part I didn't tell you. I was slitting Alice's throat."

"What?" He laughed as if he didn't believe her.

"Goat put the knife in my hand and helped me do it. I had no choice. I'm supposed to be dead as well, but he wanted me to perform some 'kink', as he put it."

"That's your fault for feeding his teenage fantasies."

"What do you mean?"

"The dickhead fancied you, anyone could see that."

She shivered. Goat looked nothing like he had in his youth. He'd grown into an ugly bastard, appearing ten or more years older than he was. "I only led him on so you'd see the green-eyed monster and bloody notice me properly."

"I know. Shit, that was mental, kicking that kid's head in while you watched. Shame we had to run after. I wouldn't have minded fucking you beside his dead body."

Oh, now she knew for sure she'd made a mistake coming here to be with him. Who had sex by a corpse? She'd have to play it by ear with regards to getting away from him. Pretend everything was fine until she could be alone and book a flight out of here. Try France or Italy instead.

A sudden need for Morgan flooded her system.

She should have stayed, persuaded him to put in for a transfer, the pair of them starting again elsewhere. He was familiar, respectful, and wouldn't dream of talking to her like this. Lydia thought of herself as a lady now, not some common tart with a boyfriend who would undoubtedly enjoy necrophilia if he had the chance. So why the fuck had she made the decision to come to him?

"What's the matter, Lyd?" He sat up, stretching his arms to the ceiling. A massive yawn skewed his wet lips.

Her stomach roiled.

"Nothing." She smiled and got on with brushing her tangled hair from where he'd gripped it in a tight fist. Her scalp still burned from the rough treatment, and he'd mentioned having another round later, after they'd had dinner and a swim.

What the bloody hell have I done?

CHAPTER THIRTY-EIGHT

For a while after Phil had left, Gary thought about spending his life back in Rushford, or even some other prison. It was clear as bloody crystal his brother didn't want to know now he knew what Gary was really like, and him walking out meant Gary would never see him again.

It was also crystal that Gary was a burden to Phil and had been right from the time Gary had learned to walk and followed Phil around the house, entranced by him. He'd grown to look up to his sibling, to want to *be* him, but he was a buffoon, a clumsy prick, and Phil had all the charm and grace handed down through the gene pool. It was like by the time Gary was conceived, all the suaveness, the good parts of a person, had been depleted by Phil the Foetus.

Gary stood and gazed out of the window, one last nose at the lane. He'd thought he'd be in the bedsit for the required time, Phil would find him a flat or whatever later on — not that it had ever been discussed but, you know, family and all that — and Gary would join a church and get involved with the community, try to make amends.

But he reckoned, even if he *didn't* get put down for his part in The Incident, people would still see him as the old

Gary. Look at how Wasti was with him when he went in the shop for his meal deal, like the stupid man still believed Gary had robbed him.

But you did rob him. The chaplain said to own your sins, not pretend they didn't happen.

Well, owning them had led to his latest decision, and it was for the best really. If he wasn't around, he couldn't get tarnished with his old brush or stand in the dock again, alone if all the remaining gang members were killed, and take the blame for either killing them or killing Everson.

No, he couldn't handle that.

He took his extra-long dressing gown cord out of the terry cloth loops and tested it for strength by wrapping it around his fists and yanking. Perfect. He draped it around his neck, the fabric dampening from his sweat. No point dilly-dallying. The time had come to admit his sins for the final time.

He dragged the chair into the centre below the light fitting in the ceiling and climbed on the seat, unbalanced for a moment, his legs going weak at the thought of what he was about to do, butterflies of excitement flickering inside him at the idea of the peace he'd get by going to meet God.

He tugged the light cord to see how secure it was, and the plastic rose wobbled. If he pulled harder, he reckoned the damn thing would come loose.

Another location then. Plan B.

He got down and, ear to the door, listened for movement out on the landing. All was quiet, so he unlocked the door to his little fortress and stepped out. He tied the end of the cord on the banister rail, the other around his neck in a noose, creating a decent knot some crim in Rushford had shown him when he'd planned to hang himself using bedsheets.

Calm descended, smothering Gary in its comforting glory, and he clambered up, clumsy as ever, onto the rail. He sat for a while, having to bend a bit because the cord had got shorter, staring at the wall opposite, grey paint, remembering his childhood before Mum and Dad died, how things had seemed so much easier then. And Phil, looking after him once they'd gone, Gary a thorn in his side and knowing it every damn day.

If Phil hadn't chosen the path he had, Gary wouldn't have wanted to be like him. Gary wouldn't have failed, wouldn't have become a second-rate criminal.

Everything was Phil's fault, and he'd know that once he read the note Gary had left beneath the loo roll on the TV unit.

He pushed off the rail, apologised to God, and waited for the noose to bite.

CHAPTER THIRTY-NINE

Morgan skidded to a stop. The killer had been here all along, right under his damn nose. He bolted out of the car with Shaz and ran up Goat's path in front of a decent house that tried to stand out from its brick-and-mortar peers, with its pretty garden and a uPVC front door, gleaming windows to match. A Fiat sat beside the kerb, nothing flashy, the dark-blue paintwork shiny enough but not in tip-top condition. It might not even be his and could belong to another neighbour or a visitor.

He remembered talking about Delia's murder to the resident, a young blonde woman, and she'd said she hadn't noticed anything down the other end of the lane on the nights Delia and Olga had been killed. And why would he suspect her of lying, an innocent-looking girl like her? Why would he think Goat would be shacked up here?

He hammered on the door with the side of his fist, calling out, "Open up! Police!"

Before setting off, Shaz had called Val to find out what the man's real name was. Calling the wife Mrs Goat wouldn't go down too well. The resulting gasp and "Fucking hell . . ." through the speakerphone told Morgan that Val knew him. Harry bloody Allerston, one of Val's customers, a fella with a nasty combover and bad skin.

"His wife's pregnant," Val had said. "And she's young. Just the right side of legal at seventeen. He told me once he has no fixed address, even though he lives there, and she didn't take his surname when they married. It's King, by the way."

What was a forty-something bloke doing with what amounted to a kid?

"Miss King?" Morgan shouted through the letterbox. "Naomi King, are you in there?"

A sob came as his answer.

"Can you open the door? We know you didn't do it, so if you could just step around the body and avoid standing in any mess . . ."

God, it reminded him of what he'd said to his runaway missus. '*Lydia, step over to me, making sure you don't tread in any blood. That's it, nice and steady.*'

Naomi's figure appeared in the slit of the letterbox gap, her coming towards the kitchen hallway from the kitchen, and she walked closer, closer still, her small belly filling the frame. She opened the door, and Morgan straightened, fetching his ID from his pocket and holding it up.

"DI Morgan Yeoman and DS Sharon Tanner. I was here before, remember? We're aware of what happened in there, so if you could just move back . . ."

She did, her face doused with tears, mascara dribbles on her cheeks, eyes bloodshot. She cradled her tummy, and although there wasn't a big bump yet, Morgan assumed she already had the maternal instinct, which was to protect her unborn child.

Morgan and Shaz stepped in, Shaz going to the kitchen to check Goat while Morgan steered the shocked woman into the living room. He urged her to sit on the sofa, and she clasped her hands on her lap.

"What happened, love?"

"A man came in through the back. Big bloke. He said I had to message Harry to come home for his dinner and to not tell him anyone else was here. I had a pie in the oven, it was almost ready, but it burnt because . . . because he wouldn't let me get it out while he was talking."

She turned to Morgan, who stood to her right, her eyes filled with tears.

"Go on," he nudged.

"He . . . he said he had a little story to tell me, about Harry and his friends. They're all murderers, killing some kid in a squat, and all I could think of was that if the pie didn't come out of the oven, Harry was going to hurt me."

Bastard. "Hurt you often, did he?"

She nodded. "He likes his food cooked nicely."

"Right. How did you meet him?"

She shuddered. "I was hooked on the brown. He was my supplier. It got so he was here more often than not, kept bringing the drugs in exchange for sex when I couldn't afford it, then when he'd got his feet under the table, he locked me in the bedroom so I went cold turkey. Said I was his now, his Lyd, and—"

"*What* was that you said?" Morgan's nerves shredded. *Goat and Lydia?*

She shrugged, wiped tears away, her nails acrylic like Morgan's wife's. "Some girl he liked years ago. Lydia. He took me to the hairdresser, the woman who does it in her house down the road, and told her to dye it like Lydia's. He said I needed lessons in cooking, because Lydia had made him and his friends the best sausage and chips once, when they'd skived off school, like."

So Goat had harboured a secret crush all these years? Morgan almost laughed. There was no way the Lydia he knew would go with a man with pocked skin and a shimmering scalp that peeped through lines of swept-over hair. She felt herself too good for the likes of him.

"Okay. So what happened next, after the man told the story?"

"The smoke alarm went off because the pastry burnt, and he told me to go and switch it off then get the pie out. All the while, he's telling me what a bastard Harry is, something about nicking money from Old Man Cossack, whoever the hell that is." She sucked in a juddering breath. "I put the pie dish on a wooden board — Harry wouldn't like it if I didn't. He had the idea of being posh, which is why my house looks like this. Said he wanted a home like Lyd's."

Morgan glanced around. Now he'd fully taken it in, the living room *was* much like his. Goat probably knew the layout from dropping coke off to Lydia, and he'd replicated it here. Why did Naomi not mind him hankering after another woman?

He asked her just that.

"I haven't ever really had anyone who cared enough to do my house up or send me for cookery classes. And it wasn't so bad — in bed with him, I mean. Okay, he likes pinching and using handcuffs and things, but lots of people do since it's been in that *Shades* book. I just thought everyone did it like that. I wouldn't allow him to him wear gloves, though, even when he begged me to let him. He . . . he was my first."

Morgan rubbed his chin. If Goat were alive, he'd smack some decency into him, but he wasn't, and that reminded him Shaz was still in the kitchen with the body.

"Hello?" Ah, Cameron.

SOCO had arrived. Good. That meant Morgan could sort Naomi with somewhere to go, then he could bugger off and find the man responsible for this.

"Come in," Morgan called. "Kitchen."

"Righto."

Morgan waved at Cameron and his crew walking past the doorway, then he smiled at Naomi. "Is there any family to stay with while the police are here? Your kitchen will be a crime scene for a while, I'm afraid."

"No family left. This used to me my grandmother's house. I took it over after she died. Lived with her because my parents are dead. I have a friend, though. She lives in Vicar's Gate." She shuddered. "That's where the man said Harry and his friends killed that boy."

"Different houses and flats now, love. They were all knocked down and rebuilt."

"Oh. Right."

"Do you know Goat's . . . Harry's next of kin?"

She took her phone out and selected a contact, then showed him the number. He wrote it down.

"Thank you. An address?"

"No, he doesn't want me meeting his mum. Said I'm just his but I can have her number for emergencies. His family didn't even come to our wedding. We just had witnesses he pulled in from outside the registry office."

Charming. "I'll sort someone to take you there, okay?" He went into the hallway, took his phone out, and quietly contacted Nigel to arrange for him to come by. Naomi wasn't in any fit state to walk there by herself. He also asked Nigel to pass Goat's next of kin number to Jane Blessing for her to get an address and visit them to break the news.

He returned to the living room.

"I tried to warn Harry," Naomi said. "I stared at him so hard, you know? But he just asked if I needed goggles, and I didn't know what he meant."

She seemed a bit dim, or maybe it was the shock.

"What did the man look like?" he asked. While Phil had told him who it was, Morgan needed to hear it from her. Phil could have lied just to get David in the shit.

"Massive."

"Okay. I know who it is and will find him, all right? He won't bother you again anyway. He was here for Harry for a reason, and that reason doesn't include you. Unless he told you he'd be back?"

She shook her head. "He said he had no business with me, just Harry, and if I did exactly what he wanted, everything would be fine, but I'm not so sure now. He thumped me in the leg at one point — he was crouching beside me behind the island."

"All the more reason to go to your friend's place. I'll get the officer to go through this again with you once he's driven you there, a proper statement — a nice chap called Nigel Stansford, someone from my team."

Sour Jane Blessing wasn't someone Morgan wanted interviewing Naomi. She had strong views on young women and pregnancy and might look down her nose at her while pretending she hid her opinions in the name of the job.

"Thank you." Naomi managed a small smile.

"You sit tight."

He left her, closed the living room door, and walked towards the kitchen. Conscious he wasn't in protectives, he remained in the hallway.

"Look at the fucking state of that." Cameron pointed at Goat.

His combover strands had flung back on themselves to one side and now rested in a pool of blood on the floor. His nose was red from booze or drugs, tiny scarlet and purple veins showing up against his greying skin. The back of the head wasn't a pretty sight, so Morgan didn't let his attention linger there. Instead, he studied the way the body had fallen, and it was consistent with how Phil had said things had gone down. He shifted his sights to the island, the pie in a red dish on a board, the top burnt.

"Yeah, a mess," he said to Cameron. "We won't hang about to wait for Lisa to give us the time of death because an informant told me when it happened."

"You and your narks." Cameron turned and instructed a photographer to take snaps of the bits of brain on the splashback, an effective dismissal.

Morgan nodded at Shaz. "We need to go."

She stepped around the body, blood and SOCOs, coming to stand in front of Morgan. "Where the fuck did Ives get a gun?"

"People have ways when they make friends in Rushford, you know that." Morgan turned to go out and wait for Nigel.

The fresh air out the front eased his tight lungs, and Shaz joined him on the path, where a PC had situated himself. Police tape flickered in the breeze, strung up across the middle of the garden as a sign to any nosy neighbours that no, they couldn't come through here.

Shaz sniffed. "I've got to get something off my chest. Leaving me with Blessing for any length of time really isn't a good idea. I know you like to go off on your own sometimes, and I respect that, but it isn't fair to me. She was moaning about you, saying how unprofessional you are."

"Sorry, but I needed some space."

"Because the case has something to do with Lydia?"

"Yeah. And she's fucked off somewhere."

"Oh. I'm sorry."

"I'm not."

"I didn't think things were right between you, although you covered it up well the last few times I was round yours for dinner. Saying that, a few months have passed since then."

"She's better off out of the way for now."

There was only her and Steve left to let the cat out of the bag regarding the murder, but then again, David Ives wasn't likely to keep quiet about it once he got caught. Then everyone would know Morgan's wife was a witness to a murder, and who knew, Ives might also say she'd killed Alice. Martin Olbey could also open his mouth. Morgan would have to make out that was the first he'd heard of it, otherwise, it'd be obvious he'd covered up for Lydia over Alice.

He should never have done it.

Nigel came to a stop in his Mondeo behind the SOCO van. He got out and ducked under the police tape. "Jane is seething at having to go to Goat's mother's, just so you know."

"Jane is always seething," Morgan said, "but she isn't the right one for this, and that's all there is to it." He explained Naomi's pregnancy situation.

"Ah, I understand now." Nigel signed the log with the PC. "Inside, is she?"

"Yeah, in the living room. Get a detailed statement off her; I just got the bare bones. We're off now. Got a man to find. Once you've finished with her, go home. You can message Blessing and tell her the same."

Morgan signed the log, waited for Shaz to, then led the way to his car.

Inside, once they'd buckled up, he drove away, turning into Elderflower Mead. He parked outside Mrs Ives' house, heart fluttering at his thoughts of David being in there. At the door, Morgan knocked while Shaz held her cuffs in one hand and her baton in the other, both things hidden behind her.

Best to be prepared for trouble.

Morgan held his ID up ready.

The door opened, and a wizened old lady stood there, her afro gone grey but her skin relatively free of wrinkles. The advantage of being black, so Morgan's mum used to say. *'We don't age, we just get better as time goes by.'*

"Mrs Ives? DI Morgan Yeoman and DS Sharon Tanner."

"Yes?" She smiled, all her own teeth by the look of it. "Are you here to check on David?"

Check isn't the right word, love. "Err, yes, is he in?"

"No. He said he was going to meet a friend. He didn't do it, you know. He didn't kill that poor boy."

"We know." Morgan smiled. "That's why we need to speak to him. Do you know which friend he's going to see?"

"I don't remember his name, but he said he met him in Rushford and they were having a meal in the pub."

Martin Olbey. The Tractor's?

"Thanks very much for your time."

Morgan gave her his card and asked her to ring him when David got home. They left, and he drove them to The Tractor's. A quick scan showed Ives wasn't there, and Morgan approached the bar and signalled for Terry to come over.

The landlord shuffled along, his foot encased in one of those medical boots. "Ended up having to go to the hospital for a cast, didn't I. It wasn't just my toes but my sodding foot that got broke. Agony, I tell you, bloody agony."

Morgan winced. "Nasty. David Ives been in?"

"You just missed him. He went off with that Martin fella after they had lasagne and chips."

He's bold enough to hang around eating after blowing someone's head off? What about the blood on him? "Any idea where he might live? I'm talking about Martin here. He left Halfway."

"That's your lot's department. He's meant to bloody let you know, isn't he? Or his probation at any rate."

"Yep, but some people are a law unto themselves. Cheers."

They left the pub.

Shaz grumbled, "I need some dinner. Haring around after killers is tiresome on an empty stomach, especially because I've smelled the food in the pub."

"I'll buy you a sodding chippy if it'll stop you moaning," he said. "We'll go to the one down Vicar's Gate." He mourned not having one of Li Wei's Chineses. Shit, he had to let Rochester out at some point an' all. The poor dog would be plaiting his legs.

There were downsides to not having Lydia around.

He hated himself for that thought.

"Shall we go now, seeing as we have no idea where Ives will have gone?" Shaz asked.

"May as well."

He twisted the key in the ignition, and his phone went off. He took it out of his pocket and checked the screen. Emma Ingles. What the hell did *she* want? Had Martin and David gone to Halfway?

He swiped the screen to accept the call. "DI Morgan Yeoman."

"It's me, Emma."

"Yep. What's up?"

"It's Gary Flint."

"What about him?"

"He's hung himself from the banisters."

CONFESSION

I was in that prison for years, fucking years, for something I hadn't done. Appeals didn't change the outcome, and I was stuck there with no outlet for my anger at the injustice. Those who'd killed that kiddie had walked free, and there was me, paying for it in their places. Better than being dead, though. If I'd given names, Phil would have gone for me, no question. So I planned, I schemed, and I knew, come release day, exactly how it'd go down. There was Martin and a man called Harry, my wingmen, and together, we'd sort it. Once again, though, things weren't plain sailing. My only regret is I've become exactly the person Mum didn't want me to be. A killer and an even bigger disgrace to my Jamaican heritage.

—David Ives

CHAPTER FORTY

After dinner in The Tractor's, a jumper covering any blood on his top, David had been about to tell Martin what he'd been up to, but the risk he'd already taken, being in the pub opposite Goat's place, meant he'd kept his mouth shut and suggested they move on to a more remote spot. They'd walked out, and a uniform copper had stood on Goat's doorstep in the light from the hallway. Yeoman's car was there along with a big white van.

Fucking hell, that had been close. David had put his head down, got in Martin's car, and hadn't looked up until they'd arrived at their destination.

So there they were, holed up in Drinker's Rest on Cobbs Moor, the darkness surrounding the pub giving David a sense of security. He'd chosen a corner table and sat facing the door so he could spot any potential trouble the minute it walked in, its body and head police-shaped, its words those announcing his arrest. Their table stood beside a door marked PRIVATE, and if he had to, he could leg it through there and find a back exit.

"So what did you want to chat about?" Martin lifted his pint of dark ale and took a sip.

David glanced around at the other customers, few and far between, but he kept his voice low anyway. "I've killed our mutual friend."

"*What?*" Martin plonked the glass down, and some froth spewed over the rim and down the side to form a foamy puddle on the table. "Did he do Lydia and Steve already without telling me?"

"No, but the more I thought about Harry letting Lydia off, the more arsey I got. There I was, minding my own, having a pint in The Tractor's before I met you there, and someone mentioned that Harry is also known as Goat. So it got me to thinking about the past. I found out where he was and popped the fucker with that gun you got for me off your mate."

"Jesus Christ. Where? And what the fuck does Goat mean?"

"Because he used to laugh like one, although he never did it in front of me in the nick. And I offed him in his wife's place opposite The Tractor's."

Martin gawped. "And we had our *dinner* in there as if nothing was *wrong*?"

"Yeah, I wasn't thinking straight."

"Clearly bloody not, which is why we agreed *I'd* do all the planning. You're too emotionally involved. You were allowed Delia and no one else." Martin shoved a hand through his hair. "Christ. What about Harry's missus? Where was she? He said she hardly goes out and spends all day cooking."

"She was there and won't cause any trouble. Thick as two short planks. She'll stay quiet — I scared the shit out of her. Better off without him, she is. So, it's time to go and get Lydia ourselves."

"What, now, at Yeoman's place?" Martin blinked. A lot.

"Yeoman's busy at the murder scene, you div." David shook his head. "Didn't you see his car? Didn't you even wonder, when we left The Tractor's, what the fuck the police were doing at Harry's?"

"No, because I wasn't aware it *was* Harry's. Blimey. Every time I've met him, it's been down alleys and shit. He never told me his address."

"Did you know he was called Goat?" David tilted his head in question.

"Did I fuck. First I've heard of that name. I met him in Rushford, remember. Didn't know him before I went inside, didn't run in those circles. I got done for hacking. Handy with a computer, as I told you before, and sending threatening emails in scams."

"Harry is *Goat*. As in, Goat, the little dick who hung around with that gang, the one I told you wasn't there that night when the kids ran away so he wasn't on my list. At least, I didn't see him."

Martin scowled. "Didn't you *know* it was the same person? Bloody hell, you must have recognised him in the nick?"

"If you knew Goat back then and saw him now, you wouldn't think it was the same kid. And don't forget, he *was* just a lad before I got banged up. Plus, he wasn't known as Goat inside, no one called him that as far as I heard, so how was I to know?" Anger surged. David was livid at being duped. Goat had to have known who David was.

"What's the problem anyway?"

"There isn't one now."

David thought back. *Had* Goat been running away that night? No. David had only seen all of the ones he'd put on his hit list, he was sure of it, but maybe there was one extra there and he hadn't noticed because that fucking Delia had got in his mug, raving on about snakes. He remembered not counting all of them, though. Well, what did it matter now if Goat *had* seen Jacob get killed? Goat was dead, and it served him right for being Phil's minion and taking over delivering to people like Old Man Cossack.

"Right," he said. "We need to break into Lydia's, catch her by surprise."

Martin scrubbed at his chin and burped. "'Scuse me. Bit too gassy for me, that. I remember Goat saying she has a key under a bush out the front, plus one on the back door lintel, so no need to break in."

"But what if she's not there and an alarm goes off?"

Martin grinned. "Harry also knew the code and told me. I made him give me every bit of information he had on the gang, and come to think of it, it makes sense now how he knew so much if he was mates with them all along. The sneaky bastard . . ."

"Who gives a fuck, he's dead, so let's get going."

They necked their drinks, then Martin drove them to Lydia's place. David whistled through his teeth at the sight of the big house. No way could a DI afford that, but then Harry had given information about Lydia coming into money, so that'd explain the massive pad. Martin parked between lampposts so his car wasn't as visible, and they walked through a small gateway to the side of larger ones that kept people off the property.

Martin used the torch on his phone and pointed the beam beneath a little ball of a tree under the front window. "It's not there. Come on, round the back."

They crept into the rear garden, and David reached up, running his gloved fingertips along the lintel. Ah, there, a key. He swiped it and held it in front of the torchlight. A Yale, for the front door, not the back. Shite. More chance of being spotted if they went in that way.

Regardless, they loped round there. David opened the place up, and Martin stepped inside to turn off the alarm. Door left ajar for a faster exit, they prowled the house together. In the kitchen, a massive dog came over, tail wagging, whining in excitement at having humans to interact with. It padded over to the back door, pawing it, so David let it out for a piss. While the dog did its business, they nosed around. And there was a note on the worktop, signed by Lydia. She'd gone somewhere. A laptop sat on the table, so he switched it on and checked the recent history.

"How do we find out where she's gone?" David pointed to a link for an airline ticket site.

Martin leant forward, his face ghostly in the light coming off the screen. "I can find out. Hacker, remember?" He tapped a few keys, bringing up some kind of data in a folder, then clicked something else. A web browser opened up. "Hotel Santuario, Spain."

"I'm going to bloody go there and sort her." David breathed deeply to calm the rage. How dare she run off without taking her punishment?

"You've been in the nick for years, and if you had a passport before then, it'll be expired now, so how the hell do you propose you'll get there?"

David grinned. "I know a man who does have one."

"Who?"

"Morgan fucking Yeoman."

David rushed upstairs, sodding it and switching on a lamp in the largest bedroom, which had open wardrobe doors and no clothes inside. One bedside drawer hung out, so he looked in the one on the other side.

"There you go," he said to himself, laughing at his new identity. "Who'd have thought you'd be a copper, eh, Dave?"

He picked the passport up and went to walk out but stepped back to check the drawer again. A credit card. It just kept getting better. And he'd even book the fucking plane ticket using the laptop downstairs.

Another ferret produced a pad and pen, so he scribbled a message.

He smiled and nodded.

"Lydia, I'm coming for you."

CHAPTER FORTY-ONE

Emma shuddered at the memory of finding Gary hanging. She'd planned to go up there to ask him if it would be okay for her to clean his bathroom today instead of tomorrow, something, anything to keep her busy since Martin Olbey had walked out. She didn't feel safe anymore with him on the streets, and she'd had the foresight to change the keypad code so he couldn't get back in, another reason to visit Gary and the others. She'd needed to give them the new ones.

But if he can bypass the system, a new code won't make a difference.

All had gone fine until she'd stood on the first stair, and something caught her eye. She'd looked up at a pair of bare feet, then legs, then a penis, and oh, Gary was hanging, naked, a dressing gown cord around his neck.

And she'd known he was already dead. His face, the shit staining the rails, and the foamy stuff around his mouth — he was gone, and there was nothing she could do for him now.

She'd screamed, and all the residents had come running. Emma had ushered them down into the main living room out of the way, then rang Yeoman. Every person gathered looked afraid, as if they'd get the blame for murder, but that was for Yeoman to determine, not her. She'd walked off into the kitchen to put the kettle on. Tea, that would calm them all. Oliver Elford had followed her, and he was still there, watching her pour boiled water into the big metal teapot.

She wished he'd go away and join the others, leave her alone so she could view the horrific images in her head in relative peace. Gary, dangling. Gary's tongue all bulbous and poking out. His hands clenched into fists. The scratch marks on his neck where he must have instinctively reached up to loosen the cord, an effort to survive despite wanting to kill himself.

Unless it *had* been murder.

Oh God.

"Didn't strike me as the type," Oliver said.

She jumped at his unexpected voice. "N-no, he didn't."

"He'd found God and seemed so happy." He came up to stand beside her.

Too bloody close. "Many people are happy, just before . . . just before they—"

The front door buzzer sounded, and she abandoned her task and rushed up the hallway. She drew the door open, relieved beyond measure that Yeoman and Tanner stood there.

"Oh, thank God you're here." *But is that because of what Gary did or because of Oliver being creepy? Or even the fact one of them could have killed Gary?* "He's . . ." She took a steadying breath. "He's just up that stairwell there." She pointed and moved back.

They came in and walked up a few steps.

"Oh dear," Morgan said. "Not much can be done for him, so we may as well get talking." He took his phone out. Phoned someone. "Ah, the lovely Miss Amanda Cartwright. Can you do me a favour and put out a BOLO for a David Ives, please. We're meant to be looking, but there's a hanging we're attending, and it's related to the case we're working. Yep, if you get wind of him, ring me immediately. Cheers." He slid his phone away.

"Do either of you want tea?" Oliver called from the kitchen.

Emma clamped her teeth. She wished he'd just get lost, move somewhere else. She didn't know why he bothered her fragile senses more than the others, but he did. Sometimes you just knew there was more to someone than they let you see.

"I'll deal with that." She strutted down the hallway, irritation lending her speed, her feet heavy with anger. "The police need to speak to you all, so the living room is the best bet."

Oliver stared at her, one hand curled around the teapot handle. She had the wild idea he might pick it up and dash the boiling tea on her, despite police officers being here.

He's not Derek. And there it was, why he chilled her to the bone. His mannerisms and facial expressions were similar, and he watched her a lot, bringing on unease.

"All right," he said. "You must have had a right shock, finding Gary like that, and I was only trying to help. Remind me not to make you feel better again."

He shuffled out in his tartan slippers, and she closed her eyes for a moment to stop herself snapping at him. No good would come of it, and perhaps he'd needed to occupy himself with the tea because *he* was affected by the death as well.

She really should stop thinking only of herself in upsetting situations.

Derek had always accused her of being selfish. That was why he'd hit her.

'Look at how you affect me when you want some time to yourself.' Slap.

'See how you make me lonely when you want a bath with the door shut.' A pinch, a kick.

'And this is your fault, me shouting at you, because you want to go to a meeting in the pub with your colleagues.' Broken bones.

Thinking of herself had got her into a mess with him, but her therapist had taught her she wasn't to blame.

So why was she slipping back into old thought patterns now?

CHAPTER FORTY-TWO

Morgan and Shaz spent a good two hours talking to the residents of Halfway, and he reckoned all of them were genuine in that they hadn't seen or heard a thing. Cameron had sent Henry out with a small team of SOCO to control the scene, and Morgan left Henry to it. What else could he do there except stand around like a spare part?

"We'll go to the chippy now," he said to Shaz in the car. "Then I need to let the poor dog out." He sped off, on the lookout for Ives along the way.

"Death at both ends of the lane," Shaz said. "Un-fucking-believable."

Morgan turned out of Mulberry at the pub end and drove towards Vicar's Gate. "I know this estate's a hotbed for crime, but bloody hell."

"Hmm. So why d'you think Flint topped himself?"

"It's obvious, isn't it? His note said he couldn't stand himself, what he'd done to Jacob, and God would look after him now."

"Not forgetting the bit about everything being Phil's fault. Sounds to me like Gary couldn't handle taking any blame for how he started off in crime."

"Yeah, we all know what Phil's about, but proving it is another matter. You'd have thought he'd discourage Gary following in his footsteps, wouldn't you, seeing as Gary was a bit . . . well, a bit of a prat."

"Maybe Phil had ideas of creating a family business, and by the time Gary showed his ineptitude, it was too late."

Morgan stopped outside the arcade of shops in Vicar's Gate. "Dunno. What are you having?"

"Sausage, chips, and curry sauce for dipping. Oh, and can of Coke."

"You teeth'll rot."

"Fuck off, Dad."

"Oi."

Morgan left the car, chuckling, and entered the chippy, assaulted by the strong smell of vinegar and fried fish in batter. He ordered, getting a can of Vimto for himself rather than his usual orange juice, and leant on the wall while the woman dished up their food.

This was a right pig's ear of a case, and he hadn't had a proper moment to think about it all. Today had been one thing after another, each one walloping into him, and he just needed half an hour, a break, so his mind could stop whirling.

The problem was . . . Lydia. With her gone and him not knowing where she was, he'd lost control. He'd tried her phone periodically, but it was switched off or her battery was dead. More than likely she was ignoring him.

He paid for the food and sat in the car, handing Shaz's over.

"I was thinking while you were in the chippy," she said.

"Steady on. You might do yourself some damage."

She tutted. "You're such a knob sometimes."

He unwrapped his dinner. Cod, chips, and mushy peas. "You only just noticed?"

Shaz opened her food, popped the lid off her curry sauce. She dipped a chip in and shoved it in her mouth. Chewed and swallowed. "Don't you want to know what I was thinking about?"

"Go on then, astound me." He broke the tail end off the fish.

"Your wife shouldn't have gone when she's a witness to a murder. Even you sending her away would be seen as wrong."

He crunched on the fish, taking a while on purpose to buy himself some time. "Look, you know what she's like. Highly strung. We have what we need from her for now, and she can come back if we need more."

"Right. One rule for her?"

"Give it a rest, mate, seriously. I'm knackered, can't be doing with you pecking at me. We've got David Ives and Martin Olbey in the fucking wind, we've got some woman strangled with a snake, two others sliced with a knife, Goat with his brains splattered all over his kitchen—"

"Christ, Morgan, I'm *eating*!"

"—and Flint dangling from a sodding banister. Forgive me if my mind isn't on my wife and what she's bloody doing at the moment, because my God, we've got murders and death up to our armpits, and all I want to do is eat my ruddy dinner and drink my Vimto."

"It'll rot your teeth . . ."

"Really? You're doing that now?"

He stared at her, intending to remain angry, but they both burst out laughing.

"Just fuck off, you daft mare," he said.

"Got you to relax, though, didn't I?"

"What do you want, a medal?"

"*How* old are you?"

They laughed some more then ate in silence. Morgan stared through the windscreen, fog from the heat of their dinner misting the edges. Nigel's car was parked outside the first house beside the parade. Naomi must be taking some time to remember everything if he was still there. Morgan wondered, but only for a second, how Jane Blessing had got on with Goat's mother and whether she'd bother to phone Morgan with any developments or be childish and wait until the morning to tell him.

He scrunched up his wrappers and took Shaz's, getting out to put them in the bin already overflowing with crap.

The drive to his house didn't take long, and he let them in, frowning that the alarm didn't go off. He'd set that before he'd left earlier, *and* he'd closed the kitchen door so Rochester didn't have the run of the house. The dog getting in the living room with all that dried blood didn't bear thinking about.

He stepped inside and whistled.

No dog.

"Something's up," he whispered.

"I'll go upstairs," Shaz whispered back.

Without turning on any lights, Morgan checked the living room, the dining room, then the kitchen. The dog wasn't in there either, so maybe he was upstairs on the bed, the little sod. A bang on the back door had him spinning to face it, and Rochester pressed his wet nose to the glass — he'd jumped up to stand on his hind legs, a silhouette in the dark.

"Jesus." Morgan went to turn the key, but it had already *been* turned, yet he swore he'd locked that. He let the dog in and fussed him. Was he losing his mind here or what? There was no way he'd leave the dog out all day.

Has Lydia been back?

The idea of that soured his guts, and he jolted at Shaz calling him from upstairs.

"Where do you keep your passport, Morg?"

He walked to the bottom of the stairs. "Right-hand drawer beside the bed."

"Well, looks like someone we know has left you a note about it."

"I fucking *knew* someone had been here." He took the steps two at a time and barrelled into the bedroom.

Shaz pointed to his bedside cabinet.

For a short while, I'll be you, Morgan Yeoman. I wonder what it'll be like on the other side of the fence? Cheers for the loan of the passport and credit card. I'll have used them by the time you realise it, so if you're thinking of finding me through them, jog on. I'm nearly at the end of my plan. Just two more to go, then everyone will have paid for what they did to that boy. I didn't do it, I said it all along, maintained my innocence, but no one would listen. Maybe now you will.

"He's going to pass himself off as you," Shaz said.

"Stating the obvious, love." He sighed. "We need a small team round here for fingerprinting. You organise that while I ring this in so Amanda can alert the airports and ports."

The idea of David Ives masquerading as Morgan set his anger on fire. The flames licked and curled their way through him, heating his skin and bringing on a sweat. This case was his worst nightmare, David one step ahead all the way.

What was he doing, fucking off to start again elsewhere now he'd caused all this damage? Or was he looking for Lydia?

Jesus Christ, no.

He legged it downstairs to the laptop in the kitchen and brought the machine to life. A screen saver, neon green with black font.

I KNOW WHERE YOUR WIFE IS. ADIÓS, PUERCO!

"That last word means 'pig'," Shaz said, coming up behind him. "Cheeky bastard."

"Spanish?"

"Yeah. I took it at school. Now there's a thing you know."

Morgan took a deep breath. Lydia hated Spain.

He nodded. She had it all worked out, didn't she. Go somewhere he'd swear blind she wouldn't.

He phoned Amanda and gave her instructions, then took a moment to steady his nerves. Somewhere in Spain, Lydia thought she'd got herself to safety, when in reality, the man who wanted her dead had probably already arrived there if he'd got a flight quickly enough.

For all Morgan knew, she could already be dead.
He rang his wife again.
No answer.
Fuck. Fuck!

CHAPTER FORTY-THREE

Lydia sprawled in bed, staring at the ceiling and enjoying the peace without Steve there. He'd gone for a swim in the darkness after 'round two', as he'd put it, something about liking the way the moon shone on the water. She hadn't taken him as a poetic sort. Apparently, he also reckoned the exercise would gear him up for a third go at her, but she ached all over, even after a shower, and her head stung in different patches where he'd grabbed her hair again.

While she'd longed for something a bit spicier, maybe the jalapeno of sex as opposed to a bell pepper, this man enjoyed a bit too much ghost chilli.

She should leave now, while he was busy with the moon in the pool. Just shove her stuff in her cases, get a bellhop to come and collect them. She'd ask them to let her wait downstairs in an office while they ordered her a taxi, away from his prying eyes.

She got up and went to the balcony doors, creeping out there to sidle along the wall so she could see him but he couldn't see her. Christ, he was down there on a sun lounger, some woman on the one next to him, the light from a nearby lamppost displaying them in all their flirting glory. Their gentle laughter floated up, and if Lydia wasn't mistaken, the insatiable bastard had movement going on in his swimming trunks, those tight Paedo-Speedo efforts she hated.

She wasn't important to him, any woman would do, that much was obvious.

Yes, she'd go now.

She lifted the phone and dialled for someone to collect her cases as soon as possible.

"It will be about half an hour, madam."

"Thanks."

That was all right. She'd stay on the balcony to check he was still down there whenever a knock came at the door. If he wasn't, she wouldn't answer. He could go to his own bloody suite with that woman. The tart was welcome to him. Lydia didn't want a man who treated her like a sex doll, someone he could treat badly in bed.

She flung some clothes on, packed her things, almost putting his grey T-shirt in there by mistake. She threw it on the bed then stood the cases by the door. Handbag hanging over her shoulder, passport and money safe inside, she leant against the wall on the balcony.

Steve and the woman snogged on one lounger.

A knock rapped out, earlier than she'd expected, and she rushed to peer through the spyhole. A man with black hair had his back to her, and he had a racing-green uniform jacket on from the hotel — the collar had the yellow strip along the edge. Relief had her crying out, and she flung the door wide.

The man turned.

David Ives stood there, and his fist came towards her face.

CHAPTER FORTY-FOUR

David smiled and walloped Lydia, her nose crunching and skewing to one side beneath his fist. What a satisfying sound after imagining it for years. She let out a grunt and staggered in reverse, tottering blindly in her high heels, her handbag thunking to the floor, eyes screwed shut where she was probably in pain.

Good. No less than she deserved.

She landed on the bed, falling back, and he closed the door and slipped the chain across. He had limited time to work, what with the bellhop coming up here in around twenty minutes. It paid to menace information out of employees in hallways, although the others would soon find the bloke he'd nicked the jacket from, slumped in a cleaning cupboard, propped against a rack of metal shelving holding bog roll and a mop bucket of filthy water some lazy fucker hadn't bothered tipping out.

His name tag read: SALBATORE.

Salbatore had given David what he needed immediately after the promise of money coming his way if he complied. David had lied about that bit — shame — and gripped Salbatore round the throat in a stranglehold until the fella had passed out. He'd tied him up and placed a rag in his mouth.

David had gained Lydia's room number and the fact she was having her cases collected, and that was all that mattered. She planned to leave — why? — and fuck, this was lucky timing to get here before she went AWOL.

He advanced on her, and in his fist, a dessert spoon stolen from a cutlery tray on a cart in one of the corridors. He could have chosen a knife, a fork, but spoons were blunt and hurt more.

She struggled to sit, her nose bloodied. Opened her eyes. They widened at the sight of him coming towards her. The silly cow had probably thought he was an employee-cum-robber or something, but now she knew exactly who he was, her expression said as much.

"W-who are you?" She rose further, acting the part of a bemused woman for some reason.

He shoved her back down. "Sit your arse on that fucking bed, and you know exactly who the hell I am, stop pretending. I'm the bloke who spent most of his life in prison because of you and your shitty little mates."

"David Ives?" She'd said it in wonderment.

"Oh, don't give me that bollocks, like you don't recognise me."

"I-I do now, it's just . . . just . . . I'm confused. I-I didn't do anything back then. And you *punched* me. How did you know I was here?"

"Friends who know their way around a computer and can find shit even though you thought you'd hidden it, like the fact you booked in here, you dozy fucking bint." He pushed her so she was flat on her back and straddled her, pinning her arms to her sides with his knees.

Being a brick shithouse had advantages.

He raised the spoon, and she winced, gasped, possibly thinking it was a knife, then her features relaxed: *Oh, it's only a spoon.*

He laughed, low and sinister, and reached across for a grey T-shirt draped over one of the pillows. He stuffed a lump of it in her mouth despite her thrashing her head from side to side to stop him.

"No point fighting. It's over, Lydia." He held her face still with his free hand, digging his thumb and fingertips into her cheeks, wishing they'd go right through the skin and she howled in agony. He trailed the back of the spoon across her forehead. Was it cold? Did it have the chill of death about it? "I heard you just watched when the others killed Jacob. You stood there and didn't give that poor kid any help. What does that make you, eh?"

She snorted mucous, nostrils flaring in her attempt to draw in enough air.

He grunted. "A bitch, that's what. And now you're going to find out exactly how much pain I felt by you watching, by them killing. Years, it hurt. *Years.*"

He lifted the spoon then speared it down to one of her widened eyes, plunged it beneath, and scooped that fucker out. She'd been blind to his suffering in Rushford and she'd be blinded by pain now. Her scream, although muffled by the T-shirt, was still pretty loud, and she writhed, trying to buck him off. He held her firm, staring in wonder at the blood pouring out of the hole, the eye dangling from something or other down by her temple. Sinews maybe. A string of optic nerve. Her neck cords rose every time she let out a rasping roar-growl, and he bent over, positioning his mouth above a pulsing vein on the side.

And bit.

Blood swamped his tongue, hot and coppery and bitter and electrifying, and he ripped, spat the skin out onto the bed. Fascinated by the red state of her, he cocked his head to better watch her suffer, her body straining beneath him, arcs of crimson spurting on the white quilt, the painting it created aptly named Pollock in the Bedroom.

He dug two fingers in the bite gash, pushing as deep as the muscles and tendons allowed, if only to bring her maximum pain while the life fled out of her. She spasmed, her one eye opening, and she stared at the ceiling, liquid scarlet gurgling in her throat.

"That's it, you choke," he said and removed the T-shirt.

Blood erupted from her mouth in a cough, spraying on his face, and he gave his fingers one extra press, then removed them to study the estuary streaming out. She stilled, teeth bared, pink-streaked veneers if he was any judge. Her tits stood proud, no dragging down to the armpits for the likes of them, and he supposed you could buy whatever you wanted if you had money.

Except freedom, in his case.

Except life, in hers.

He got off her and found the bathroom, washing his hands and face, his neck, sluicing his hair where tiny droplets of blood had anchored there. He took the dirty jacket off and left it in the bath, dried his hands, laughed.

Someone knocked on the door, and he reckoned it'd be the hop coming for the cases, although why they didn't question Lydia wanting to leave at this time of night, he didn't know. They'd probably think he was some bloke Lydia had picked up at a bar.

David walked through to take the chain off and opened the door so he stood behind it, unseen.

A man strode in, just swimming trunks on, stopping three paces inside and staring across at Lydia, a whispered, "Fucking hell!" coming out of him.

David shut the door, and the man spun to face him.

Steve? Was that *Steve*? Had to be — same eyes, same nose, same weird-shaped ears.

"What the fuck?" Steve said.

"All right? Long time, no see." David smiled. "Looks like I've got myself a bargain. Two for the price of one."

CHAPTER FORTY-FIVE

Taina took the lift to the third floor. She loved working the night shift. The quiet, the lack of hard work, suited her better than scurrying around after holidaymakers, catering to their every privileged whim — and people here *were* privileged, no package holidays for them. Jobs like taking painkillers or cups of tea to rooms where people couldn't get to sleep were preferable, easier after a lifetime of the frenetic day shift. She wasn't getting any younger, and rushing about left her breathless these days, but she never shirked her responsibilities.

Not like Salbatore. He was pushing it by always disappearing the way he did, and she'd have something to say about it if he wasn't back by the time she returned downstairs. He liked to smoke cigarettes, leaning on a palm tree out by the pool, one leg crossed over the other, the toe of his shoe pointed to the ground. She hadn't seen him for over half an hour since he went on one of his many breaks.

He should be doing this task, getting Mrs Laura Smith's cases, although that wasn't her real name. She wanted to be called this while here, but her passport said she was Mrs Lydia Yeoman. Many people who stayed at Santuario chose different names, mainly Smith or Jones or Brown, and Taina could guess why Smith had. She'd been friendly with a permanent resident since her arrival earlier, so she must be one of those wives who came here for a dalliance while the husband remained at home, working to provide such luxuries for her. Well, more fool her, because the resident was Steve who picked a different woman every two weeks from the revolving carousel of beauties who glided in and out on exclusive deals.

He'd been out by the pool with a black-haired lady tonight, so perhaps that was why Mrs Smith was leaving. It wasn't Taina's right to ask why, although speculating was fun and, over the dinner table, she often regaled her family with tales about the foreigners' antics.

Some people acted terribly while away from home. Flirting, flaunting, having affairs. Once, a man had trapped his penis in a drawer, and an ambulance came. All the tanned elites had stood around the bar afterwards, discussing the blood at his midsection as he was carted away to hospital. The tip of it had . . .

She didn't want to think about what had happened to that.

Never a dull moment in Hotel Santuario.

She shuddered at the memory and leant forward to inspect the wrinkles beneath her eyes in the mirrored lift wall. Ah, she had a few years left in her yet, then she'd retire in the hills, her children and grandchildren all around her if they chose to follow her there, but if they didn't, there were always holidays.

The lift dinged and lurched to a stop, and the door glided open, a faint whoosh of movement and sound so as not to disturb those sleeping.

Every whim was catered to here.

She stepped out into the corridor. Mrs Smith was in thirty-eight, so Taina walked down there. She knocked on the door and, with no answer after a couple more taps, slid her access card down the slot beside the jamb and went inside.

Blood, so much blood.

Two bodies. One on the bed, the other on the floor beside it. Mrs Smith had one eye missing, and her neck had a big laceration, and Steve, oh God, Steve had a pair of swimming trucks around his neck, his face a mass of bruises, and he was *naked*, his hairy privates on show.

Taina's head swam.

She clutched her chest and fainted.

CHAPTER FORTY-SIX

Morgan and Shaz drank tea in the kitchen at his house while SOCO got on with fingerprinting. He'd received a call that David had landed in Spain and had been caught on CCTV hopping onto a shuttle that took him to Hotel Santuario. Now, they waited for someone from Spain to call back with any news that Lydia was also at that hotel — Morgan had given in, unable to hide shit for her anymore, and contacted Doncaster and Sheffield to see if his wife had departed for Spain, too.

She had, much earlier in the day.

With her life in danger, he could no longer keep quiet about her involvement in the gang, and he'd admitted all to Shaz, minus the part about Lydia holding the knife and slicing Alice's throat. He'd let Goat take the blame for that murder, and with him dead, no one would question it.

"So they kicked the shit out of that lad and she didn't do anything about it?" Shaz sipped her tea.

"Apparently so, although she did run away for a week, something I had no clue about until her dad told me."

"What *did* she tell you about her past? Like, aren't we supposed to share shit in relationships? Doesn't that come under the 'getting to know you' phase?"

"Now I think about it, she told me sod all. She deflected a lot, changed it round to ask about me instead. I thought she was stunning, confident, and let that overrule everything."

"That's a shit thing to do for a copper. For anyone. What I mean is, you know the risks, how people's pasts can affect your future, yet you let it slide. You had access to background checks and didn't use it, albeit it's against the rules, but that hasn't stopped you before."

"I get that now. I got it soon after she received that money off her dad. She wasn't who I thought she was. I only saw what she wanted me to at the beginning. Suppose I felt lucky someone as pretty as her was interested in me. Punching above my weight, see."

"Fuck off were you. I'd do you." She blushed and looked away.

He laughed, although a sprig of hope flourished. "Pack that in."

His phone rang, and he was thankful for it. The conversation was getting deep, too revealing, and Shaz implying what she had with SOCO listening in wasn't his cuppa.

Amanda's name came up on the screen, so he answered.

"Yep." He scratched the side of his nose.

"She's in Hotel Santuario, but it's not good news. The Spanish police have been in touch."

Morgan's heart rate scattered. "What sort of bad news?"

"I don't like doing this over the phone."

"Well, I do, so get on with it. Give it to me plain and straight, no fucking about."

"She's dead, sir."

He stared at the floor tiles, in shock, even though he'd told himself she would be dead. How could she not be when David Ives had flown over there?

Morgan hardened his heart. Had to. Couldn't function otherwise. "Right. How?"

"Someone gouged her eye out with a spoon and bit some of her neck off. She bled out."

"Bit some of her fucking neck off?" Imagining the mess of that, the act of doing that, weakened his knees, and he leant on the worktop to steady himself. Nauseated, he swallowed bile. Let out a long breath through pursed lips. Stuck his professional head on, although it was a loose fit and likely to fall off if he wasn't vigilant. "Okay, what about Ives?"

"He fled the scene. But there's something else."

"Fuck me. Go on."

"A Steve Tomkinson was also deceased in the room, beaten and strangled by a pair of Speedos. It's the man you're after. He left his wife, Val Hoskins, and went dark for a while, then he surfaced in Spain with a load of money and has lived in Hotel Santuario ever since. I let Jane know all this about him earlier. Didn't she say?"

"Excuse me?" His chest tightened, and his jaw ached from him clenching it. *That fucking Jane Blessing . . .*

"Yes," Amanda went on, "after you left here with Shaz. She asked me to track him while she looked into other people, and I sent her the information via email. She got it, because she replied with 'thank you'."

Morgan would have Blessing for this. The little cow had deliberately withheld vital information, and had she passed it on, Steve would have been apprehended, and Lydia might still be alive.

"I have to go." He cut the call and stared at Shaz. "Um, give me one minute." He went outside into the back garden and punched the shed, too many things swirling in his head.

One, Lydia had gone to be with Steve. How long had she known he was there? Had they been in contact all this time? Were her shopping trips in London a disguise for her meeting him for a few fucks over the weekend?

Two, Jane had hampered the investigation. Morgan would let the DCI know first thing, fuck hiding this to save Blessing's arse. He'd always thought her the type to follow the rules, never had he imagined her doing something like this. She'd allowed a man to meet his death, for what, so she could feel justified a child killer was off the streets?

Three, David was in Spain somewhere, an alert out at the airport in case he checked in — he'd bought an open-ended return ticket, so it was highly likely. Morgan had cancelled his credit card after checking his account via his phone app. Only the ticket had been purchased. If Ives planned to buy anything else, he'd be shit out of luck.

And four, now Morgan had to visit his in-laws. By rights, with it being his wife, he should pass this on to someone else, but he wouldn't put Lydia's parents through that. *He* was the best person for this, him and Shaz.

He went inside. "Come on, we need to go." Heart hardened even more, because shit, his wife had buggered off with another man, had perhaps been having a long-term affair and that was why they'd drifted apart, not his job, which she'd probably used as a convenient excuse, he got in the car and waited for Shaz.

She sat in the passenger side and put on her seat belt. "She's dead?"

Morgan nodded. "He took her eye out with a spoon, Shaz. A fucking spoon. Then he bit her neck open."

"Christ. I'm sor—"

"Don't." He gunned the engine and peeled up the road. "Steve Tomkinson was there, been living at the hotel for years, apparently. Jane knew that, but she didn't think it important enough to tell me, even though, before us two left, I put a list of all gang members, apart from Lydia, on the damn whiteboard for her to document — friends, family, haunts, habits, spending, phone calls, social media, all the usual."

"What a bitch. I knew there was a reason I didn't like her."

"Same here, *and* she passed the job of searching for Steve to Amanda, would you believe, as if she doesn't have enough to do on the front desk. Amanda passed on the info to her, but Blessing never said a word to me." He swerved round a corner. "She can't have told Nigel either, because sure as shit he'd have said when he came to collect Naomi."

"What are you going to do?"

"Tell the DCI."

"Aren't you going to speak to Jane first?"

"Yep, and she'll wish she'd never been born. Shh, now. We're here."

"Where?"

"My in-laws' place."

"Oh, Morgan, no . . ."

"It's got to be me, mate."

They left the car, and Morgan stared at the large property standing majestically in its own manicured grounds. All of it wouldn't mean a thing once he'd stepped over that threshold. Their baby girl was gone, and her husband would be the one to ruin their lives.

He walked up the drive, Shaz by his side, and she reached out to catch his hand. Only for a moment, but it was enough. She was there, his work rock, and they'd get through this. He'd be broken, angry, and confused for a while to come, and maybe he'd punch a few people under the cover of darkness if things overwhelmed him, but he was alive and had a job to do, and by God, he'd fucking do it, no matter how much it crushed him.

CHAPTER FORTY-SEVEN

David held the passport in his sweating hand. He'd boarded the shuttle along with a snaking line of waiting holidaymakers leaving the next hotel along for a late flight. Prior to its arrival, he'd stood hidden by a cluster of palm trees at the edge of a curving road, observing everyone chattering, their luggage parked beside their tanned, flip-flopped or sandy-espadrilled feet.

Now, he waited in line at check-in, conscious he looked odd without a suitcase, but he'd shucked that thought off on the way here so would do so again. Maybe they'd ask him why he'd flown in then wanted to fly out again so soon, and he didn't know what he'd say. He was on parole, and part of his conditions meant he couldn't leave the country yet.

But he was DI Morgan Yeoman, he must remember that, not David Ives.

He stepped up to the lady behind the counter. Handed the passport over.

She stared at it, then at him, then back at the passport. "One moment, sir."

She typed something on a keyboard, one-handed, and stared at her screen wide-eyed, then reached beneath the counter, and he knew, fucking knew she pressed some kind of alert button.

Blood pounded through him, his pulse manic, the rush of the *thud-thud-thud* creating a cacophony of sound inside his head, hissing water mixed with TV static. His breathing quickened, and he gazed at his feet in order to compose himself.

Blood streaked the toes of his boots.

Deep breaths.

You can do this.

He'd completed the list, all his years of planning coming to fruition.

But he hadn't got away with it.

The hand clamping on his shoulder told him that.

CHAPTER FORTY-EIGHT

Delia danced to the music on Steve's little tape player, her head swimming from the booze. She'd had four shots, two of gin, two of vodka, then Goat had produced a small bag of coke. That was some serious shit, but the drink had sent her silly, her inhibitions vanishing, so why not give it a try?

The others went first, taking thin lines one by one off the windowsill through a rolled-up fiver of Steve's, and she was last, her heart pounding in anticipation. What would it be like? A rush? A sweep of exhilaration flowing through her?

She sniffed it up, everything going strange after a minute or so, her vision cloudy, everyone vague shapes, although their voices alerted her as to who was who. She made out Lydia and Goat fucking about by the wall, getting off with each other, and that confused her. Didn't Lydia have a crush on Steve?

Delia shuddered. Steve was the last person she'd fancy.

"Let's play dares," Steve said.

He carried on talking, saying something about hanging off the balcony outside and not having to pay a share of the sweets and booze money next week if you dangled there the longest. She followed everyone out, their figures sharper now, clarity rushing in quick, heightening all Delia's senses. This was better, and she floated onto the walkway, sucking in the fresh air, her lungs expanding, her horizon clear.

"There's that Jacob kid." Goat.

"Let's fuck the little shit up." Steve.

"Hey, Jacob!" Olga called.

A man sitting on a bench turned to look, that weird David from Elderflower Mead, Delia reckoned. He scared her a bit, loping around the way he did, scowling at anyone he passed.

"Come up here," Lydia shouted. "We've got some sweets."

David faced forward.

Jacob stopped walking.

"Hurry up then!" Alice said.

Jacob stared at David, who reached out to touch the kid's crappy satchel, tugging the boy closer. Were they talking? Was David a pervert, one of those kiddie fiddlers Mum had warned her about?

Then Jacob came running towards the flats, and everyone on the balcony whooped. Delia had no idea why she did, it just seemed the right thing to do.

While Steve dished out instructions regarding giving Jacob a few punches, Delia zoned out, picking up the clatter-thud of footsteps on the stairwell. They were so loud, unusually so. Had the drugs and drink enhanced them?

A massive spider scuttled towards her, bigger than a tarantula, and she squealed, rushing inside to get away from it. Where had it come from? Was it poisonous? Why was it so big?

She pressed her back to the living room wall beside the cupboard and stared out into the hallway to make sure it hadn't followed her.

Olga entered the squat, and she retched, closing her eyes, a hand to her chest.

"Did you see the spider, too?" Delia said.

Olga opened her eyes and came into the living room. "Spider?"

"Doesn't matter." Delia felt silly now. Maybe she'd imagined the bloody thing.

Olga hugged herself. "It's what Steve said that did it. I feel sick."

"What did he say?"

"Stuff about what he wants us to do to that kid."

"What, beat him up? I heard that bit."

"It's more than that. I don't want to do it, but Steve said if we don't, he'll fuck us up instead."

Delia didn't like the sound of this. "We should go. Steve's cruel. Remember when he took that penknife to school and slashed Lee's arm, that kid who has asthma, then made out it wasn't him?"

"I saw him do it."

"Me, too."

They remained pressed to the wall, the shakes gripping Delia. The sound of laughter wended in, and Jacob's sweet tones, no rough-and-ready teenager with a breaking voice but a child, one who hadn't matured yet.

"We really should go, now, while we can," Delia said.

"Yeah. Hang out in the park until we sober up. Come on."

They pushed off the wall, and Olga took the lead down the hallway. But Steve came in, frowning, his cheeks red, the heads of all the others bobbing behind him.

"Where d'you think you're going?" A demand for an answer.

Delia's stomach bowled over, and she clutched the back of Olga's top, whispering, "Say we need some fresh air."

"We need some fresh air. We both feel ill." Olga took another step forward.

"You can fuck right off on that one." Steve came closer. "In the living room, go on."

Olga turned and widened her eyes at Delia, as if to say: Shit, what do we do now?

Delia retreated, going back to her place beside the cupboard. Olga positioned herself next to her and grabbed Delia's hand, giving it a squeeze. The air had turned funny, like it had razor blades in it or something, catching in Delia's throat every time she inhaled a breath. This wasn't going to go well, picking on Jacob, she just knew it deep in her bones.

She whispered to Olga out of the side of her mouth, "Wait until everyone's in here and busy, then we'll run."

"Shut the front door," Steve called back to Alice, the last inside.

"Fuck." Olga closed her eyes and swallowed.

Fear pounded in Delia's chest, adrenaline speeding into her veins, and the fight-or-flight urge pushed her to make a decision: Leave and risk Steve hauling her back in or remain and watch a lad get a kicking?

Everyone crowded into the living room, Jacob lost in what seemed a sea of people. Steve whispered something to Lydia, and she nodded, moving to plant herself on the other side of the cupboard. Goat followed her, loitering close, Alice stood by the door, while Steve and Flint pushed Jacob away from them so he stood by himself, a lonely target.

"Why have you got the satchel?" Steve asked him.

Jacob shrugged.

"What's that?" Steve tilted his head. "I didn't catch it. Or maybe you didn't say anything at all, which isn't good, because I asked you to fucking speak. That's what questions are for, they need an answer, and I don't think you gave me one. So . . . Why. Have. You. Got. The. Satchel?"

"M-my . . . my mum got it for me." Jacob was bricking it, that much was clear. The poor kid shivered all over, and his eyes watered.

"M-my . . . my mum got it for me," Steve mimicked.

Flint laughed. Goat joined in with his strange, bleating giggle. Lydia tinkled her usual trill, the one she must have thought sounded sexy and womanly, but it didn't, she just came off as a prat. Alice bit her bottom lip.

Delia and Olga remained silent.

Steve spun to face them. "What are you two doing over there? Come here."

Delia glanced at Olga, who shook her head a tad. But what did that mean? No, she wasn't going over there? No, they couldn't run now? No, Delia should stay there and Olga would do as he'd asked instead?

It was so confusing deciphering that gesture, and Delia had the crazy urge to either laugh hard or cry until she sobbed. She didn't feel right, all that shit she'd allowed into her body crowding her system, and apart from Olga, everyone seemed so . . . so big and menacing, like that horrible spider.

She looked around at them all, each probably in different states of mind, and the disgusting mess of the squat appeared more so now, with bits of paper and debris on the floor, the peeling wallpaper, the damp creeping up from the skirting, dirty paintwork, and the closed door that, if opened, meant freedom if Alice moved out of the way, a reprieve from fear, but only a reprieve, because if Delia walked out, Steve would catch up with her at some point, then that fear would come back.

"Well?" Steve glared. "Why are you still over there? You heard what I said outside. If you don't do what I say . . ."

But Delia hadn't taken much notice, she'd come inside, hadn't she, so what the hell did he want her to do? Did they all have assigned roles? Was that why Lydia and Goat were over there? Had they been told to just watch or something?

Steve took the small vodka bottle out of his pocket and stormed over, thrusting it at Delia. "Drink."

She took it and unscrewed the lid, all the while maintaining eye contact with Olga, who shrugged and bit the inside of her cheek. There was no help from that quarter, and Delia had no choice but to neck a swig.

"More," Steve commanded and glanced over his shoulder. "Do you want some?"

Delia flicked her attention to Jacob. He shook his head, tears falling.

"Crying, are you?" Steve marched over there. "What a fucking cock. What a baby."

Steve's fist shot out and connected with Jacob's nose. The lad stumbled backwards, then lost his footing and landed on the floor. He cried openly, little sobs catching.

Steve turned to Delia and snatched the bottle and cap, putting the lid on and returning the bottle to his pocket. "Kick him in the head."

The extra vodka had skewed things, turning wrong into right, the need for acceptance and to keep herself safe from Steve a high priority. She knew what she was about to do wasn't kind and she'd get into all sorts of trouble if they got found out, but her need to prove herself as a viable part of the gang surfaced, shunting her forward.

She ran across the room.

And kicked.

Then Steve lit a cigarette. "Let's see how much he squeals when I burn him with this fucker."

CHAPTER FORTY-NINE

Morning dawned, and Phil reckoned there was a chance of sustained sunshine, going by the sky. Few clouds, and those were white, puffy, pretty blue expanses between them. He stared through his living room window. People played out their lives in Regency. Folks taking kids to school or leaving for work. Billy loading his van. Must have an under-the-table job on again then. What's-Her-Face opposite watered her flowers, and Phil'd bet she'd give her windows a good spray of Windolene later, something she did every week. Didn't matter whether it was raining either.

"The windows need washing no matter what," she'd once told him. "My mum said a tidy house means tidy windows, because they're the things you see first."

Daft cow. Billy would wash them for a fiver, save her the job.

Phil thought about Val and smiled. At last, they were in the right place, together. Patience on his part had paid dividends, and now she was just his. She'd stayed at her gaff last night, and although he didn't like to be parted from her anymore, that was a good thing. He hadn't wanted to taint her with his feelings about Gary, to warp her idea of him — or the idea she'd come to know lately. He shouldn't be pleased his brother was out of the way for good, unable to balls things up now Phil had a new life on the horizon, but he *was* pleased.

He didn't know how he was supposed to feel about that. Bad?

Some copper had come round to break the news about Gary hanging himself from the banister in Halfway. There was a note: *We have to keep the original for evidence at the moment, but I've got it written in my notebook. Do you want to know what it says, sir?*

No, he hadn't wanted to bloody know and still didn't. Gary had always been unable to own his issues, his choices, the nasty quirks in his personality, and his reason for suicide would be blamed on Phil, of that he had no doubt.

There'd be a funeral to arrange once the body was released, like the note, held by the authorities for now, what with Gary being part of the murders, reduced to nothing but a piece of evidence in a riddle, a puzzle that had been solved as far as Phil was aware. He hadn't heard from Yeoman and didn't expect to until the detective had something he wished to say. There was still the issue of Steve but, as with Val, Phil had patience, and he'd wait until he knew where the prick was, then go after him.

Billy drove off, a pole of scaffolding clanking in the back of his vehicle.

Phil turned from the window and went for a shower, thinking beneath the spray of hot water. The stuff for Karl's flat had been delivered early this morning. Phil had bought top-of-the-line gear for the kid, everything a home needed, including new bedding, towels, and he'd even got his secretary to nip to that posh shop to buy Karl some fancy shit for the shower, men's grooming products and liquid gels, deodorants and the like.

All for Val.

He'd do anything for her.

Including killing her ex-husband.

He got out of the shower, dried off, and texted her to let her know about the bedding, just so they didn't lug Karl's round there. Phil's secretary had also washed it all. His nan had told him to always do that because unwashed new sheets gave you shingles.

Val replied with a love heart and: *You're so good to me.*

He nodded to himself and replied: *And you're so good FOR me. We'll be brilliant, you'll see. Everything will be okay now.*

Val: *How are you today? About Gary?*

Phil: *I'll live. Don't you go worrying over me. Get on with settling your lad in the flat.*

Another love heart in response and: *Thank you.*

Christ, he really did fucking love her. She was such a decent, gentle soul. A brief thought came, of whether he deserved someone like her after what he'd done in his life, and he decided yes, he did, because he was putting all that shit behind him. She'd set him on the straight and narrow, no problem, help ease him into forgiving himself for the stuff he'd done. To own it, unlike Gary.

It was time to move on, get to grips with his new self, his new life, and to start it off, he was going to visit someone about buying the drug business. Lunchtime. A pint and some grub in The Tractor's. He reckoned Terry, the landlord, would do well running the patch.

Good job Phil was handing over his drug runners as well. No way would Terry be able to go out chasing people who didn't pay. Not with that broken foot at any rate.

CHAPTER FIFTY

Val stood inside Karl's flat, amazed at everything around her. It was a classy place, all the mod cons, and the furniture, well . . . "Make sure you look after this stuff. No shoes inside — that cream carpet will get grubby in no time if you do. And watch your jeans on that leather sofa. Those brass bits on pockets. They might rip it."

Karl laughed and pointed to his grey trackie bottoms. "Don't think I have a problem there. Haven't worn jeans in ages."

"Your mates' jeans then."

"Haven't got a problem there either. Not until I find some new mates anyway." Karl ran his fingertips along the mantel.

She studied his face in the mirror hanging above the fireplace. "We made it, kid."

He turned to her. "We did. I think he really loves you."

She nodded. "Hmm."

A part of her was still afraid of falling into complete love with Phil. She'd kept five per cent of the hundred free, a reserve she'd cling to until she knew for sure she could give herself fully. Look what Steve had done, and look what Phil used to do.

But Phil's changed.

Had Steve? Had he matured over the years, become less mean, less perverted with regards to leering at women?

Her phone blipped Yeoman's tone, and she sighed. Smiled at her son. "Won't be a sec." She left the living room and entered the kitchen, going to switch a kettle on but remembering Phil had one of those taps installed that let out boiled water. Funny how he'd done that here but had a bog-standard kettle at his own place. He must really want the best for her lad.

She accessed the message.

Yeoman: *Got something you need to know. Where are you? I'm at your house.*

Val: *In Karl's new flat. Come to the end of Vicar's Gate. I'll meet you there.*

Yeoman: *Yep.*

She called out to Karl, "Just got to see what Yeoman wants, then I'll be back to help make the bed and whatever."

"All right, Mum."

The sheets and quilt covers Phil had bought were high-thread Egyptian cotton but felt like silk when she'd touched them. Someone had already removed them from the packets and washed them, and the scent of Lenor, the blue one she used, had wafted up.

Phil had sent a text to say if Karl smelled home, he wouldn't feel so out on a limb.

Christ, she really did fucking love him.

She left the flat and, glad the lift was working, took it down to ground level and walked up Vicar's Gate. Yeoman was already there, sitting in his car outside the chippy, and she waved, wondering what he had to say. A lot had happened in a matter of days, so many changes, so much upheaval, and too much death.

She needed a break.

Maybe, now Karl had his own place, she could take Phil away for the weekend once he'd paid her first wage. Nowhere fancy, just a little bed and breakfast, perhaps in Skegness as it was so close by, over in the next county, what with Nottinghamshire and Lincolnshire being neighbours. They could walk hand in hand by the sea, listening to the waves joining in on their laughter.

Life was good despite the recent heartbreak.

She reached Yeoman's car and got in the passenger seat, sensing the eyes of the street on her. People on this estate all knew Yeoman, all knew she'd been his nark, and it was funny, you'd think they'd give her a wide berth, but they didn't. Many of them 'let slip' things they wanted her to plant in the DI's ear, revenge against someone who'd pissed them off.

Yeoman glanced across at her, and bloody hell, he looked rough.

"This case is taking it out of you," she said. "You need some sleep."

"It's over. Been one of the worst, personally."

She nodded. Must be hard to cope when your wife was involved. "So what did you want? I've got nothing to pass on at the minute."

"It's Steve."

His words snatched the air from her throat with clawed fingers, and she clasped her hands tight to give her something to focus on other than her heart beating too fast, her stomach clenching in spasms.

"What about him?" She stared through the windscreen at the block of flats Karl lived in. The outside had been painted recently, nice and white. She idly pondered whether Phil had arranged it with the other homeowners, footing the bill.

Yeoman cleared his throat. "We located him."

"Right . . ."

"And Lydia. Together," he said.

Oh no. Lydia had left Yeoman for *Steve*? Yeoman must be going through hell. No wonder he appeared ragged and exhausted.

"I'm sorry to hear that," she said. "For you, I mean. Have they been . . . you know, for a while?"

"I expect so." He paused. Reached out and gripped her double fist in her lap. "They're dead, Val."

She continued to stare ahead, refusing to whip her head around to face him. Couldn't handle seeing any devastation crafted onto his face by fate's cruel hands. While he'd admitted to her once that things between him and Lydia had gone so far south they'd ended up in Hell, he must still be crushed. She knew that feeling. Steve's behaviour had brought it on a million times. All those looks, those women, his wandering cock.

As for Steve . . . Relief pounced on her shoulders, pushing them down, taking away the burden his mere existence had placed there, something she'd thought had vanished long ago but clearly hadn't until now.

"I'm sorry," she said. "For you, not for me. Steve died in my heart the day he walked out."

"I don't know what to feel."

She remained looking ahead, absorbed in the heat from his palm sinking into her skin. "Maybe just allow yourself to be honest. You were in love with her once, you fell out of it, and it turned into caring instead. She didn't treat you right, you already know that, and while someone being dead isn't a good thing, perhaps you can move on now." She thought about one of his confessions. "Remember what you said about her sticking around with you because she said she was safe if she was married to a copper?"

"What about it?"

"Despite you two drifting away from each other, her treating you badly with her snark and spite, she remained in the marriage. Okay, it seems she may have met up with Steve, more fool her, but she still needed the safety you provided and, not being funny, and I think you can take this, she used you. She was involved in that gang, and it seems to me, right from the start she chose you for a reason. A selfish reason. Can you mourn someone like that?"

"What you've said is nothing I haven't already thought."

"So you're on the way to getting over it already."

"Yeah. Sounds cruel, doesn't it?"

She shrugged. "It's how things are sometimes. People hurt you, and you sit there and wish bad things on them, feel guilty for it, then wish it all over again anyway. I did that with Steve. Hoped he'd fall off a cliff or just happen to get nudged onto a train track, and let me tell you, imagining his body all mangled up from that . . ." She'd never admitted this to anyone and never would again. "Doesn't make us bad. We're only bad if we act the thoughts out."

"I get you."

"Thought you might." She let out a long breath. "So how did they die? Let me guess. Murder?"

"Yeah, in Spain of all places. That's where Steve's been, by the way, living it large in some posh hotel on the proceeds of a big job he did that set him up for life."

"Why doesn't that surprise me?"

"Because he was an arsehole."

"And Lydia was a bitch."

They laughed then, letting all the tension out, and finally, Val looked across at him.

"It'll be fine, you know that, don't you?" She blinked back tears — of hilarity, relief, or secret upset, she didn't know and wasn't going to investigate it.

"Yeah." He smiled. "You're a good sort, Val."

"I know, and so are you."

"That's debatable with what goes on in my head sometimes."

"Like I said, it's only bad if you act it out."

He sighed. "And therein lies the rub."

CHAPTER FIFTY-ONE

In the early hours of the morning, Emma had breathed a massive sigh of relief as Flint's body had been taken down and away. She'd stayed in the kitchen while they did it, unable to stand seeing a stretcher with a sheet over the top, or even one of those bags they put corpses in. She hadn't slept, preferring to sit at the table once the residents had gone to bed, leaving the police to do their thing. Yes, a suicide note had been left, but they'd stuck around and did all the things they usually did in these situations, in case it was murder. Or someone had forced Flint to do it, so technically, still murder.

Her eyes itched, and she stared around the kitchen at the mess cooking the breakfast had made. She'd opted, when she'd taken over Halfway, to provide meals, thinking it would help ease people into life outside Rushford. After all, they'd had three squares a day while in there, and worrying about dinners and whatnot was extra on top of settling into a world that was far removed from the one they'd known upon entering their cells.

Now, she wished she hadn't done that. She was tired, in need of a good few hours in bed, but she had to clean first, then maybe she could lock herself in her flat this afternoon and kip on the sofa.

She scraped stray baked beans and a couple of toast corners into the bin, moving on to stack the dishwasher. A cup of tea and a ginger biscuit might settle her tumultuous stomach after, and then there was the job of hoovering the stairs and landings.

A buzz fizzled in her ears, the hairs on the back of her neck stood on end, and she knew Oliver Elford had come in. She turned, a plate held midair, and smiled at him despite not wanting to. She needed to grin and bear his presence.

"Want some help with that?" He came to stand beside her.

She *could* do with some help, but not from him. "Um, no, it's fine."

"Thank you."

"Pardon?"

He stared at her. "It's fine, *thank you.*"

She shivered at his nearness, his tone. "Yes, sorry. Thank you. I'm tired, so I apologise." *Please go away.*

"You should have gone to bed last night then." He sniffed and stared through the kitchen window.

"I couldn't. Not after . . . that." She placed the plate in the dishwasher and put a tablet inside. Door closed, machine on, she straightened and went to move around him.

He moved, too.

"Excuse me," she said, voice shaking.

"Maybe I don't want to be excused."

She sighed and dredged up the speech she'd prepared ages ago, just for this sort of eventuality. "If you don't move out of my way, I'll have no choice but to think you're breaking the terms of your agreement here, crowding me, being obstructive, threatening. I'll have to contact your parole officer."

Oliver nodded, as if contemplating the ramifications of that. "No need to get shirty. I only came down to pass on a message anyway and thought I could help you tidy while I was at it."

A message? "What sort of message?"

"Doesn't matter, it'll keep."

He walked out, saying something else, and her whole body went cold. No, he couldn't have said that, could he? Not that . . .

She stared at him rounding the newel post, and he winked.

"Did you hear what I said?" He stopped at the bottom of the stairs and stared through into the kitchen.

She nodded, biting her bottom lip. Yes, she'd heard him.

He'd said: *Derek sends his regards.*

CHAPTER FIFTY-TWO

Jane Blessing, that was what he always called her, and she knew it was because she called him DI Morgan Yeoman, no matter what. She did it to make a point: *You are the lead detective around here, so remember that, will you, instead of acting like a bully in plain sight?*

He hadn't twigged, she was sure of that much. Too busy stuffed inside his head, dealing with his own needs, like punching a criminal or two.

Deary me.

He'd gone out alone again this morning, apparently to see one of his narks, although if truth be told, she reckoned he was sloping off to lick his wounds in private. Why lick a cut if it hurt, though? Or, if she had her suspicions right, the only wounds he had were the ones Lydia had inflicted with her sharp tongue, deep scars that would never heal, because words had the power to hurt more than any blade or bullet.

Everyone knew how Lydia had ridiculed him. She'd done it on a couple of occasions when she'd joined them for drinks after work. Jane had also caught her sniffing a line of white off the vanity unit in the ladies' and looked into where she'd bought the gear. Of course, Jane had kept quiet about it, filing it away as a spear to throw at Morgan should he annoy her too much.

Ah, here he was, with that swagger, rolling into the incident room and casting his steely gaze about. Who did he think he was, bloody Luther?

She almost giggled at her wit.

"Jane Blessing," he barked. "In my office."

Oh, that was a shame. He'd probably found out what she'd done. Time to face the Grim Reaper, in his mind anyway, the person who represented the death of their jobs if they didn't toe the line. *His* line.

Irritating man.

She followed him down the corridor and entered his office. He stood behind his desk, the window at his back, sun streaming in, and she imagined that sun was Jacob in Heaven, beaming because all his bullies were in Hell, burnt by the flames of retribution.

Fanciful.

She closed the door and approached the desk.

"Sit." He pointed to the spare chair.

"I'm not a dog, DI Morgan Yeoman."

He gritted his teeth. Well now, it really *did* get on his nerves when she called him that. Good. She'd keep doing it — providing she had a job after this, but she had a fair old idea she wouldn't be going anywhere.

"And besides," she went on, "I prefer to stand. It seems you're rather annoyed and have something to say where you'd prefer to be above me, looking down, showing me how senior you are, a DI against a mere DC, and therefore showing me my place. But I won't bow to your demands in this instance, *sir*, if that's all the same to you."

"You're a fucking piece of work." He stared at her, probably to cow her.

She remained straight-spined, unafraid. Let him say what he had to say, then she'd let him know what was on *her* mind.

"Fair enough." He folded his arms. "You dropped the ball, which meant my wife died."

"Oh, is that how you're going to play it?"

He frowned. "What are you on about?"

"Nothing. Go on." She folded *her* arms, too, not to give herself comfort, but to show him she was on equal footing, rank be damned. He wouldn't know until she told him so, but there was time enough for that.

He grunted. "You knew Steve Tomkinson lived in Spain and never told me."

"No, I didn't. I can't fault your powers of deduction there."

"Give over with the superior act, for fuck's sake. Just for once, be normal."

"Normal?"

"Instead of snippy." He paused. "You received that information from Amanda Cartwright, and you replied to her, saying thank you, so don't go denying you were told."

"I wasn't going to deny it."

"What?"

"You heard me."

He sighed, possibly wanted to slap her, but she hadn't heard of him hurting women on his travels.

He rubbed his chin. "What you did — or didn't do — resulted in my wife going to Spain to see Steve, and David Ives followed her out there. He then murdered them both."

"I know this, so why are you repeating it to me as though I'm thick?"

"I'm stating what happened so we're both clear on why I'm now going to go to the DCI and report you for it."

She let out a manic laugh. Nodded. "Interesting."

"What is?"

"You going to the DCI about a police officer doing something wrong. *You* do things wrong all the time."

"I bloody well do not!" He had the grace to look sheepish while he lied to her face.

She hadn't expected anything less. "So you not reporting your wife, who bought quantities of cocaine and stored them at your house, enough to be classed as possession with an intent to supply, isn't doing something bad?" She smiled at him. "Or how about the way you mess with people, how you punch them in the face in order to scare them into giving you what you want? I mean, we all know it's so easy for someone who's been arrested to fall over from the shock of it and scrape their face on a fist, and oh, they just happen to have a broken, bleeding nose, the poor things, but as often as *your* arrests produce? My, you apprehend some seriously clumsy people."

His eyebrows formed a monobrow. "What the *fuck* are you getting at?"

"You know what I'm getting at. I did you a favour withholding that information. Your marriage was on the rocks a long time ago. If you think your little chats with Shaz in the kitchen go unheard, you'd be wrong."

"You've been *listening*?"

She shrugged. "Can't help it sometimes. Words carry." She studied him, wanting him to be uncomfortable. Then her reveal: "Jacob Everson was my best friend."

His eyes popped wide. "What?"

"Hmm. No one knew, because if they did, I'd have had the piss taken out of me as well for hanging around with him. I felt bad about that, after, so decided to join the police, right the wrongs. Isn't that the cliché reason? Something bad happens to a person, so the person or their friend becomes someone who can fix it all?" She laughed again. "And a bit of advice. If you're going to menace people, do it with more finesse."

"What do you mean?"

"Like me. A slip of the memory. Oh, whoops, I forgot to pass on the information about Steve because I was so tired after being stuck on CCTV, which I hate, and you only ever put me on it to let me know where I am in the pecking order."

"Christ, get it all out why don't you."

"That's the intention." She told him about her times going out into the dark, getting results all by herself, hidden, no one knowing who she was, whereas he allowed himself to be seen, to have people pointing fingers at him. "You're a gauche little bastard, and you need to learn how to get what you want without those fists of yours getting in on the act. Now, if you'd like me to go to the DCI and explain about Lydia's drugs, about your imperfections, I will, because there are so many. I especially like the time you threw that man in the river, held his face under for a while, then pulled his head up. He did whatever you wanted after that. He claimed he'd tripped after running away from you and fell in the water."

"I don't know what you're talking about."

"Of course you do. So, shall we?" She gestured to the door.

He let his arms flop to his sides. "Fuck me, you're a dark horse, Jane Blessing."

"I know." She smiled again. "Maybe we can be cowboys and ride those horses together."

He shook his head, not in the negative, but in bemusement. "I underestimated you. Blimey, you've got me by the short and curlies."

"I do." She moved to open the door. "About time, too, before you fuck up your whole career. Now, let's get back to our jobs. Watch and learn, DI Morgan Yeoman."

CHAPTER FIFTY-THREE

Everyone gathered in The Tractor's after work. There was still a fair bit of paperwork to do, and everything needed filing, all the info Jane Blessing and Nigel had gathered from CCTV, social media, and their behind-the-scenes enquiries while Morgan and Shaz had been out there among the masses. They always had a bevvy or two with the closing of a case, and while he'd had that disturbing yet enlightening interaction with Blessing earlier, Morgan had still agreed to go out. Had to put a brave face on it, but fucking hell, he'd be watching her closely in future. She knew too much in all respects and had kept it to herself, waiting for her moment to reveal all.

A dark horse indeed.

They sat around the largest table in the corner beside a window with dusty bull's-eye panes, their glasses full, and Morgan assured them all there was no need to act maudlin because of Lydia being dead.

"She'd been in that gang, same as all the others, and she needed pulling up for her part in it, no matter who she was." Shame he hadn't thought that when he'd been prepared to cover up for her.

He'd seen the error of that this morning. Blessing could so easily have dug deeper and found out what Lydia had done to Alice. Could have used it against him later down the line.

He swigged some of his pint. "Although death is a bit much for an ending, but I can't do anything about that, seeing as I wasn't told where Steve was." He stared pointedly at Blessing.

"I didn't read the email Amanda sent, just said thank you to her." Blessing gave a sickly smile.

Conniving bitch. But she'll prove useful. "Can't change the past."

She seemed to get his meaning: *You can't right the wrongs of your friend's childhood just by being a police officer, no more than Lydia could by marrying one.*

"No," she agreed, "but you can alter your future and change your behaviour accordingly."

I hear you, woman.

"Hark at her." Shaz shook her head. "A right philosopher all of a sudden. What have you done, swallowed a bloody old-fashioned book or what?"

Morgan wondered whether he'd ever tell Shaz about Blessing. Probably not. "No, she's a wise one, and we're only just noticing it."

Blessing dipped her head in acknowledgement.

"She's all right underneath it all, aren't you, Jane?" Nigel said. "Bit of a prickly pear, but I think you mean well."

"Thanks, Nigel, I like you, too."

Titters went round at that.

While the others talked, Morgan cast his attention elsewhere, namely, inside his crowded head. He had a shitload to sort out, getting Lydia's body back, handing everything over to her parents, as was their wish. Morgan would be a hypocrite — *no surprise there then* — if he arranged things for a woman he'd stopped loving properly years ago. Better that her mum and dad give Lydia the send-off they thought she deserved, with all the bells and whistles. He'd attend, pay his respects, but he'd never forgive her for standing by and letting that lad get killed, nor would he forgive her for duping him into thinking she was someone else.

Come on now, you let yourself be blinkered.

Yeah, he had.

Steve's parents were dealing with his body. Morgan had spoken to Val at lunchtime, checking in to see if she was okay, and she'd said she was, but she wasn't letting Karl know his father was dead. It'd bring upset to the lad, and he was so happy being in his own place. Val didn't want to ruin it. Said Karl deserved a bit of stability after ditching his shitty college mates.

Morgan had been glad to hear that, and he'd keep an eye out in case those mates decided to give Karl grief. He'd maybe get Blessing to go after them in her black outfit, waving her knife around, the dangerous, creepy bitch.

He still couldn't get over that. What did she fancy herself as, Catwoman? Fucking hell . . .

The landlord called out, "Are you here for the duration, you lot? Only, having coppers sitting in my gaff might put people off, know what I mean?"

"We've parked our arses and we're staying put," Shaz said. "Bog off."

Morgan smiled.

Terry didn't.

What's up with him? Maybe his foot was giving him gyp.

The door swung open, and Morgan turned to check who entered. Val and Phil, arm in arm. Val smiled to say hello, walking to the bar and getting her purse out. Terry shuffled along to serve her, his cheeks going red. Did he have a little crush, or was it Phil's appearance that sent Terry jittery?

Morgan looked at Phil who jerked his head and disappeared down the corridor where the loos were. Morgan got up and followed him. Inside the toilets, he found Phil nosing in the stalls.

"What are you bloody doing?" Morgan asked.

"I don't want to be overheard."

Morgan pressed his back to the door so no one could come in. "Out with it then."

"About Steve."

"What about him?"

"I wish it was me who did it."

"You and me both, but it wasn't either of us, so deal with it. He's out of Val's life for good, that's the main thing."

Phil danced from foot to foot, unusually iffy, nothing like his usual self. "Right, I've got something to say, and I hope you don't do me for it."

Morgan frowned. "No assurances."

"Didn't think there would be, but for Val . . . Can you just mind your own for her?"

"Depends."

Phil took a deep breath. "I've sold the business."

"What, the car lot?"

"No, the other one. Going straight now."

Morgan laughed. "I see, going straight by living off the proceeds, eh? Don't you feel bad that people have got hooked because of the likes of you? They've died, for fuck's sake."

Phil shrugged. "Like I said to my brother, or words to that effect: *They have a choice to buy it, I've never insisted they buy.* That was one of my rules, see. Never did like the term drug pusher. Pusher means you forced it. No, I provided, they purchased. What happened because of their decisions isn't my concern."

"You're viewing it that way to absolve yourself of any guilt, like Gary did with Wasti's and every other shitty thing he did. 'It wasn't me, Officer!'"

Phil flinched. "Don't compare me to my brother. I'm nothing like him."

"Oh, really?" Morgan lifted his eyebrows. "You sure about that?"

"Fair point." His shoulders slumped. "Fuck it."

"We all need to take a long hard look at ourselves, sunshine, including me, and while it stings, finding out there are parts of yourself you don't like, there's still time to do something about it. Take care of Val, otherwise, I'll get all the info I need from your old drug runners now their allegiance is elsewhere and have you put down for life, got it?"

"No worries there. Now, are you going to move or what? My tongue's gagging for a pint."

Morgan stepped aside. "Good luck, and stay clean."

"Same to you." Phil paused in opening the door. "You're going to need it with that woman on your team."

"What woman?"

"Jane something or other. I didn't realise she was one of yours, just thought she was a mental-case copper. She's a fucking scary bitch behind the scenes."

Morgan laughed, shaking his head. "She's had a go at scaring *you*?"

"She did. A few years ago now, but blimey . . ."

Phil walked down the corridor, leaving Morgan to wonder just what Jane Blessing got up to when darkness shrouded Pinstone.

Maybe, now they were cowboys together, he'd find out.

He walked back to his seat and sat beside Shaz. Blessing and Nigel stood at the bar, talking to Terry, who said a bit too loudly that he wasn't up for anyone doing drugs on his property, so if 'you coppers' think I am, you're mistaken.

He doth protest too much.

Jane turned and widened her eyes at Morgan. Yep, he got it crystal clear. Phil had sold his bloody business to the landlord.

Shit a fucking brick.

"Everything okay?" Shaz elbowed Morgan's side.

"Yeah, it'll do."

"What will?"

"How things currently stand."

"Right . . ." Her frown said she didn't know what the hell he was talking about. "So, Lydia . . . Need help with the funeral?"

"No, her parents are doing it."

"Okay. Need help with anything else? You know I'll cook you some food batches if you want. Saves you sitting on the bench outside the Chinese every night with Rochester."

"But I like Chinese and I like my dog."

"Do you like me?" She appeared hopeful.

The air turned stagnant.

"Too soon?" she asked.

"Just a bit, but thanks."

"For what?"

"Letting me know I haven't got a face like a bag of hammers."

"What, you mean letting you know I fancy you and your wife didn't know what she had when she had it?"

"Yeah, that." He sighed. Shaz was a good woman, but really? Him and her? He'd often wondered what it would be like but had dismissed it as a crush on a workmate. "Probably wouldn't pan out, you know that, don't you."

She huffed out a breath. "Rubbish. Look at Tracy Collier and her Damon. DI, DS, working and living together."

"Hmm. Maybe one day."

She squeezed his arm. "I'll be waiting. However long it takes."

"I know you will." He pecked her on the cheek. Didn't hurt to be affectionate to a mate, did it? Or was he leading her up the garden path by doing that? *Shit.* "But don't wait too long. I might not come round to the idea."

She shrugged. "Even so. I'm here."

And she always had been, right from the word go. And she wanted more. How had he never seen that?

Sometimes, you just didn't see the woods for the trees.

And sometimes, you forgot to take evidence out of your boot and fucking burn it.

Shit!

THE END

THE JOFFE BOOKS STORY

We began in 2014 when Jasper agreed to publish his mum's much-rejected romance novel and it became a bestseller.

Since then we've grown into the largest independent publisher in the UK. We're extremely proud to publish some of the very best writers in the world, including Joy Ellis, Faith Martin, Caro Ramsay, Helen Forrester, Simon Brett and Robert Goddard. Everyone at Joffe Books loves reading and we never forget that it all begins with the magic of an author telling a story.

We are proud to publish talented first-time authors, as well as established writers whose books we love introducing to a new generation of readers.

We won Trade Publisher of the Year at the Independent Publishing Awards in 2023 and Best Publisher Award in 2024 at the People's Book Prize. We have been shortlisted for Independent Publisher of the Year at the British Book Awards for the last five years, and were shortlisted for the Diversity and Inclusivity Award at the 2022 Independent Publishing Awards. In 2023 we were shortlisted for Publisher of the Year at the RNA Industry Awards, and in 2024 we were shortlisted at the CWA Daggers for the Best Crime and Mystery Publisher.

We built this company with your help, and we love to hear from you, so please email us about absolutely anything bookish at feedback@joffebooks.com.

If you want to receive free books every Friday and hear about all our new releases, join our mailing list here: www.joffebooks.com/freebooks.

And when you tell your friends about us, just remember: it's pronounced Joffe as in coffee or toffee!

Printed in Great Britain
by Amazon

61290176R00173